The Fortunes and Vicissitudes of Stern Whitman

The Fortunes and Vicissitudes of Stern Whitman

Derek Burnett

FIVE STAR
A part of Gale, a Cengage Company

LIBRARY OF CONGRESS CATALOGING-IN-PUBLICATION DATA

Names: Burnett, Derek, 1970– author.
Title: The fortunes and vicissitudes of Stern Whitman / Derek Burnett.
Description: First edition. | Farmington Hills, Mich. : Five Star, a part of Gale, a Cengage Company, 2020.
Identifiers: LCCN 2019034188 | ISBN 9781432868017 (hardcover)
Subjects: GSAFD: Western fiction.
Classification: LCC PS3602.U7633 F67 2020 | DDC 813/.6—dc23
LC record available at https://lccn.loc.gov/2019034188

First Edition. First Printing: May 2020
Find us on Facebook—https://www.facebook.com/FiveStarCengage
Visit our website—http://www.gale.cengage.com/fivestar
Contact Five Star Publishing at FiveStar@cengage.com

Printed in Mexico
Print Number: 01 Print Year: 2020

To Sam Clemens, who raised me from a pup

Chapter One

The awful end of the Tsar—I notify Green—The Blackfoot sisters puzzle the camp—A risible congress—Factions—Drawing lots—The missionaries smell trouble—Resolving to depart.

It wasn't any strain to recognize Peter the Great even with his head stove in and caked all over with half-dried blood and sawdust and dead leaves and the like. He was a cinch for the biggest man in camp, and his trousers gave him away, patterned as they were with stripes where nearly all of us others wore plain blue jeans. It was a fine morning after a wild hurricane night; the sunshine hung wet on the air, the puddles gave off sweat, and the mosquitoes breezing along over the mud knocked heads above Peter the Great's blood-blackened face, if such a wreck as that could anymore be deserving of the name.

I was the first to spy him, being the first man to stir in camp that morning. I discovered him while on my way back to our tent after moving my bowels, having taken a turn past the laundry shed in idle hopes of catching a glimpse of one of the Blackfoot sisters, and there he lay, on his belly almost but with his back hunched so tight that one hip cleared the muck and only his right shoulder touched the ground.

Take it all around, it was an awful funny way to lie in state. I'll tell you the impression he gave: it looked for all the world like he'd been fired out of a cannon from some tolerable distance off and landed hard just inside the little slabwood kiosk that Jeff Bill had slapped together to sell trifles out of. Which just goes to show you what a disappointment death can be; how you might look forward, for years and years, to the grandeur it affords, only to be let down in the moment. Peter had never been a dandy, but any man who respects himself even a little takes a pain or two to hold himself a certain way, present himself to the world after his own notion of what dignity consists in—and now it was the sorry luck of poor Peter to have come to rest in nine inches of mud with his face mashed in and his rump plying the air like a busted coal chute.

Well, I never received any schooling in the medical arts, but I made shift without it to conclude that Peter the Great had drawn his last, on account of his skull having been turned inside out and his brains being slathered all down his shirt. Our camp had existed for just three weeks now, outside of any established mining district, a wholly unincorporated and entirely makeshift entity without the first hint of an authority to whom I was obliged to report this finding. So I did the only thing right and necessary, and trudged over to the tattered tent of Peter the Great's partner, Michael Green, to break the unglad tidings.

There wasn't anything but a few strips of canvas still clinging to the willow poles of the shelter—the night's storm had shredded every stitch of cloth in camp, it seemed—so you just about couldn't help but see inside. Green was sprawled back on the pallet he and Peter the Great normally shared, spread-eagled, fully dressed but for his hideous hat, looking so ash gray and somber that I judged his health to be in the same neighborhood as Peter the Great's this morning. His hands were bloodied up into scarlet gauntlets to the elbows, and streaks and flecks of gore dappled his clothes and face and beard. He was snoring, though, which the dead seldom do—snorting, gabbling, choking on his own spit.

Along the boards of the pallet beside him lay two of those

brown bottles that had held a portion of the corn whiskey Compass had carried into camp the previous morning. I imagined it was lucky for Green there hadn't been a third such bottle, for I believe it would have seen him and Peter reunited, some other place that never wants for warmth.

"Hi, there—Green."

Soft talk wasn't much use, I could see that straight off. I fetched him an ungentle kick at the sole of his boot with the rounded toe of mine and hollered his name again, and at this he muttered and smacked and exhaled so rotten it offended me even at a distance.

"Up, damn you, Green." I delivered him seconds, and this time his eyelids came open, but not as fast as I've seen some other eyelids work before, and I didn't reckon those bleary eyes of his let through much more light than did those brown bottles, they were that glazed and clouded. "Your pard is come to naught," I said.

This had no effect.

"Peter the Great's taken his one-way ticket," I told him.

Green peered at me hard, then growled low and confused and dragged himself up to spit. "The hell?" he said.

"Peter, I'm talking about. Expirated. Fully. Foul play."

He sprang for me, but I was expecting him, and he wasn't in any condition for that kind of extravagance anyway. I took an easy step backward, and he flopped into the mud at my feet like something you turn with a spatula, a messy pile of sobs.

"Over yonder by the laundry is where you can collect on his remnants," I said and waded back to my tent.

Johnny was gone to the shitter when I returned. Well, I say "shitter," but that makes it sound a good deal fancier than what it was, which was only a low place a couple dozen steps from camp where a fellow could get everything but the top of his head out of view of his companions when he had to take a squat. Unless those companions were there squatting, too, in which case nobody had the advantage. You couldn't get complacent about where you set your feet when you were down in that hollow, that's sure; and you can bet that venturing there with a belly full of whiskey was a risky enterprise every time.

When the Blackfoot sisters first came to camp, Johnny and I had proposed to build them a proper, respectable shitter, for the sake of their feminine modesties etc., in which no male member would be allowed to intrude on pain of banishment; but evidently these wildwood flowers couldn't compass the thought of defecating indoors, because they gave us to understand that such a chivalric gesture was not only unnecessary but rather unwelcome and distasteful.

Thus, inevitably, in the days that followed, certain members of the group fell prey to the burning mystery of just how, where, and, eventually, even *whether* the sisters conducted the solemnities that any of us previously would have sworn amounted to medical necessities. It had been the generally accepted understanding among us that women had not fewer, but a power more, such considerations in that line than did men, but neither sister was ever seen heading toward the shitter nor for any other sacred spot we knew of.

One evening George Auburn had taken his supper with us, and during a quiet spell Johnny had sighed and laid his spoon across his plate full of beans and said, "Well, *I've* about had it with this not knowing. I don't believe I can bear up under it another hour."

"Not knowing just what, Johnny?" George said.

"About those Blackfoot sisters."

"And where they . . . manage themselves?"

"There, you've hit on it direct. I see it's worn on your mind a little, too."

"Oh, I reckon *not.* Only every time I glimpse one of them. Mark me, I'd a lot rather think of *other* things when I look at 'em, but this keeps on intruding. I do wish they'd take pity and clear matters up for us."

Johnny shook his head. "So do I. So do I."

George says, "What I wish, really, is I wish to the Lord they'd give me a good reason not to think they was witches."

"Oh, it ain't witchcraft, George—is it?" Johnny says.

"Blamed if I know. But it don't hardly seem natural."

"It isn't witchery," I said.

"Well, it isn't very mortal of them, either, carrying on so."

There followed a lengthy symposium in which several explanations of a more scientific nature than witchcraft were held up to the light, examined carefully, and set back down. Did they retain it all day and steal off in the dead of night when all the rest of the camp was sleeping? Had they constructed some secret chamber within the laundry shed special for that purpose? Were they in possession of some esoteric system of nutrition and hygiene that rendered such activities unnecessary? I cannot claim to have been entirely immune from curiosity myself. What made it even more confounding to me was that they were cleaner and better groomed than any white women I'd known, even the frilly, quality set that takes tea and so on.

After a time, Johnny says, "Do you reckon they'd mind a great deal if we was to *ask* them?"

"Ask them?" I said. "Ask them hell. You don't ask a woman a thing like that. Even a half-wild Blackfoot woman."

"Oh, I suppose you say that on account of how well acquainted you are with such a great number of Blackfoot women. I reckon you're a famous expert on their manners."

"Well, a woman is a woman, seems to me."

"Well, I once thought so, too. But a Christian woman will excuse herself and take to the shitter once or twice a day, like a creature of flesh and blood, won't she?"

I had to admit that she would.

"And won't a plantation slave, same way?"

"Far as I know, yes, she will; though I can't claim to have studied it."

"See? These ain't natural women, and so if we was to ask them where they do it, they might just yawn and answer us same as if we'd ask their names."

"True," George said.

"Still, it's a bad idea," I said. "They don't have enough English for that conversation to go smooth. Remember how it was when we offered to build the shitter? Remember the sign language we had to use?"

Johnny nodded solemnly. I hated to see him consternated so, and I was glad we had talked it over lest he feel all alone with his troubles. By and by he said, "Why, I think I've hit on the thing, Stern. I'll write to Mama and ask her what she knows."

"Why, she'll keel over in her tracks, Johnny."

"Oh, she can bear it, I reckon."

"*I* don't."

"Well, here's something you don't know: night before I was married, she took me aside and told me a thing or two about this and that."

"*Mama* did that?"

"She did. She comes off squeamish and prim, and if there's such a thing as angels, we have one in her; but it just goes to show you that even angels have got to keep a foot on the ground sometimes."

"Hell, write to her, then, Johnny. I didn't know you and she were that close."

And so right on the spot he scared up pen and paper and did so. We were still waiting for Mama's answer and didn't expect one for many months to come; but Johnny said over and over that knowing help was on the way took a sizable chunk of edge off the mystery, enough to where he reckoned he could abide with the uncertainty.

Anyway, when Johnny came back from the shitter, he said, "Peter the Great is laying over there all smashed to flinders."

"*I* know that. I was fixing to tell you the self-same thing."

"Why, how'd he come to it?"

"I do not know, Johnny. I do not know. Except that Michael Green was likely mixed up in it somehow."

"You think 'twas he who done for him?"

I shrugged. "I never said he *did* the thing. 'Mixed up in it' is what I said. But he was pretty well pickled from yesterday noon, and this morning his pard is gone out of print, and him laying there sleeping it off while the blood dries nearly up to his armpits."

"Well, he's over there right now kneeling in the mud and bawling like as if the man had been his bride."

"That's about to be expected either way," I said.

Johnny nodded. After a minute he said, "What do we do if it *was* him?"

"Same thing we do about whoever it was, him or no: hang him up."

Somehow, even though I'd known it deep down, I hadn't as yet really thought of it until I heard myself say it aloud: though it had initially seemed an entirely private matter between Green and the Russian, the fact was that the camp would need to hold some kind of inquest, and then a hanging—and I could foresee my own deep involvement in all these procedures. This beautiful day would go to waste, and maybe days and days more, all thanks to a pair of chuckleheaded ruffians who couldn't stomach their tanglefoot.

On the other hand, maybe there was opportunity hidden somewhere in all this . . .

We breakfasted and climbed up to my claim, where Johnny helped me work on the shaft I'd started the day before. But it was foolishness even to have bothered, because quite soon enough here came Willie Shaughnessy and Tiny Paul Maddock up the hill, with Sing walking between them speaking faster English than anybody else in camp.

"Mornin', boys," I said as natural as anything, though I knew they were here for no nobler purpose than to wreck my day.

"Mornin'," says Willie. "Say, what do you fellers know about Peter the Great?"

I didn't even look up. "I know he's used up pretty final as of today," I said. "That's the main fact I'd offer."

Tiny Paul cleared his throat. "We heard you was the one found him," he said.

"Far as I know, yes."

"Well, do you know who done for him?"

I shook my head and pried at a stone with my pick.

"Well," said Willie, "have you any ideas?"

"Precious few, as a general thing," I said, stooping to lift out the stone.

Sing said, "What about you, Johnny Boy?"

"I didn't know the three of you all had taken up police work," Johnny said.

"We ain't," Tiny Paul said. "But there's more than the three of us down there figure somebody'd better swing for this, or it'll be hot times around here once some of these boys sees they can kill whoever they want to with no fear of reproach."

"It's a fine enough principle," I said. "But I don't know that our little gaggle has got the expertise or the authority to pull the thing off."

"Well, it's been decided that we're going to try," Willie said. "So you ought to come out and tell us what you know."

"Who elected you three prosecutors?" I said.

Willie shook his head. "You're having the wrong idea," he said. "We've only come up the hill to fetch you back to camp."

Tiny Paul said quietly, "Everybody's gathered up down below. Think you boys is best off coming down off the hill with us. Some might take it as strange, y'all being the only two not participating, and you claimin' to have been the one that found him, Stern."

"*Claimin'* your granny. I saw him, and I told his pard. That's as much as I claim."

"Still," Sing said. "You come down now."

We did. We put away our tools and joined the other thirty-odd miners, who had all bunched up around Michael Green's pallet. I could see as we approached that things had already got heated, and to myself I began cursing anew the bad luck that had brought this pack of coyotes onto what had until recently been Johnny's and my own private claim.

To anyone fortunate enough not to have had a stake in it, it would have been a scene to bring down laughter: such a passel of ignoramuses puffing themselves up, struggling to speak the way they imagined professors of law to speak, breaking their spines to straighten up to their fullest heights the better to be heard and respected, some of them teetering atop overturned pails and chunks of firewood to elevate their stature, only everything sinking into the mud and them toppling. But I wasn't much for laughing at that moment, because I would live or die by how well this farce went along, there being little in this world more dangerous than fools deluded by righteous conviction.

Johnny and I listened for a moment and saw right away that two factions had already arisen, each accusing one miner and adamantly protesting the innocence of another. Roughly half the camp had it in for Michael Green, who was plunked down on his pallet with his face in his hands looking like a baby hiding behind its mother's skirts; that half said it was only too obvious that Green had got to quarreling with his partner sometime during the night and had taken advantage of the Tsar's more advanced state of impairment to belabor his head in with a hammer "or something" and had awakened fairly steeped in the Russian's blood.

The other set swore these were vicious lies and outrageous fictions: at first light, one of the twelve Mexicans, a boy named Joaquín (standing wide-eyed among his countrymen like a schoolboy who's thrown a rock through a window), had been discovered down at the creek *washing his hands,* a thing (it was said) no Mexican would ever undertake of his own volition; everybody knew that Peter the Great had despised and abused the Mexicans regularly, and any fool could see that, out of pure vindictive hatred, Joaquín had anointed the Tsar's face with a heavy stone "or something," which he had disposed of in the stream before rinsing the blood from his fingers.

I will insert here a clarification of perhaps no interest to anyone but myself, which is that those beings referred to around camp invariably as "Mexicans" were, in fact, an amalgamated group of Spanish speakers, the greatest concentration of which were Venezuelan. I had once or twice attempted to point this out to my fellow Americans but threw in my hand once confronted with the inevitable response: "I don't give one continental which *part* of Mexico a man is from, whether 'tis Venezuela or any other. Ain't he still a Mexican? Don't he still answer to a king and worship a pope?"

Anyhow, alternative explanations to those involving Joaquín Caracas and Michael Green—even the possibility that alternatives could ever exist—had diminished in prominence and then vanished entirely away, these two competing theories hardening like amber in the unpracticed brains of our cohabitants. The rapidity of it was astounding; just moments ago, these floundering intellects had not known what to think and had clutched at whatever meager evidence had suggested itself. From that flimsy evidence they had fashioned crude possibilities, which morphed into complex hypotheticals, which soon took on the cast of solemn theories and then had, like magical beanstalks, flourished suddenly into full-blown legal arguments, then received doctrine, and finally irrefutable articles of faith. And anyone who opposed them must have been heretics, scoundrels, the blindest of imbeciles.

Amid the increasing din, Johnny said to me, aside, "I'm surprised anybody but Mexicans is standing up for old Joaquín. Still, there ain't all that many. I reckon that's the side we should join, don't you?"

"We aren't joining any side," I said.

"No? I believe it's the weaker faction."

"Weaker in number, maybe. But the Mexicans come well armed, and these fellows know what'll come if they try and string up Joaquín."

Johnny's eyes widened. "Jesus. It's war, ain't it, Stern?"

"Surely looks headed that way."

I listened to the foolishness for a while longer ("How do you explain how clean that Greaser's hands is?" and "How do you explain Green's sleeping so late this mornin'?"), until things got so hot that the two sides had physically sorted themselves and were faced off against each other, tearing at their own clothes and pulling out their knives and revolvers. Another moment and things would boil over. My time had come. I shook my head and spat and stepped in between the two groups and held up my hands. To my surprise, the men hushed themselves up instantly.

A pretty fine speech bubbled up out of me from somewhere. "Now listen to me, boys," I began. "We've got a situation here that nobody was looking for, but it's found us. It's a conundrum, and it's a sorrow. One of our own has been done for, and another of our own is the killer, only we don't know who. If we aren't careful in our words and behavior, we'll be burying a lot more than just Peter the Great. We'll be burying a good deal of his friends, right along with a good deal of his enemies, and our honor to boot. Boys, a war is the last thing we need. There's a heap of ore scattered along this river, and as sad as this all is, it would be an awful crying shame for anybody to get himself killed, sitting right on top of his fortune, over such a little thing as this. Now, when a tragedy like we've seen falls upon a camp like ours, the men will sometimes set up a miners' court to settle the thing. But look around. That isn't going to work for us, for we're too split down the middle for it to come out fair."

They all seemed to agree with that much, so I pressed on. "Another way would be to put it before the wisest and most educated men to be looked into and decided out. And you'll have to excuse me, but there ain't a single one of us qualifies for that line. I've met educated men in the mines, but I haven't seen one fetch up in our gulch, to this date. No, friends, what we want is outside help. And so what I suggest is this: we let there be a truce; we allow Peter's friends to plant him in peace, unmolested; and we let off all discussion of this matter while one of our number goes over the mountains to fetch a by-God Placerville judge who can come in here and resolve this."

The rabble held their tongues for a good long minute, thinking over what I had said, as Sing translated for the Chinese and Juan Pablo put it into Spanish. After the interpreters were done, I waited for the obvious question, and it was long in coming, but at last Willie says, "But who would *make* that trip?"

"Well," I said, "first we'd ask if there's a volunteer. Anybody care to step forward?"

Unsurprisingly, no one did, for the reason Tiny Paul was now drawling out: "You ain't going to get no volunteer, Whitman. What man in his right mind is going to leave off his claim to traipse over the mountains on such a fool's errand as this?"

"I don't like to hear it called a fool's errand," I said. "More like a solemn duty. But if nobody volunteers, why, we cast lots for it."

There was a general murmur of assent, but I wanted it codified some. "Raise your hands if you think casting lots is good."

"What is casting lots?" Juan Pablo said.

"Selecting by chance," I said. I tried to remember the word, and somehow it came to me. "*Aleatorio*."

He nodded and put it into better words for his fellows, but I noticed that I'd raised the hackles of some of the Michael Green faction by using Spanish.

I *had* blundered. Of course they took it for an indication of my sympathies, as well as an ostentatious show of learning. I'd lived in the democratic west for years now but still forgot myself from time to time and spoke more intelligently than I should have; a man must always take care about his speech, suppressing his education when discoursing with some, and inflating it with others. If I tell you that caution in this regard is a matter of life and death, you'll find it hard to swallow, but with my own eyes I've seen men die for forgetting themselves and talking too *high and starchy* amongst the wrong company. And so we all generally cut it as low as it would go and still grow back, which wouldn't have made our schoolmarms happy to hear us, but at least allowed us to go on shunning the grave.

From what I could see, all hands went up in support of random selection, but to make certain, I said, "Now raise up your hands if you think casting lots is a *bad* idea."

No hands.

"Good. Now, if you promise to abide by the outcome, even if it's your name comes up, raise your hand."

All hands.

And so we wrote all names on scraps of paper and dropped

them into a hat.

It appeared we were on our way out of trouble now, right until Isaac Ford scratched his belly and growled, "Who in hell's going to *draw* the name, though?"

I shrugged. "Anybody," I said. "You can do it yourself, Ford, if it's fraud that's got you worried."

"The hell he can," George Auburn said. "I don't trust him."

"Now just a minute," I said. "We're all standing right here watching. What kind of a magician would he have to be to fool us when all eyes are straight on him?"

"No deal," Auburn said. "He's for Green, and it ought to be a neutral party."

"Well, Johnny and me we're neutral. One of us will pull the name."

"No deal," one of the Green men echoed. "You it was first accused Green, if I ain't mistaken."

"Well, you are mistaken, then, friend. I never *accused* anybody. I woke Green up to tell him his friend was dead, which is the very long and the very short of it."

I didn't like how warm it was getting. I looked around the camp for some kind of solution and saw that the Blackfoot sisters had quietly retreated back to their laundry shed. I slopped over to where they were working. The younger of the two looked up at me, not at all unkindly.

"I'm in a pinch here," I said to her. "I need your help." I tried to make a motion with my hands in front of my chest that appeared like supplicating, but it felt more like I was offering her something. She smiled warmly at me, and hell if I didn't start blushing like a redheaded schoolboy.

"Will you draw the name?" I said, pantomiming the reaching into a hat, but doing it so exaggerated that I could have been feeling around down a well or helping birth a calf. She was a smart Blackfoot, though, and she nodded and walked with me back through the muck to where the hat was set on a log.

"What's this, then?" Willie Shaughnessy said.

"She's going to pull the name," I said. "She hasn't got a stake in this. She's a perfectly neutral party. Probly don't even know what this row is about."

"I won't speak for others," Shaughnessy said, "but the very last person I'd trust is a Injun."

"Anyway look at her," Tiny Paul said. "She's moony for Whitman. Looks like she'd follow him clear off a cliff. That ain't no way neutral."

This was enough to turn most of the others against the idea.

I shook my head sadly and turned to the Blackfoot sister. "Thank you just the same," I said. But she'd already understood and was slogging back toward her shed.

There was only one thing left to try. The missionaries, too, had snuck back to their tent early in the discussion, and I could see now that the wife had fetched their mule and that they were hastily stowing their plunder, making ready to flee the impending bloodshed.

"Well, how about we have the parson pull the name, then?" I said loudly. "*He* hasn't picked a side, has he?"

At my words, the missionary, one Philemon Gray, straightened his bony back and froze in place for a moment, then went back to tying his bundle, letting on he hadn't heard. His wife, though, holding the mule, looked me directly in the eye before turning away. It wasn't the first glance she'd ever given me, either.

"Come with me, Johnny," I said.

The two of us tramped over to the Grays. "Parson," I said in a low voice. "Your services are needed."

"Not here they aren't," he said without looking up.

"All I want you to do is pull a name out of a hat," I said. "Isn't that a simple enough thing?"

"One might think so, mightn't one?" he said. He looked me in the eye now, and I found myself rather wishing he hadn't. For pure complacency and smugness, no artist could have out-designed that China-cat eye and drooping, thin-lipped mouth, and for about the three hundredth time I found myself wondering how in the Lord's creation a fine woman like Clarissa could have hitched herself to such a snake as this.

"These men are ready to kill, every one of them," he said. "They'll kill the first person who they feel has wronged them. And to pull a slip of paper out of that hat is to wrong one of them. Ergo, to draw a name is to invite violence against oneself. Ergo, to participate in your efforts is no 'simple thing.' "

I should have been used to it by now, but I was so put off by his pedantry that I was momentarily speechless. Johnny spoke. "Aw, hell—excuse me—*heck,* parson," he said. "There's some rough ones in the bunch, but I don't believe there's any so far gone as to lift a hand against a man of the Lord."

Gray sniffed and rolled his eyes. "That is your assessment," he said. "Mine differs."

"Ma'am?" I said. "Would you pull the name?"

"No she most assuredly will not," Gray snapped. "How dare you even ask, sir?"

But I wasn't looking at him. I was looking at his wife. Camp life would have run a lot of women right into the dirt, but the open air seemed only to elevate her. Her left temple was swollen where mosquitoes had bitten her, but her red hair was glossy beneath her bonnet and her eyes gleaming with health, and she filled out her dress as well as any woman I'd ever looked upon. Two mud-daubed mosquito welts down on the side of her neck stirred something in me. She didn't answer my question, but I enjoyed imagining that the look in her eye meant she would have been happy to draw the name if her husband hadn't been such a low, contemptible worm.

"May I ask where you're packing to?" I said.

"Away from here," Gray said. "Good day, gentlemen."

"Good day," I said without stirring. "Are you crossing the mountains?"

He ignored me, but Clarissa silently nodded behind him.

"I think you're crossing those mountains," I said. "Which means you could just as well fetch us a judge to handle this."

"Well, you're wrong," Gray said. "We've been called to Las Vegas. It's south we're traveling, not west."

"Called?" I said, chuckling. "Called in an almighty hurry. Since breakfast, it would even seem."

He unfurled that bland reptile smile of his that was so much worse than his grimace. "The Lord hires no express, nor has need of one," he said.

I couldn't help myself; I snorted right in his face. "Let's go, Johnny," I said. "This man is the very beatenest for lowdown yellow cowardice and shames the cloth by wearing it." I didn't even look back to see his reaction.

The mob had gotten back to its feuding during our absence, and as we walked back over to where they were snarling and yipping at each other, I said to Johnny, "You keep a good eye on things around here and keep a level head. Don't trust any of these men, do you hear me?"

He never got a chance to answer me before we reached the gaggle, where I lifted the hat off the log and dumped the slips of paper into the mud. A kind of religious silence fell over the crowd.

"I leave in one hour to fetch us a judge," I said. "Meantime, disperse, and keep away from each other until we can get this thing settled out."

Predictably, there arose some clatter about whether I was to be trusted. I held up a hand and spoke quietly, as if I was right at the end of my tether. "If you want to keep me honest, damn you, then send one of your number with me," I said.

And as my wretched luck would have it, the man they gave me for a traveling companion was Stormy Isaac Ford.

Chapter Two

Brief sketch of Ford—Johnny wins the rifle—The Christians depart—Teasing a stripling—Belated departure—A tagalong—I name Stormy's mule—Lectured by Ford—I learn the Blackfoot's name—Screams in the night.

Now Stormy Isaac Ford had been one of the original Forty-Eighters, and he didn't ever for a minute let that prized biographical chestnut slip anyone's mind. You see, in that time and place, to have been a Forty-Niner was to be a sort of king, and no paltry one either; but Forty-Eighters? They were popes. Curious pope this one was, too, forever laughing after his rancid, eggy farts, drawing his bowie knife at the slightest hint of quarrel, spitting every few seconds heedless of bystanders, scratching gratuitously at his flea bites, and chewing his pitted yellow tongue as he cogitated over the very plainest facts and propositions.

Yes, landing in the California gold fields at just the right time would have been something to admire in a man with brains and gumption enough to have got him there; but Ford had only to open his mouth and you knew that anything good that had ever befallen him had been the undeserved blessing of a merciful Providence and should in no wise be construed as any feat of the intellect. I have known on this earth men of nearly every stripe and caliber; and I will not stand here and tell you that I found Ford to be the dullest-witted of the lot—but I couldn't recall any that surpassed him in that line, either.

Some others may have wondered why he would leave his stake to chance (for he was without a partner) and chase over the mountains with me, but I thought I knew: despite it having been his professed livelihood for more than a decade (mixed liberally with profitless gambling and low-grade thievery), Ford knew next to nothing about mining. How could he? Even his grasp of the hands in poker was tenuous, so for him to know where to stake a claim or how to work it was asking a goodly sight too much. No, Stormy Isaac Ford was never more comfortable than when drifting along, buffeted by chance into this or that circumstance, never having to tax his mind with details or plague his serenity with aims. It was just as easy and comfortable for him to go fetch a judge as it was to stay put and try to make something of a mining claim.

I had known him a little in California, and once or twice in Colorado I'd chanced upon his company the way a shin chances upon a chair in the dark, and now three weeks ago he'd washed ashore here at the strike I'd made with my brother, about as welcome as the syphilis and only a little bit uglier. It remains a mystery just how word had got out about our strike; it could only have been Johnny, though, running his loose lips while out prospecting downstream, for I never breathed a word of it.

I suppose I shouldn't disparage poor Johnny; for all I know, sometime in his life he'd kept a secret, and I just didn't know about it. But he denied ever running his mouth about our claim, and anyhow I've never put much stock in grudges, especially where kin is concerned. So I more or less held my tongue as the mass of miners came streaming up to the foot of the slope: first Ford and George Auburn and Tiny Paul Maddock and Green and Peter the Great and their lot, then half a day later a troop of near-silent Mexicans or "Mexicans"; and finally that inexplicable admixture of Irish and Chinese, singing and jabbering like it was Babel all over again. Others had straggled in during the days since, and through it all I'd cautioned Johnny against attaching too much jealousy to what we'd found, since I've seen more than a couple of miners enjoying what was rightfully theirs from the inside of a shallow grave.

No, I told him, we'll hold onto what we've officially laid claim to and nothing more, and we'll come out pretty enough all right in the end. Rich is rich, I've always said, and if you can show me a man who sees a practical difference between owning one million and owning ten millions, I'll show you an avid old billygoat who thinks he can't get along on just one stomachful of dinner.

Well, Johnny came now and stood beside me as I sorted through our belongings, laying out my share onto the manty I'd spread out on our pallet. I worked in silence, letting him sulk there until he was ready to talk. Finally he comes out and says, "Why, would it have been such a hard thing for you to have consulted me?"

"Well, I reckon I could have, Johnny," I said. "But what good would that have done me, though?"

"Dang it, Stern, you're the very last man should leave this camp. You know that."

"The last shall be the first. It's even wrote down somewhere."

"It ain't a joke, Stern. We got us a fortune here, and you're waltzing off and leaving it."

I paused and held up a slab of bacon. "Is this enough to keep you fed, Johnny? I don't want you going hungry."

"Take the blamed bacon, goddamn it."

I wrapped the bacon, shaking my head. "I'm not walking away from our fortune, Johnny," I said. "Who knows? I might just have some aim in mind for you and me to profit considerable from this trip of mine."

"Now, just what can you mean by that?"

In a low voice I said, "Better for me not to say at present. Meantime, I've got you here to see that we hold onto what's already ours. All you've got to do is keep working what we've claimed for the next fifteen days. These old-timers are kind of scoundrelly, a lot of them, but they know the rules and live by them, and there isn't one among them is ornery enough to stand idly by and watch you get robbed of your property."

"Well enough. But what about that tiff over the Tsar?"

"What about it? Let the fools tiff."

"And just suppose they drag me into it?"

"Don't drag along."

"Suppose they insist?"

"Then insist right back."

"Yeah? With what?"

"With wh—?" Oh. Now I saw what he was after. I shook my head. "Sorry, Johnny," I said, "but I kind of need to have that rifle with me. That or starve to death, one," I said.

He sighed like I'd sat down on his chest. That boy missed his calling on the stage, I swear to it. "Well," he said, "I wish to Christ I had me a good revolver—or any revolver, really."

"Well, I'm sort of glad you don't, hearing you talk like that."

He was so mad he stamped his foot, and pegs of mud came splashing up and landed on the manty like a spray of stubby little fingers. "Hell, Stern," he said. "Just because we're in a fix don't mean you have to let on there's no danger here. The whole damn reason you're leaving is because you see as clear as I do that these men are fools, like as not to start shooting at each other any minute. And you're leaving me in the midst of it, unarmed, which is a deeply irresponsible thing, and nothing our mother would approve of."

This comment had its desired effect, but he wasn't done yet, for something new had occurred to him. "Say," he said, "hasn't Isaac Ford got him a rifle?"

I didn't like that. "You know that he does," I said.

"Then let *him* hunt up your trail grub, and leave our rifle with me."

I'd been afraid he'd think of that, not least because the logic of it was invincible, and the only thing that made me more uncomfortable than traveling the Sierra unarmed and at the mercy of an old blackguard like Ford was leaving my brother unarmed in this tinderbox.

"Fine," I said. "But don't you for a minute think of starting anything. You use that thing to defend yourself from mortal danger, and not for one thing more. You mark me?"

"I mark you. Thanks, Stern."

The missionaries had cut out minutes after I'd spoken to them. I'd watched them stride resolutely away without so much as a rearward glance at the holy work they were abandoning. As an admirer of the woman, it disappointed me some. Even Lot's wife had fetched a wistful look back at what she was quitting, though perhaps Clarissa was taking to heart the hard lesson learned by that storied antecedent of hers. They led the mule south out of camp, as though I was gull enough to believe them headed anywhere but San Francisco.

I hitched my manties up on my mule and tied him by the halter to our pallet and trudged across to where Ford, days ago, had laid out a single layer of bent and twiggy logs into a rather seasick rectangle, which improvement he insisted upon referring to, with an appalling sense of his own cleverness, as his *cabin.* He'd absorbed that gambit in some mining camp years ago where it had been the law to build on site in order to secure one's legal claim. Now, whatever camp he landed in, he flung together his haphazard version of a "cabin" as a critical first step in fending off competitors, even in districts where such action was no consideration.

He slept on the mud within the contour of this crude and roofless eccentricity, using one of the logs for a pillow, and any kind soul who believed the arrangement to be only temporary was granting an unwarranted compliment to Ford's ambition—and to his architectural gifts, which had been depleted in the placing of the logs into something resembling a square.

Right now, the southeastern "wall" of his building was serving him as a pretty low bench. He was sitting on it with his legs stretched out into the mud before him, jawing at a young miner named Benson who'd only been in camp for a couple of days, haranguing him on the only topic under the sun that could rouse him to enthusiasm: women. "Right up and down the side of her leg, like so," he was saying as I approached. "Say, how many whores you been with, boy?"

Young Benson's eyes widened just slightly at the question, but then you could see in the next half an instant his decision to lie.

Well did I recognize this strain of young manhood, which, if it isn't the only one, has got to be the most common: self-consciousness and self-confidence rolling all over each other like two bears fighting, and you never knew which would spend a moment on top. Your average young bravo knows deep inside that he's got just all manner of strength and ability. He *knows* it, but it's as yet unproven, and he cannot trade on credit for it in any store, and therefore he cannot, for the moment, enjoy true self-confidence. And so he goes about his awkward way blushing and boasting and fuming and groveling and thrusting out his chest and demurring and acting out, each of those in turn, sufficient to make a body wonder just how many souls can inhabit a single set of skin.

Yes, the trouble comes of his refusing to rest until you—all of you—know of his embryonic heroism, all the while that powerful social law insists that he defer to those with *real* achievements to boast of. This state of things wrecks his confidence, spoils his balance, renders him perpetually uneasy, leaves him with a desperate thirst to get onto the black side of the ledger, puts him on constant lookout for auspicious situations from which to forge his reputation. Which, of course, is what makes young men so dangerous, and so useful to the generals.

And it may have been even harder for this particular specimen than for most, cursed as he was with long, curling lashes and the kind of lips that quite a lot of women will paint liberally onto themselves in defiance of short-shrifting nature. In physical appearance he was not very dissimilar from Johnny, though being a few years older Johnny had gained a little experience, and with it the confidence to live down his beauty.

Right now Benson was looking over at me trying to disguise his hopes that I'd arrived to save him from himself. But I was not in the saving vein today and was curious to hear his response besides.

"Don't let me interrupt," I said. "Go ahead and answer the question."

He gulped. He shouldn't have, but he did, regretting it instantly, I knew, and said, " 'Bout eleven."

Ford emitted a grating noise somewhere roughly halfway between choking and smirking. "Eleven whores. That's a tolerable heap of 'em for a child of your age."

Aw, hell. He'd had to go and call him a child. Now, all the boy had to do was laugh off the insult—couldn't he see that Ford wanted him for an audience and wasn't looking for real trouble?—but what I'd seen so far told me that he wouldn't. Sure enough, the youngster out and says, "*Child?* I don't think I'm the *child* you take me for."

There, I'm thinking, *that's sufficient, and nicely put, too.*

But now he unwisely tacks on: "And if you're not careful about things, you'll learn all about it."

Ford didn't get up. He sat there leering at the boy, his pig eyes gleaming with what could easily be mistaken for lust. He didn't draw his bowie, but he did rub theatrically at its smooth butt with his fat thumb and forefinger.

I knew that from Ford's point of view, this was a delicate, even difficult, moment: he had challenged, and been met with challenge, but even he understood the hollow idleness of it all, the predictableness of the boy's response. I watched his eyes slide back and forth as he plumbed the recesses of his entrammeled brain for just the right words—there was, after all, some correct and proper way for escalating this sort of thing one notch at a time—but it was taking too long, and after an awkward beat or two, I saw my chance and intervened.

"*Kid* is all he meant to say," I said. "Not child. And there ain't any shame in youth. I wish to God anybody called me *kid* anymore. Besides which," I added, "there's been plenty of bloodshed around here for now, and Stormy Isaac's got to be picking himself up and shoving off with me for Placerville. That's important business. Hey, Ford?"

Ford hauled himself up off his log seat with such decrepit ponderousness that I hoped it didn't give young Benson any false notions; men like Ford have a way of developing a tiger's agility when riled, and they display a most disheartening carelessness when it comes to losing fingers, teeth, and ears on their way to disemboweling you. But the kid made no move, and when Ford got to his feet he only said to the boy, "You keep in mind who you're talking to, and you'll find that you live considerable longer."

The stripling opened his mouth to speak, but I stuck my hand in front of his face and said, "Enough. Whatever you're thinking about saying, plug it up with the fattest cork that'll fit. It wasn't right of Ford to call you a child, but he's giving you wise counsel now. You'd be a fool not to take it to heart."

Poor kid was steaming up—the twin bears of self-consciousness and self-confidence snarling and slashing each other over—but I couldn't fault him that. Every such meal a man is forced to eat is a kind of soul-poison. But a goodly part of longevity is deciding which is more likely to do you in: an accumulation of those small doses of poison or one lavish helping of bowie knife? The kid lifted a finger, half threat, half proposition, and sputtered, "Well, all right. But the thing cuts both ways. You ought to be careful who you underestimate, too."

Before the rusted machinery of Ford's derelict works could churn out any kind of response, I said, "True enough. A good lesson all the way around. Now if you'll excuse us, Mr. Benson, we've got that business to attend to."

He stomped away through the mud like someone who means to go tell his mother. I turned to Ford and quickly said, "You about ready to push off?"

He shrugged. "Can't seem to find my mule," he said.

This wasn't the thing I most wanted to hear. "Christ Jesus," I said. "And did you think you'd find it by sitting here on your cabin jawboning at that tenderfoot? Hell, it'll be dark before we can leave. I'll give you one more hour, and then I'll go without you, and you can explain to your friends why it is you're still here."

The younger Blackfoot sister was waiting beside the tattered ruins of my tent. On her back she bore a loaded pack basket, and I saw that she was wearing moccasins, where normally she barefooted it around the camp. I reckon you've gathered by now that she was a beauty; at least I thought so. Her only fault that I could see was she was missing two or three toes, but I'm not one to get bogged down in trifles, and now her feet were covered anyhow.

Living mostly in mining camps and lick-skillet settlements, a man can't be very particular about his women, and yet it does happen to just about all of us that we develop our pet tastes and preferences, whether or not we'll ever have the luxury of exercising them. To my eye, a lot of those Indian women are rather flattish and squared-off in places where you want some padding, but this one was different in that regard, and she had a kind, intelligent eye besides.

More than one night I'd stared up into the darkness and entertained a hotly argued mental debate as to the competing merits of this girl and those of Clarissa Gray, the missionary's wife. Generally the Blackfoot came out the winner, which in the end had as much to do with her character as anything else. Not that I wasn't drawn to Clarissa's character—she was spirited, and I like a spirited woman—but there was at times a little too much challenge behind those eyes, a bit too much flare about the proud nostrils, which might have been her husband's complacency spilling over some. The Blackfoot had just as much brass, as I estimated it out, but she wasn't afraid to cast a kindly eye your direction, which I liked a sight better than Clarissa's haughty sneer. Right now this Blackfoot looked just as pretty as I'd ever seen her, but she wasn't smiling. Nervous, I guessed, which touched me some.

"Looks like you're fixing to travel," I said to her and walked the first two fingers of my right hand across the palm of the left: a spindly-legged man hightailing it across a desert.

She nodded, not two or three times like we do but once, as if the gesture settled everything for good.

"Where?" I asked, shrugging broadly and scanning my surroundings like a country Jake who's lost his bearings at the fair.

She touched her hand to her breast and then opened it toward me.

"With me?" I clutched at my heart: seizure, genuflection.

Again, that one solid nod.

I opened both hands, palms toward each other, and waved them in exaggerated confusion. "Why?" I said.

She nodded again.

Well, it was too many for me. Other than offering to build her a shitter, all I'd ever done is smile at her and mumble incomprehensibly as I handed her either my dirty britches or payment for her having washed them. If she was offering herself to me, I couldn't fathom it, certainly not with Johnny around. Women were generally hard put to remember of my existence once Johnny came on the scene. No, it must have been something else. Likely she had some errand over the mountains, and this was her chance to travel in the company of men. Well, if she chose to tag me, then far be it from me to object; it confused me a good deal, but I was more than reconciled to it in an instant. I knew the resourcefulness of Indian women, knew them to be invaluable traveling companions; and, besides, a good-looking woman could go some way toward compensating my having to look upon Stormy Isaac Ford all day long.

I offered her a seat on the pallet, but she declined, preferring to stand there straight as a steeple as I checked over the mule's load and then sat and watched the camp returning to its normal activity. The two rabid crowds had dispersed; most of the men were up on the hill shoveling, or carrying loads of dirt down to the stream, or squatting in the water swirling their pans. Off to the east a little, just above the shitter on a small rise, Michael Green and a few of the men had the remnants of Peter the Great rolled up in a torn tent canvas and laid out on the thin grass like an enormous bullet. They were digging his grave, and I couldn't help but notice, even at this distance, the furtive inspections they made of each spadeful of earth they moved, checking for color, to be sure they weren't squandering opportunity.

By and by Ford trudged over to us, leading his scrawny mule, which was so haphazardly loaded that already it had its ears laid back like skids and its eyes stretched wide with discomfort. Ford glared at the Blackfoot sister and growled, "The hell's this?"

"She's coming along," I said.

He stared at her a good long while, his craving eyes traveling all up and down her curves. As much as I love to look at a woman, I usually can't bear to see another man do it. I've always wondered if it makes me look half so ugly as a lot of them do.

"Good," he grunted at last.

"All right," I said. "Say, Isaac, what's your mule's name?"

"Name? Hell, hasn't got any name."

"No? Mind if I name her?"

"*I* don't give a continental. Name her after your mother for all it plagues me."

"All right, then. Let's call her Jezebel."

"Jezebel. That's your mother's name?"

"No, sir."

"Jezebel's good," he said. "Do we shove off now?"

"Well, if it's all the same, I'd just as soon we make Jezebel a bit more comfortable. You mind if I shift her load a little bit?"

"Well," he said, "I'd have set her up better myself, but for you've been in such a pison hurry to shove off." But as he said it he plunked himself down on my pallet and waved his hand in consent.

The instant I stepped over to the mule and reached for the pack rope, the Blackfoot woman was there on the other side, uncinching and rebalancing the load. It took us all of two minutes, and then we got under way.

A few feet down the trail, Ford twisted around and called out, "Say, there, Whitman. What's *your* mule's name?"

"Ahab."

"Ahab. And what'd you say mine's name was?"

"Jezebel."

He wasn't chewing, but he spat a jet of yellowish liquid off to the side. "Well, Christ Jesus Almighty," he said. "You might have come up with a set of names that warn't quite so god-damned *secluded.*"

By now it was early afternoon, the sun high and broad in the world, but not overheating it any. The night's storm had cleared the air nicely, and now it fairly sang with freshness and promise. With the camp at my back, my feet rejoiced in my boots to be moving again. Ah, woe to the young man who falls in love with movement! For fifteen years now, I'd been incapable of staying put anywhere, such was my lust for the trail, and nobody gets very far ahead in this world if he isn't able to hold still and get a thing or two accomplished somewhere.

We followed the river along and unspooled a few miles of easy travel before the slope increased. Our little troop plodded along in the sunshine, everyone glad to be out of the mud, right down to the mules. The woman walked in front, Ford and Jezebel in the middle, and me last to keep an eye on his load—and on him. I put precious little trust in the man. There was a pretty well-known story of his having beaten a fellow nearly to death back in Colorado, and that wasn't the worst of what I'd heard.

The Colorado anecdote was as senseless as it was predictable. Ford's victim, a timid little rack of bones named Cornwall, had committed the unpardonable sin of waking Ford from a sound sleep at a time when Ford would rather not have awakened. I say Cornwall was timid, but only when sober; and that night he was spreeing it awfully hard and got to be about fourteen feet tall, and no amount of pleading and coaxing from his fellows could rein him in. After Cornwall broke a glass lamp right beside where Ford was sleeping, Ford bolted up like he was spring-operated, vomited profusely into his own lap, then leaped onto his unsteady feet to locate the source of the racket.

Well, Cornwall couldn't decide which was funnier, the sitting up or the vomiting. Two of his chums clutched hold of him and began trying manfully to steer him clear of Ford, but Cornwall was in a hectoring mood, fired up by liquor and thrilled to be slinging insults at a man three times his size. Even though he was on his way out the door, he didn't get more than six or seven loud words out before Ford came crashing into him like a bull buffalo.

Cornwall needed his friends more than ever now, but they were newly absent, having all just remembered prior commitments of one kind and another; and for the next five minutes Ford had his way with Cornwall. It was two solid weeks before Cornwall's eyes came open again, and he wasn't right in the head afterward. Still, he was lucky: Ford had gambled away his bowie just hours before the incident, and had had to resort to his fists. If he'd had the weapon at his belt as usual, every single stroke he'd delivered Cornwall would have been sharpened metal and not just dull fist. There had been a not-dissimilar incident in Taos, I'd heard, in which Ford had swung his bowie, underhanded, up between his victim's scrawny legs from behind, burying it to the hilt—and that had merely been his opening salvo.

Yes, Ford was a caution, but for now all was quiet. Here on this side of the Sierra the snow had gone weeks ago, and we strolled easily among girlish pines with needles so new and fresh they felt like leaves between your fingers, and among scattered boulders long since whitewashed by unfathomed centuries of sun.

But this kind of peace can never last. By and by the hushed and pure solemnity of the forest must have begun to chafe at Stormy Isaac, who felt he had to talk filthy or die. Where the clearing was wide enough, he halted his mule and waited for me to draw alongside, and when I did, he said, "What's your claim on that woman, Whitman?"

I said, "What makes you ask, Ford?"

"Well," he said, "it ain't every man could put up with her wigglin' around beneath that doeskin as long as I have. If she's your woman, out with it, and I'll either pay up or leave off. If she ain't, I aim to help myself."

"Well, what if I said she wasn't my woman, but she wouldn't have you, Isaac? What then?"

"Well, I don't see where that could be any of her concern."

"*She* might think it is, though. And I reckon she knows how to use that knife on her belt."

He grinned. "You'd be afeared of a little old thing like that?" he said.

"It might just deter me, come to think of it," I said.

"Haw. That's only for show. These squaws ain't like our Christian women. They *like* it."

"Well, it doesn't matter, Isaac, because to answer your question, yes, that's my woman. And she ain't for sale, nor rent neither."

Ford's eyes widened with a wounded sense of camaraderie, and he spat in genuine disgust. "Thunder and lightnin'," he said. "I never remembered you to be so stingy and unneighborly back in Californy. You've put on considerable airs over the years, that I can see."

"Maybe I have. So what?"

"So what? So it makes your society powerful unpleasant, that is just what. Lord Christ Jesus Almighty God, it does just about beat the Dutch, you takin' on so back at camp, ordering around men nearly twice your age, bullyraggin' true-blue Forty-Eighters like they was so many schoolboys; naming mules; and now! Now you've got yourself set so high up that you can't see your way clear to let one of your betters enjoy a scrawny seven-toed squaw for a few minutes, all because . . ."

He trailed off there, sputtering ineffectually. Evidently he'd been retaining the speech for hours, but once the sluice was opened, the contents wouldn't slide clear of the trough quite the way he'd hoped; something was clogging it. It *was* a pretty solid chunk of oratory, anyway, and glossy enough, too, for the likes of him, but somehow it left me untroubled. In fact, I found it heartening, for it amounted to nothing more momentous than idle grumbling, to bootless complaint, and when a man chooses to grumble it's because he's already decided not to fight.

So I was plenty happy to let him expend himself with words. Which he set out to do, with hell's own fury. Even after Ahab and I passed him silently by he came stumbling along behind, roundly damning me, the mule, and our forebears alike.

Yes, he was merely grumbling for now, but I knew I'd have to watch him.

By evening we were leaning hard into the slope, beating steadily uphill, sweating even in the cool shadows, while down behind us the greensward lay in damp, rich shade, and beyond it, out on the storybook plain, the desert still rippled in the late-day heat. Twice now, on encountering flat spots suitable for bedding down, the woman had turned back and fixed my eye questioningly, and twice I had motioned for us to continue.

As pleasant as the journeying was, I did not mean to draw it out any longer than was necessary. I hated to think of Johnny back there among those ignorant savages. Even the best among them—take the Benson kid—lacked all judgment, and there was still a smart quantity of liquor in camp, thanks to that bastard Compass, who'd slunk off to other precincts once he'd done his damage and amassed his pile. But soon it would be dark in earnest, so when a third level clearing presented itself, I nodded to the woman and began unloading the mule. When I slipped free my hatchet, she held out her hand for it and set to work gathering firewood.

Stormy Isaac had fallen far behind. By the time he came hobbling into camp I had bacon curling in the pan, and the woman was browning a long strip of dough twisted around a green stick.

"Thunder and lightnin'," he said, dropping the mule's lead and throwing himself to the ground beside the fire. "What is the everlastin' rush? I never see anybody run up a hill as fast as the two of you, without they was being chased by Injuns. What's that? Bacon? Good. Serve me up a panful, pard. I'm nation hungry."

"We're all nation hungry, Ford. What did you bring to eat?"

"Oh, I'll cook tomorrow. Breakfast."

"Fine. Unload Jezebel and get you something to eat."

"Unload? Unload hell. What the deuce for? Just to turn around and load her back up again come morning? That ain't the way this old child travels, pup."

"You prefer traveling with a mule that's sore-backed and lame, is that it?"

"Hell. I reckon she can stand it one night."

"Aren't you going to need to unpack to cook us breakfast?"

He was pulling off his boots. "Cross that bridge when I come to it," he grunted. "Right now, I aim to set here and eat some grub unmolested, and I don't need you nor anybody else's grandma to tell me how to cross country."

He swallowed a full plate of bacon and two generous helpings of bread, demanded more, pouted when I refused him, and from somewhere on his person produced a wretched old pipe and a greasy pouch of rancid tobacco that might have come down from Walter Raleigh himself. He puffed sulkily two or three times and abruptly plummeted off to sleep with the pipe laid over on his belly, whisping its last.

In the new quiet, the woman and I cooked for ourselves, and despite my good breeding I set my portion aside to warm until hers was ready so that we could eat together. Normally I would never have exercised such bad form, but I suppose the events of the day had defiled my judgment. The unspoken spirit of unity against Ford had colored my feeling toward her to where I'd quite foolishly begun to think of her as a proper woman, and no mere squaw. That shows you the danger of keeping bad company. To her credit, she at first tried to insist that I eat before her, but she might easily have shown a bit more decorum and *gone on* insisting. Instead, she half smiled and, when her food was cooked, lifted her bread as jauntily as some drawing-room petticoat wishing *bon appétit,* and brazenly took her first bite almost while I was still chewing mine.

In the moment, I didn't care. I liked the way she looked in the firelight, the way she set her square white teeth into the bread, the steam moistening her upper lip, the way her brown throat moved when she swallowed.

"What's your name, anyhow?" I said.

She answered me something indecipherable, and I pointed at myself and said, "I'm Whitman."

She nodded her one-per-customer nod and said, "Stern Whitman."

"Hell! You have it. That's it, right there: Stern Whitman."

I pointed at her, then, and said, "What's your name?" and she made the same sounds she'd made before, which meant she'd known the first time what I was asking.

I tried to imitate the syllables of her name, but it just about split her sides to hear me do it, and I feared for her health if I tried it again. After a minute she stood up and began circling the fire, making a humming sound and flicking her hands rapidly by her sides, mimicking wings.

"Hummingbird," I said.

She stopped and cocked her head, and I repeated: "Hummingbird?"

"Bird. No," she said.

She took two more flying turns around the fire and then, seeming to settle just beside me, she stretched out one wing and pinched me hard just above the elbow.

"Ow," I said. "Hornet?"

She hesitated, with what I took to be a Blackfoot-style shrug.

"Hornet," I said. "Hullo, Hornet. Or else Yellow Jacket or Wasp or Bumbly-Bee, one. Lands sake, I hate to think how you might have come by that kind of a name."

But she wasn't done. Now she was a human again, dipping her finger into some invisible substance and smearing it onto her tongue, which operation appeared to bring her no small measure of delight.

"Honey!" I said.

She smiled then like a roomful of children, bigger than I'd reckoned it possible for an Indian to smile.

"Hell, I don't know why we went through all that," I said. "I reckon I'd have come onto that name for you all on my own."

A man says some almighty dashing things to women when he knows he can't be understood.

When it was time to sleep, I pushed all the coals together and stretched out on the ground, taking care to place myself between Isaac and Honey. I stared up at the patch of stars burning behind the haze of wood smoke and thought about Johnny down there in the valley.

I hated to think of him there all alone among such men. Somehow my mind got onto how Johnny had been as a boy—just about as honest and earnest and happy as it's possible to be—and then I thought of all our wanderings, how he was always there by my side, helping me not to be so selfish, how good he was to children and dogs and widows and the like.

How happy he'd been to get married, and how heartbroken after his woman had died. How one January day in Wisconsin we'd squandered the whole morning helping a doe and her fawn that had broken through the ice; by the time we'd got them out they'd been in the water so long their eyes were glazed and their legs had stopped working, and I was all for eating them. But Johnny insisted we build a fire, and we rubbed their limbs until they could walk, first the mother, who stood off waiting, and then the youngster. And we could have used the meat, too.

Now I had a sick feeling, a gnawing notion that I would never see Johnny again in this world. It lasted a good long while, so real and so awful that I almost woke that woman just to seek cheer in her pretty, smiling face. But by and by that feeling slacked off, and I reviewed all the decisions of the day and concluded I'd played my hand the best possible way, and that Johnny would be just fine. I had some notion of lying awake to see whether the woman Honey, who hadn't left my sight all day, would steal off to take care of her needs—just as a favor to Johnny, you understand, and not to satisfy any cheap curiosity of my own. But fatigue outmatched my generosity, and at last I drifted off to sleep.

It was screaming that awoke me an hour or two later, the kinds of screams you'd just as soon go a lifetime never hearing: screams that tell of mortal terror, of savagery and blinding pain. In an instant I was on my feet, hatchet in hand. In the gloom I could see the whitish shape that was the woman Honey's doeskin floating beside me, and now to my right I heard Stormy Isaac Ford breathing hard through gritted teeth: "Hell's doin' all that screaming?"

Somehow I knew, even in all that disjointed confusion. "Hell,"

I said, "it's those damn fool missionaries, getting torn up by Paiutes."

Chapter Three

An uneasy night—We find the Grays—Carelessly unsaid prayers—Raised by porcupines—Strange Diggers—Religious error—A hasty raid.

The sky held clear, but the moon had come and gone, and now the riverbed and its clumps of willows lay clothed in an almost perfect darkness. There was nothing we could do for those missionaries until first light. Maybe you've read dime novels about scouts who can flit through such obscurity like so many cats, but I can tell you that when it's too dark to see, a body with sense will stay put, no matter how many tribes have made him honorary chief and insisted he marry their princesses. Yes, we knew the missionaries must be directly upriver of us, and, yes, it's a simple enough matter to chase upstream when you can see the bank all laid out before you and the sunlight glistening in the riffles. But at night, things and their results have a way of magnifying, such that to step into a gopher hole is to plunge down a well, and to walk over a three-foot drop is to plunge headlong down a precipice. And I didn't consult the others but just presumed that such catastrophes were in nobody's plans.

No, there wasn't anything for it but to smother our coals and to sit up and wait for morning. The one glimmer of hope for the missionaries was that, after considerable of that infernal screaming, a rifle had been discharged, once—after which the screaming had abruptly quit. Now, our hope, of course, was that the shot had been fired by Philemon Gray, and that it had driven off the Indians; and that was no unreasonable hope, either, since few Paiutes carried firearms. But few isn't to say none, and it was just possible that the screamer had been done for by a single shot from a Paiute rifle. In the morning we would hunt up the scene and learn what we could.

And my, but wasn't that one long, uneasy night! If the Paiutes had detected the missionaries, we ourselves could scarcely hope to have escaped their notice, for we had taken no caution in building a handsome fire and filling our stretch of valley with the scent of cooking bacon, the Indians in those parts being less inclined toward brazen raids than to smouching your belongings while your back was turned.

Now, I'll not stand here and denigrate the gallantry of Indians, but I will say that it's a rare one who isn't judiciously mindful of his odds, so it seemed likely they had chosen the missionaries as the weaker of the two parties. But if they had been successful in plundering the Grays, then they might feel emboldened to make a run on our camp, as well. So we sat up the livelong night, wishing we'd picketed our mules closer, repenting of our bacon, and silently chewing on our apprehensions.

Yes, wide-eyed and blindly we sat, each contemplating his estate, recounting despite himself the most merciless Indian depredations contained in the lore, and rehearsing what he would do if three Paiutes should attack from this direction, or two from that, or one from here and four from there. If a breeze rubbed two soft aspen leaves together in the canopy overhead, we felt the cacophony explode in our blood the same as if we'd been standing beneath the whistle of a steamboat when it went off. And if, a hundred yards away, a rodent working the night shift grew careless about his footing and caused a twig to grate for an inch or two over the forest floor, why, we wished we could have died and had it all over with. Fortunately, we only needed to endure about four million of these alarms before the washed-out purple of dawn began to show between the trees.

Not that we were out of all danger yet, for what the dime novels do have down correctly is that Indians adore to attack just at the very first light of day. So we waited still, while the mists faded off and our surroundings came back into view. Presently the growing light showed Honey, sitting smartly with her back to what had been our fire, her little bone-handled dagger unsheathed and pointed toward the treetops. And over here on my other side sat Ford, scowling and wretched, rifle across his lap and bowie drawn. And there where we had picketed them stood Ahab and Jezebel, lounging indifferently alongside each other, muzzle to ham, like old friends. Nor did they appear so very far off as we'd remembered them being, after all. In fact, the soft light streaming down between the trees bathed everything in such a golden beneficent hue that the thought of our nocturnal fears was cause for embarrassment.

I stood stiffly and chuckled, and though I intentionally shaped that chuckle to be the low and quiet kind, still it seemed to ring like thunder in those silent woods. "Some night that was," I said when I'd recovered a little from the chuckle. "What do you say we beat around here and see what we can find of those missionaries?"

Ford groaned his way up to his feet and farted and coughed and hawked and spat, and I realized this was likely the longest stretch he'd ever gone without making one or another rude bodily noise, and I felt for him some. "There ain't going to be nothing left of 'em anyhow," he said. "But I don't mind casting around for their leavin's for a short spell, so long as it don't take all morning."

Honey rose to her feet just as spry as if she'd only plunked down there a few seconds ago, belted her knife, and looked at me, jabbering in her language and pointing west up the river.

"You reckon so, do you?" I said.

Heavy nod.

"Honey says this way, Stormy. Seems right to me."

Ford shrugged massively. "These Injuns is seldom mistaken. I reckon they can smell things a Christian can't."

I nodded at Honey, and she went and fetched the mules, helped us load them in a twinkling, and set off along the riverbank with the carefree bearing of a schoolgirl. As we followed behind her, I began shouting Gray's name.

Although it startled all five of us anew to hear my nerve-jangling yells after such a night of stillness, I reckoned it was better than sneaking up on the missionary and being shot dead for my troubles—if he was alive, that is, and if he could hit anything on purpose, both of which I somewhat doubted. But we hadn't searched for more than a minute before we heard a man's voice calling out in reply.

Honey stopped and waved me forward, evidently level headed enough to know he'd shoot immediately upon seeing an Indian—any Indian—coming through the trees. I called again, and Gray halloed back, and we found the pair of them, alive, cowering up against one of those white boulders, scared as a pair of rabbits set down in a kennel of hounds. Gray was clutching at his rifle, and his wife was hugging herself all over and trembling like to come right out of her skin.

"Well, Gray," I said, stepping forward. "It's good to see the two of you alive."

"Praise God in heaven, Clarissa. We are saved. Our friends are here."

I didn't guess it was appropriate circumstances to be correcting him as to who was and wasn't friends, so I let it slide. He was wearing what looked to be a pretty respectable gash across the base of his neck and on down his shoulder, and the woman's face was a good deal bruised up, her dress tattered and filthy. Both of them were shaking as though the attack had just finished up instead of adjourning so many long hours previous.

"How bad hurt are you?" I said.

Gray tried to stammer something out, but after his initial outburst words would not seem to come, and his wife appeared as dumbstruck as a trout. Rather than trouble them to talk, I began looking over their wounds. Gray's injury was long but shallow, more scratch than cut, and had already left off bleeding. I motioned for Honey to pour water over it, and then I had a look at Clarissa.

Her right eye was so purple and yellowed that I feared the bones were smashed around it. The asymmetry of that expressionless pulpy eye next to her uninjured left one was uncommonly disturbing, and more so since all the proud fire had gone out of that left eye, replaced by an awful film of fear mixed with resignation. When I reached out my hand, she yanked back her head like a horse that won't take the bit.

"I'll not hurt you," I said to her. "I just mean to look you over and see to your wounds. Where does it hurt you the most?"

I saw that this confused her; I really believe that until that moment she hadn't known herself to be injured. This sounds like a curiosity indeed, but I have observed more than once that the excitement of circumstance can blot out a person's sensitivity to even the most excruciating bodily pain. She let me probe around that eye a little, and there wasn't any give to it, so I satisfied myself that the bone there lay intact.

But around her lips and chin was smeared a little too much blood for me to feel satisfied. "Can you open up your mouth for me, Mrs. Gray?" I said. She obeyed, and I saw she'd lost an incisor and that the tooth beside it was dangling by a thread. Her tongue was awful cut and swollen.

"Give her some water, Honey," I said.

Gray had sat down beside Ford, who had wasted no time making himself comfortable, and the two were watching proceedings, Ford likely with prurient interest in this beaten, vulnerable, semi-clad woman, and Gray with the blank stare of the victim.

"I'm going to touch you a little now to see where else you're hurt," I said, looking over to Gray for permission. But he just went on staring like a storekeeper mentally tallying his accounts at suppertime. "Let me know if I hurt you."

I ran my palms along her shoulders and down her arms, then over her back and ribs. She winced a little at the pressure against her right side, but I calculated she was only bruised up there, and nothing fractured. I dared not venture further in my examination.

"Well," I said, "it may not feel like it, but neither one of you is badly hurt that I can tell."

Turning sidelong to Gray, Ford spoke for the first time: "What become of your mule?" he growled.

"It . . . the savages . . ."

"Yes," I said. "I reckon that's mainly what they were after. What'd you do, put yourself in their way? Well, can't say I blame you, after all, and it's no matter besides. We'll travel on together one big party. Ford, how about you scare up some breakfast for us all?"

He looked at me as though I'd asked him to dance a hornpipe or recite a sonnet. "*Me?* Well, why the hell don't *you* scare up some breakfast if you're so pison hungry?"

"Why, Christ Jesus Almighty Lord, Stormy, it's because I fed you last night. And because you swore up and down that you'd cook breakfast for me and Honey this morning."

Ford sniffed and crossed his arms where he sat. "Wahl," he said. "I ain't above cooking for my betters. But you was still tuggin' cow tits in Missouri when I was panning the color up in the Sacramento Valley. And as for *her,* I'd admire to see the day when Stormy Isaac Ford cooks bacon for a smutty little seven-toed Blackfoot."

He did just about beat all creation for pure obstinate gall. But I decided to follow his line of argument to see what else he might turn up. "Why, Ford, are you telling me that this man of God and his vessel are not your betters?"

This stumped him for just a moment or two. But with the peril of physical labor all around him, he dug deep, sifted his pan, and came up with a nugget: "Now, that's a close one, I'll admit it," he said, with a scholarly frown. "He's got me beat on upbringin', and on education, and on religion." He held up a filthy finger to represent each of these points. "But we ain't in no drawing room, nor school, nor church. We're in the by-God Sierra mountains, and the bare fact of it is that this man don't know enough to protect his mule and his pelt from a couple of moth-eaten savages. So, no—no, sir, he *ain't* my better."

A part of me was kind of proud of him, a little, for sticking with it and for building out an argument that had some structure to it. Anyway, Honey had already started a fire, and before very long we had some coffee and bacon going. The Grays were still too stricken to eat, and it would likely be a day or two until Clarissa's mouth was sufficiently healed to allow her to endure any chewing or swallowing. But we got Philemon to sip some coffee, and over the little meal he began to come to his senses and to look around at his surroundings a bit less like a sheep in a slaughterhouse.

I could tell he'd be all right in a day or two, but I wasn't so confident about the woman, and I'd have gladly had it the other way around. That missionary and I had clashed daily ever since he'd come snuffling into camp looking for souls to save, and not a syllable from his lips had ever sat right with me. I'll come right out here and admit straight off that I'm not the missionarying type; my idea is to let a body alone and see but what he doesn't come around to your way of thinking all on his own. But to harangue and hector and petition and threaten, all in hopes of winning people to your creed? I've never put stock in that.

Of course, that's because my own religious training never took hold, and that's not any fault of my mother, I hasten to say. No, for her it was morning prayer, evening prayer, prayer at every meal, and prayer ad hoc as needed, which when you tallied it all up was pretty close to constant praying. And a lot of the responsibility for it fell upon me, too, for each of us has but one jaw and one tongue, and with such an overwhelming pile of praying to get through daily, and Pa run off, everybody had to pitch in to keep from falling behind, even the littlest ones. I'm proud to say it was done with scarcely any complaint, for we all understood the importance of keeping our accounts squared.

There was only one time we ever went into arrears, and you couldn't blame Mama, for she was laid up with a fever so hot that she was out of her mind for days and days, unable to pray or to oversee the praying, and we feared to lose her outright. Oh, we certainly did pray, all of us, and did it by the minute, too. But we never consulted one another as to *which* prayers were getting taken care of. As it happened, we were all praying *after Mama's health,* and letting all the other prayers slide! Well, at the end of eight days, when Mama could sit up and sip a little broth, the shock of seeing that heap of unsaid prayers just about laid her flat again. For they had smothered the yard, and buried the woodpile, and capped the fence posts, and drifted up to the very window sash of her bedroom! And all of us too blinded by concern for her to have noticed.

She didn't waste one second setting things to right, even in her reduced state. She divided us up into committees and had us go right to it, and we laid into it like we meant it, too, and sometime around dawn of the next morning you could see the yard again, and by noon we were in the clear. It was a close one, though, and a lesson to us all in wise management.

Anyhow that's what I told Philemon Gray on his first day in our camp, and I don't fully believe he took me at my word, for he said to me, "There'll be a place in the great hereafter for those who would mock the righteous, and I wouldn't trade places with you for all the riches on earth."

I thought that was ratcheting things up rather abruptly, and so I smiled and said, "You'll have to excuse me, Reverend. It's my blamed upbringing that's fashioned me so, and I allow that if I'd ever had a mother or a father, or seen the inside of a Sunday school, I'd be a different man today than the impious wretch that stands now before you. But you never see a child as kicked around and cast off as I was, and it's been hard times for me straight from the cradle. Well, I say 'cradle,' but only as a figure of speech, for I never enjoyed that mode of luxury. I've heard tell of lost youngsters that was raised by wolves, and I've always envied them considerable, for it was my lot to be suckled by a mother porkypine, which was better than starvin' to death and dying; but it did smart like blazes to have to yank out the quills after every meal. Still, it was the only tenderness ever showed to me, and what little good there is in my heart I owe to that porkypine, and to all her collaterals who contributed to my upkeep. And to this day when I see a squaw with a fine pair of moccasins all done up with quillwork, I can't stomach it somehow, for I know what's behind it, which is the sacrifice of the distant relations of my only kin."

"But I thought you had a brother here in camp?"

"Oh, I do, but we warn't raised together. No, 'twas badgers brought Johnny up, which accounts for his all-fired haughtiness, for there isn't a mammal on the American continent puts on airs like a badger does. And if you think Johnny will ever let me forget of his superior fostering, then you don't know the ways of badgers. Now, the funny thing about it is that the badgers condescend to the porkypines, all the while the porkypines are looking down their noses at the badgers. The badgers believe themselves to be the quality because they ain't studded all over with quills, of course; but the porkypines know that a badger ain't anything more than a naked porkypine, which makes him a low, inferior thing. To them. This is a debate that goes back millions of years, of course, without resolution, and I wish I could say that Johnny and me was above hashing it out now and again.

"And yes, as far as religion goes, we come up through with some of what you likely would consider some peculiar notions. For my side, I took it early on that Jesus Christ was a hickory stump—a particular one, you understand, not just any—and I never had anybody to correct me in that until I was nearly forty. And by that time the false idea had set there fixed in my head for so long that it's awful stubborn to try and shake loose, though I have tried and tried. So to hear you talk of Jesus Christ, try though I might, all I see is a hickory stump."

"Sir, your facetiousness is abhorrent."

He thought so—but Clarissa was doing everything she could not to laugh as hard as the boys.

And now here she was beat up awfully bad, hugging herself as though that were all the comfort to be furnished by this cruel world. But then I saw Honey come up and sit behind her and put her hands on Clarissa's shoulders like you would a child's, and after a minute Honey fishes down into her pack basket and comes out with a genuine hair brush, and she sets out to straightening that rat's nest that Clarissa's hair had become overnight. Well, old Philemon, he doesn't like this one bit, so he emerges from his dumbfoundedness to blurt out: "You there. Quit that!" and hisses at Honey as though she's a mangy cat come prowling round church during service.

Honey freezes and looks over at me sort of wide-eyed.

"Gray," I said. "Let her be. Can't you see your wife needs a kindly hand?"

"Well, not from the likes of *her* she doesn't."

"Why, look around you, Gray. Who else is going to comfort her? You? Have you ever even touched her?"

At those words Gray set in to trembling again, this time with impotent fury, and I saw I'd let my mouth run off without me, a habit which will one day deliver me my Waterloo. In my favor, though, I'm quick to correct things when I can see I've overplayed. "I had no call to say that, Gray," I said. "I apologize for it. But Honey's only trying to help, and I believe it'll do your wife some good to be petted by her a little."

That placated him, some. Just enough and no more. "She'll be looked after well once we reach Placerville," he said with a voice not untainted by malice. "The best thing is for us to begin moving."

"There's where we agree, right there," I said.

In a few minutes we were crossing country again, snaking along with the river ever higher and closer to where the ancient snows of those iron peaks glowered fiercely beneath a fine midmorning light. Now and then we passed beneath cool sheltering groves of ponderosa pines, the smell intoxicating, the stillness divine; and when we emerged out the other end, it was often enough into a world of high meadows and wildflowers bursting with daylight and birdsong and the chatter and flutter of contemporaneous insect civilizations plying their various economies. I led the way now, with Honey behind me walking alongside Clarissa, Gray next, and Ford straggling in the rear.

I would like to have seen Clarissa Gray do anything besides stumble mutely along with that awful vacancy in her good eye, but I was gladder than ever to have Honey there, to nurse her through. A time or two as I turned around to check on everyone's progress, I caught wind of Honey babbling softly to Clarissa, a kind of mothering tone that I calculated could possibly do the stricken woman some good and anyhow couldn't hurt. Still, I hoped Philemon wouldn't hear it, for it seemed the kind of thing to fluster him, and maybe some folks are agreeable enough when flustered, but Philemon Gray never was.

We nooned in the shade of a cottonwood a few feet above a pleasing little rock-strewn flat along the river where the tule grass wasn't too thick. I couldn't help, sitting there, thinking what a fine thing it would have been for me and Honey to have been traveling alone and to have found that spot. Instead I had a surly missionary, his dumbstruck wife, and a half-witted miscreant along to spoil the beauty of what would have, in the world of my fancy, been a magical setting.

Not just a little bit disgusted, I sought to distract myself by rambling up the stream bed looking for the color and saw behind me that Ford had done the same—opposite direction—though I wondered if he'd know gold if he felt it crunching amongst the pebbles beneath his boot soles and saw it gleaming in the sun already fashioned into coinage. I turned up some flecks that appeared to hold some promise, but I only took a sample or two and made no move to tuck them into my pocket but held them secretly in my palm until I was certain Ford's attention was directed elsewhere. I took good mental note of the place and resolved to return alone or with Johnny at a later date.

We had all finished our dinner and were rising to depart when Gray cleared his throat and commenced to telling us what had befallen them the night before. We sat back down and listened.

He and Clarissa had made good time after leaving camp but

late in the day had been accosted, he said, by a family of Digger Indians.

"I believe you're mistaken there, Gray," I interrupted. "What you want for this story is Paiutes; your Digger hasn't got the gumption nor spite to have brought you to such grief."

"No, Whitman," says Gray rather coldly. "I know my Indians, and these were Diggers. I even speak a word or two of their language. It will be a sorry day indeed when I mistake a Paiute for a Digger."

"Pardon me, then, and be on your way," I said.

Well, to continue, this was the sorriest, most godforsaken set of Diggers Gray had ever laid eyes upon, which is saying something indeed, for the Digger disenjoys a reputation as the most luckless pauper who ever walked upright. He is a perennial starveling; an injured, slouching, friendless pilgrim who gets the better part of his nutrition by grubbing for roots, munching insects, and shooing buzzards off of carrion. One of this passel, the *pater familias,* had recently lost both ears—or only nearly so, to speak accurately, for he was not yet fully quit of them: they dangled down either side of his face by two thin strips, blackened and leathery, and swung liberally each time he turned his head.

His woman had lost most of her hair and was so diminutive and scrawny as to be easily misplaced among the children, with two of whom the pair was traveling. The only clues to the woman's sex and age were her shriveled, droughty dugs (serenely exposed) and her mask of profound wrinkles. As for the youngsters, Gray was instantly convinced that malnutrition or perhaps some backwoods accident had rendered them both imbeciles. They drooled and stared at the ground and made silent poking gestures heavenward at strange intervals, sometimes moving their lips as if conversing with spirits.

Not being without compassion, the Grays had taken pity on

this vision of earthly misery and had fed the family handsomely from their already scant provisions. Through signs and a smattering of common language, the man had conveyed to the missionaries the strikingly singular fact that he and his family were dead. They had (the story ran) been killed by marauders two or three days prior, and each had walked the pole above the raging river which features in the Digger's idea of an afterlife similarly to a Christian's notion of standing before St. Peter. They'd slipped off the pole and fallen in, all of them, failing the test of their goodliness and proving that they had lived immorally. Now they were condemned to trudge up and down this barren, inhospitable, comfortless realm for all eternity.

So shocking was this account, and so jumbled its delivery, that Gray and his wife had stepped aside and consulted one another to be sure that each had come to the same understanding of the man's signs and utterances. Indeed, each concurred with the other's interpretation.

Now this was such a thicket of religious error as to present months and months of hard work to any conscientious missionary, and the Grays instantly resolved to halt their travels and set about leading these children out of darkness and confusion and into the warm light of Christ. But Father Digger was not done yet with his unsettling news, for he wished to inform the Grays of an even more startling thing: namely, that they, too—the missionaries, I mean—were dead. The world had ended just yesterday, the Digger said, and Philemon and Clarissa would soon find themselves facing the narrow pole over the whitewater. With everyone on earth dying at once, it seemed, things had gotten sort of swarmy along the river bank, there being only one pole to serve all humanity. But the Grays would get their chance as soon as an opening came available.

Plumbing their recent recollections, the Grays could produce nothing to suggest any possibility of their having died. In fact, they were even more certain of their own continued existence than of that of the Diggers. And so they set about trying to dislodge these strange notions and cure the Diggers of their bewilderment. But it was awful hard going with so few words at their disposal, and such a hardheaded audience to boot. Try as they might, they made little progress in their argument over the course of two or three hours, during which time the Digger woman dropped off to sleep, the indifferent children wandered off up the river, and the father stood with his arms crossed, stubbornly swishing his ears in stolid dismissal of what was good sound Christian doctrine.

Now, what sounds laughable in broad daylight and at sufficient distance is often another thing entirely when encountered in the flesh, and with night coming on, too. Despite being cloaked in the courage of the Lord, as it were, the Grays felt an awful creeping fear washing over them. I can scarcely blame them, myself, for by the mere description of those otherworldly wretches I believe most anyone meeting them would have felt his neck hairs prickling. But to hear the confident assertion that the family was *dead*? And on top of that to have them stand there and argue that *you, too, were dead*? That would be an uncommonly dread-inducing thing, even for such favorites of God's as were the Grays. Capping the climax was a fact I have hitherto left unmentioned, which is that this family bore about them the unmistakable scent of death! If there was room at all in the Grays' philosophy for walking, talking corpses, here were some prime candidates for the role.

So the missionaries begin to lose heart for the work, and to make their excuses, gathering up their truck and readying the mule. At the sight, Father Digger thrusts his hands out for more food; this Clarissa grants him, despite their shortage; and soon they're on their way with the sun sputtering low in the sky and all four Diggers now suddenly standing awake together in the little clearing, reaching after them in unabated ghastly supplication.

No one followed, so far as the Grays could see. Still, wishing to place the greatest possible distance between themselves and the Diggers they pushed on, through the golden hour of sundown, through the gloom of dusk as bats ruffled overhead and the low trees hunkered into human shapes, and on beneath an early moon gleaming like a fang. At last, exhausted, they had bedded down at the spot where we had found them in the morning, making a cold camp lest they reveal themselves by building a fire.

Gray had meant to keep watch, he said, but the events of the day had so thoroughly fatigued him that it proved impossible to stay awake (At this Ford snorted like a hog over a trough, and though I'd never soldiered with the man, I thought it rich irony for such a loafer as he to cast aspersions on another man's camp discipline). He was awakened sometime after moondown by the horrified screams of his woman and the feeling of his weapon being steadily extracted from his hands.

There followed a lengthy struggle in which Gray and Father Digger (for Gray harbored no doubts but that it was the family that had attacked them; in the utter blackness he could taste that sepulchral odor on his tongue) rolled over and over one another, exchanging blows, butting heads, snatching back and forth the rifle. Clarissa had never had time to rise and fight. She was beaten by the woman and children where she lay, pummeled with fist and foot and club, unable to do more than ward off blows with her crooked arms and shriek like the very hell.

Sometime during the scuffle over the weapon, Gray had received the long scratch down his shoulder, although he could not recall seeing a knife on any of the Diggers earlier in the day. This development spurred in him an even greater sense of urgency, and with a violent burst of strength he wrenched the rifle free and fetched his adversary a vicious kick in the middle. Despite the darkness and confusion, this shift in fortunes appeared to have registered instantly with the rest of the party, for they summarily left off their beating of Clarissa and vanished into the night. Gray fired one shot directly at the spot where the father had taken the kick to the stomach just an instant ago, but the ball racketed off into the trees to harmless effect.

"The whole thing," Gray said, "was over in three minutes."

"Haw," Ford growled. "Three seconds, more like."

I said nothing, though I tended to agree with Ford.

"Sir, were you there?" Gray challenged.

"Nope. Didn't have to be," Ford said. "Because I've been in a heap of other such quarrels, and they don't never last as long as you imagined they did. Besides, if a set of Injuns—dead or otherwise—had whaled on your pelt with clubs for three whole minutes, you'd still be collecting bits of her from around your camp site."

I thought we'd have a problem now, with Ford having referred to Clarissa as a pelt, but evidently the other content of his utterance had set Gray to more sober thinking.

We shoved off again, and the next night was even more eventful than the one just described—but I'll reserve that account for the next chapter.

CHAPTER FOUR

Lovesick—A sonnet—Lizard and Pockmark—Gray loses his temper—The truth about my claim—Twice blessed by Providence.

About midday, Honey told me she expected rain sometime during the night. Not in so many words, of course, but that was what she gave me to understand, through a pretty alluring histrionic turn.

"Pshaw," I said when she had finished. "There isn't a cloud anywhere about, Honey. Where's all that rain meant to come from?"

She wouldn't budge, though. Insisted that it would rain, and rain big, looked like, if her gestures were anything commensurate with her idea.

"Well. I suppose it won't do any harm for me to act as though I believe you, Honey. Only I don't."

I smiled winningly as I said it, to mask the import of my words, but this was piling layer on layer of deception: at the bottom of it all, it wasn't Honey being hornswoggled but me, for the better part of me believed that if Honey said it would rain, it would by-God rain; and all of this supposed doubt of mine was cheap show, drummed up to convince myself that I was still a reasonable man.

For you see, to tell the truth, Honey was unraveling me but good and wasting no time about it, either. I could tell I was about to make a world-class fool of myself with her, could see my ruin coming at me nice and steady from a mile off, but still felt helpless to stop it. It was the old dream where you stand idiotically on the tracks watching the train bear down, knowing you ought to sidestep out of harm's way but lacking the simple sense to do it, somehow. I'd already been in love a time or two, in younger days, so I knew the symptoms when they first presented and doubted not of the seriousness of the affliction. But if there's a physician alive who can stop a disease just because he knows he's got it, I'd admire to make his acquaintance, for I imagine he has other tricks equally diverting, such as walking upon water.

It was something awful, though, what was befalling me: when Honey wasn't looking my way, I yearned for her eye to wander back to me and warm me with its gaze. I delighted in the smile around her eyes. With no justification I ascribed to her an impossibly long and variegated list of virtues, virtues no Indian ever held all at once, nor white person either. In my increasingly lovesickened eye, she had blossomed into a paragon of patience, good humor, stalwartness, thrift, tact, cunning, tenderness, insight, honesty, managerial skill, bookkeeping prowess, medical wisdom, political instinct, and, if she ever cared to try her hand at it, city planning.

The most telling symptom of all was this: my healthy white man's regard for the female savage had got lacquered over with notions of modesty, of chastity, of chivalry and tenderness, concepts entirely incongruous with her race. And when a man sets down that path, only trouble lies ahead. Indeed, I should have said just now that I was about to make an *even worse* fool of myself with her than I already had. For again at breakfast I had abstained from eating until her plate was filled, as if she were the daughter of some hidalgo, and had done it right under the surly gaze of Stormy Isaac, and in full view of those high-born missionaries. Every time she blessed me with a word or a glance, I felt my helpless face lighting up like a soaker's when the whiskey is poured, like a child's at the sight of candy. When our hands lightly touched over our work I was a calf set loose in the barnyard after a long winter, the way I fairly cavorted and kicked up my heels. I wanted her, yes, but not in the simple, respectable, traditional way that's come down to us from generations of good, healthy squaw men. No, I wanted her in the way a man stands before God and declares for a woman. Awful? Why, I actually dreamed of *bringing her home to Mama;* of seeing the two of them sitting on the step hulling beans while our little half-breed youngsters turned somersaults in the grass. It was patent and disgusting and misplaced and absurd, and it threatened sorely to wreck my reputation for decency and sobriety of mind.

As still further measure of my lunacy, I had taken to probing the dim recesses of my scant learning to pull forth some scattered fragments of one of the sonnets that seemed ready-built for the occasion, and with them I quite gratuitously stimulated my infatuation as I plodded along beside Ahab, attempting to piece the particles back together again. Today, of course, in the comfort of my study, I have relearned the poem and can recite it clean. But I set it down here just as I dredged it up on the trail, that you might know me as an honest narrator not afraid to let his warts show. The bits and pieces fell into place as follows:

My mistress' eyes are nothing like the sun.
Corrals have dun, far browner than her lips' red.
If hairs be wires, brother, they grow there on her head.
I have seen Damascus curtains, red and white,
Yet no such curtains wears she on her face . . .

I was stuck there for now, but the loveliness of the imagery and the richness of the language floated me along up the trail, doing precious little to suppress my elation. I was throwing fuel on the fire, and I knew it, such is the foolishness of love. As for the old matter of how and whether she took care of her private needs, that question was finally settled, thanks to the last remaining shard of the poem at my disposal, which I was struggling somewhat to locate within its lines:

I grant I never saw a goddess go. . . .

That was it, right there: she was a goddess, and that explained everything. Goddesses don't stoop to that sort of thing.

Now, I know I needn't lay out how dangerous a thing it is when a semi-educated white man elevates in his thinking an illiterate squaw to the rank of goddess. And a Blackfoot, to boot, as if it all wasn't shameful enough to begin with. I told myself that I must put an end to this folly, and for several hours I sought to banish her from my mind. But she wouldn't banish, not even a little. She'd bend to drink from the stream, and I'd fall to wondering how it was no artist had ever thought to get down her image, just there, just in such a posture and in such a light. To watch her at her pantomiming was pleasurable in the extreme, and I confess to hauling out pretexts for conversation, just so I could watch her work her fine fingers and shapely arms, with that self-conscious twinkle playing about her dark eyes.

At last I thought I had a cure in view. "See here, Stern," I told myself. "What you suffer from are the rather predictable effects of excessive abstention. She is only a squaw, and the sooner you treat her like one the better off you'll be. Yes, take her tonight, get it out of your system. Treat her the way a white man treats a squaw, and you'll relieve yourself of all these confounding impulses."

Late in the afternoon, when the mules needed water, Honey led us off the ridge we'd been traversing and set our party down nearly atop a couple of miners working their rockers in the streambed. Isaac knew the men. I didn't, and I didn't care much for the idea of so many prospectors plying this slope of the range. Nor was I eager for Ford to flap his jaw as to where we'd come from or where we were going.

He greeted the miners with a grunt, and they didn't delay but set right in to asking questions, so I cut in straight away and say, "We're for Placerville, and we've got a woman hurt, and her husband here in the party."

They ignored me just the same as women do when Johnny is about. "How's the color downstream, Isaac?" said one of them, a lizard-looking fellow about two inches taller than Honey.

"Where all the two of you been pannin'?" I said.

"How's the color, Isaac?" he repeated.

"Good color, boys," Ford said. "Whitman here hit a pretty good strike about a day's walk downriver, and I got my claim in. You better get there quick, though. It's filling up fast."

This information must have cast me in a different light, for now both men turned and fixed their eyes on me as if Ford had suddenly conjured me. The second prospector was pitted all over with pockmarks, and his broad front teeth were lined with vertical streaks of green, like mold up a slabwood fence. "You hit you a vein?" he said.

"Well, I reckon the vein's up there," I said. "But hell. If you've found a single piece of float right here, there's a vein somewhere about." My hope was that Ford's friends were as ignorant about geology as he was. "Anytime you've found gold, there's a vein."

"He find a vein or not, Isaac?"

"I don't reckon he did. I believe he thinks he's found him a pocket."

Hearing this remark, the lizard fellow shot me a strange look, then turned back to Ford. "Y'all carrying in samples for an assay, I reckon," he said.

"That ain't it," Ford said. "We've run to fetch us back a judge."

"Sakes," Lizard says. "What, lawsuits already?"

"Nah, it ain't lawsuits. Young greaser killed one of our number, and there's a passel of softheads standing between him and the scaffold. Whitman here figures we need a judge to settle it. He's chief softhead, come to think of it."

"Who are them two?" Pockmark says.

"Missionaries. Got themselves near et up by Paiutes last night."

"Diggers, Ford," Gray puts in.

"His pelt there took quite a piss-pounding. Hasn't spoke a word since it happened."

"Good-looking woman, ain't she, though? Or was," said Pockmark.

"I don't see nothing out of place from the neck down," Lizard said. "Which is all that matters to me. Woman like that has plenty to keep a man distracted from a busted-up face. Say, that your squaw, Isaac?"

Ford spat. "Nah," he said. "Whitman's."

"Well, looking at her ain't no kind of hard work at all, either," Lizard said. "And I'd wager by the looks of her she knows enough to milk it clean out of a man. That right, Whitley?"

"It's Whitman," I said. "And if you think you're free to speak however you choose about these two women in our presence and theirs, then you're mistaken."

Lizard tossed back his head and laughed and threw a look over at Pockmark. "Whitley here roams the mountains without so much as a stick in his hand, and he wants to threaten *us* over how we speak of a broke-down pelt and a filthy squaw."

I was fixing towards a properly-calibrated rejoinder when in a flash Gray burst forward and drove the muzzle of his rifle so hard into Lizard's throat as to nearly puncture it through. Lizard flopped into the stream on his back under the force of the blow, and Gray followed him down with the tip of the barrel, pressing it hard into the bone-notch at the base of the windpipe. I saw with alarm that Gray's finger was laid over the trigger—a mighty dangerous practice during those kinds of antics, and a thing that's landed many an unintentional killer up on the gallows. Lizard's right hand groped around in the stream for the sidearm at his leg. But he'd set apart most of his energies to the pressing object of drawing his next breath and wanted for accuracy, so that he missed it on the first couple of passes, and by the third I'd already splashed down and snatched it clear and stood pointing it at the ground between myself and his unarmed partner. Ford never flinched, just stood there with his rifle across his arms the same as if the conversation had continued peaceably along.

"Breathe another word," Gray was grunting through thickly clenched teeth. "Say one thing more about my wife."

Lizard opened and closed his mouth silently, his eyes bulging worse than ever, the water tugging at his stringy hair. His wreck of a hat had been knocked off, and it spun and bumped slowly in the current past his feet, one edge of the brim slanting down against the rocky bottom.

"Best leave him be, Gray," I said quietly, "lest our judge have double duty to perform."

We left Lizard lying there gulping, and Pockmark gaping with the current spilling over his boots, and continued on up the river. I carried Lizard's revolver along for a half mile or so, pocketing the cartridges as I went. I deposited the empty weapon on a rock in the middle of the stream, where he wouldn't have any trouble finding it.

"Gray," I said at last. "For a man of God, you showed but little forbearance back there."

"The man still lives," Gray seethed. "So there's your forbearance."

It was quiet for a few minutes, and then, lest there be any surfeit of peace, Ford spoke up, allowing that he'd never seen the likes of Gray for losing his temper over a trifle. I could have said something just then about Ford crippling a man for having awakened him when he'd rather sleep, but I didn't.

"Thunder and lightnin'," Ford continued, chuckling low. "The man only said he liked the looks of your pelt. That right there's a compliment, where I come from. A man's pelt is his—"

Gray didn't drive the rifle barrel into Ford's throat, but he surely did aim it there in a hurry, and up close, too, where he couldn't ever miss, and I saw that his finger was on the trigger again. I doubt Ford missed that detail, either. "If I hear you refer to my wife as a pelt once more—just once more in your lifetime—then so help me God I'll kill you in your tracks," Gray said. "Is that understood, sir? Sir?"

Ford betrayed not the slightest trace of fear, but his face was the very picture of bewilderment. "Now what in every kind of hell do you have against me calling her that?" he said.

"It's a filthy, disrespectful epithet," Gray snapped. "And I won't tolerate it an instant more."

With a smooth, unhurried motion, Ford reached up, grasped the rifle barrel in his fat fist, and pulled it downward till it was pointing at the dirt. Somehow his bowie had also appeared and was glistening an inch or two away from Gray's right eye. "Listen close now, parson," Ford said. "If a word itches you so, then the clean thing is to come out and tell a body as much, so he can leave off saying it, rather than go around pointing guns in everybody's faces. As a general matter, I try and make my speech delightsome to all. I'm the very first to check his tongue when there's ladies present, or youngsters, or the quality; and if I sense that a word of mine brings pain to any creature, I'm first in line to repent of it and expectorate it from my dictionary. Christ Jesus Almighty Lord and Savior, there's been many and many a time when I myself has had to clean up the speech of others, for the sake of respectability. So if you was hunting up some kind of argument about this, you've failed every time, damn you, for whiteness of speech is policy for the likes of me. But where you run foul is in thrusting your gun up my snout, for no man has ever tried it before you and lived, up to this date. You're green and foolish, and you wear the cloth, elsewise we'd be diggin' you a shallow one already."

He released his grip on the gun, which remained pointed humbly earthward, sheathed his bowie, and, turning to face the still-stupefied Mrs. Gray, doffed his hat with a broad flourish and bent himself nearly double. "Sincere apologies, ma'am," he said. And then: "No need to reply."

He chirked his mule and continued on up the path without another word. Oh, he did cap the climax, Stormy Isaac Ford did. He was grizzly bear all over, right up until the rattlesnake showed itself—or the turkey.

Well, about now I began to feel I'd erred sorely in leaving my rifle behind with Johnny. As best I reckoned, Ford had brought along very little in the way of food, nor was he to be counted on to share what little he had packed or to hunt up more. And, since the Grays had been robbed of their provisions, they represented two additional mouths to feed, a net draw on our stores, and no minor one, either. I calculated we could make it down to Placerville if we rationed, but that we'd not be wanting for appetite when we got there.

But a food shortage didn't get to the heart of it, except insofar as an empty stomach makes a body irritable. Philemon Gray's run-in with the Indians had knocked something loose upstairs, anybody could see that, for twice in twenty minutes he'd threatened another man's life, putting his own into serious jeopardy, whether he knew it or not. It was a miracle that Ford hadn't already used him up, and I wondered what would happen once it was dark and Gray's back was turned, for I little doubted of Ford's assertion that no man had ever got so far in threatening him and lived. In other men, such a claim would have rung out as hollow boasting, but given Ford's legend I took it as sober fact.

The first chance I got, a little before we made camp, I let the others go on ahead a piece until Jezebel and Ahab were plodding along nearly in tandem. "Ford," I said nice and quiet. "I believe we have a piece of trouble on our hands."

"How's that, then?"

"Well, I reckon Gray has fairly lost his mind. Don't you?"

"Wahl, he's always been a little tetched, by my lights."

"Well, it's worse now, isn't it, since that Indian raid? That temper of his is like to get him killed."

"Yes," Ford said slowly, stroking his chin. "I reckon I *will* parbly put him under if he speaks harshly to me again."

"That's just it, right there. You've put your finger on it directly now," I told him. "We don't need any more of that kind of trouble. And so my idea is this: tonight while he sleeps, you and me we wrench that rifle away from him, and we don't give it back till he's deposited in Placerville, and we're shut of him once and for all."

Ford reckoned that was a good enough plan and gave his subscription without argument. I considered asking Honey for help, too, but I knew it would be a dangerous business, and I couldn't bear the thought of her coming to any harm.

★ ★ ★ ★ ★

Honey convinced me to halt our little train while there were still several hours of daylight remaining, on account of the coming storm, of which there was still not the slightest sign. Ford must have calculated that it would not be too great a strain on his ambition to end the day's exertions and loll about while others saw to his comfort, for he made no objection to the early halt. But Philemon Gray demanded to know the reason for it.

"Well, Mr. Gray," I said carefully, "there's some belief that we're in for a spell of weather, and we'd best hunker down and make ready."

"*Some belief,* do you say? On the part of whom, precisely?"

"On the part of me, if you must know."

"You, or your consort?"

"Me *and* my consort, if that's what you want to call it. We think it'll rain."

"Oh, you do, eh? And what exactly makes you think that? There's not the faintest trace of a cloud in the entire firmament. And so by what mysterious sign do you come to this belief?"

Oh, he knew how to sicken a man in short order; he could have instructed the diphtheria in that game. "Gray," I said with a sigh, "when I lose my mule to a set of rag-picking Diggers and become dependent upon you for my bread and my safety, then you may take every decision as you see fit. But until that day, when I halt the train, the train halts."

We had climbed in earnest all day and were now hard against the edge of sawtooth country. The river fell faster here, and the land lay broken up by foothills that were stacked close one upon another. What with my strange feelings toward Honey and my distaste for the company of Gray and Ford, I thought to while away the time before supper by rambling a ways into the surrounding hills. I grabbed my tack hammer, in case the land was good for crevicing nuggets out of the clefts in the exposed rock. I threw one more yearning look over in the direction of Honey, who was at that moment inspecting Clarissa Gray's injured mouth, hoping she might follow me. But if she wanted to, she managed to restrain herself, and I turned my back on the camp.

Within minutes, I had put four respectable-sized hills between myself and the others. I always walk quickly when I'm deep in thought, and today my mind was reeling. I was worried about my brother, worried about what was happening in camp down-river, worried about Clarissa Gray, worried about finding a judge who could be convinced to haul himself away over into Nevada over anything as foolish and trifling as the murder of Peter the Great. I was worried about falling the rest of the way in love with Honey. And I was worried about one thing more, which I haven't mentioned yet.

You see, Lizard and Pockmark had hit directly on the secret I'd been hiding for two weeks now: the strike that Johnny and I had made along the river was indeed a "vein," and no small one, either. I'll explain, in case you've spent your life's energies on something profitable: most prospectors are "placer" miners, who do exactly what all those idiots at our camp had been doing, which is to scoop up sediment from the soil or streambed, run water over it by one method or another, and take out whatever gold has already been separated, by the work of nature, from the minerals it so often insists on adhering to.

But, you see, the *main body* of gold resides in the earth in veins, in subterranean seams within the rock, and only makes its way, in flecks and nuggets, down hills and into streambeds through the unfathomably slow forces of geology over eons. That is, nothing more momentous has happened than that those flecks or nuggets have broken free of the rock and plashed into the creek, to be gathered up by simpletons who begin to imagine themselves possessors of the wealth of Croesus. Meanwhile, the great mass, the vein, the lode, lurks nearby in its secret place undisturbed. And to squat in ice water up to your ankles, picking away at placer tracings, while behind you lies what could very nearly be described as a mountain of gold, is the same as rejoicing to have hunted up a robin's egg in the shadow of a chicken farm, or delighting in having collected a dipperful of rainwater when you might have parted the bushes and revealed a bottomless lake.

So, yes: before the others had arrived to spoil our good fortune, we had found the vein. Or *I* had, to be frank, for while Johnny's goodness knew no end, his understanding most assuredly did. We had had a nice placer strike along the river, and Johnny was all for getting out of it whatever we could. I made no great objection, but I had seen too many men squander their sanity on the belief that some streambed pickings were going to make princes of them. I had, over the past couple of years, made careful study of the topography around some of California's richest lodes, and I liked this land by comparison. So I left Johnny to collect the float while I spent my days toiling up and down the hillsides, breaking my back with shovel and pick, sinking narrow shafts, pulling samples, ciphering out the geology, and drawing in my mind's eye a more and more complete portrait of that vein.

The day before Stormy Isaac and the others had burst into our little valley, I had satisfied myself that I had located the very apex of the lode, which meant that, at least by California law (which likely applied here), in claiming it I owned the entire vein, wheresoever it proceeded underground. At my best measurement, I was in possession of a gold streak that extended some eleven hundred feet, at an average width of eighteen inches. Now, the richness of the ore—that is, the percentage of it that contained gold—was another question yet unanswered, as was the problem of the types of inferior metals and other minerals from which that gold must be separated. While I had educated myself somewhat in minerology during two San Francisco winters, I was not equipped to make those assessments out in the field.

With others now come on the scene, we'd needed to stake our claim or have it taken away from us, and I'd faced the impossible task of convincing Johnny that our piece should be the site of the apex, up on the hill, rather than the very most prolific section of riverbank we'd found, which was his quite logical preference, even his demand.

Now, I said before that I hold no grudges where family is concerned, and I stand by that. And yet, since Johnny had already let slip about the placer strike, I dared not explain to him about the apex, since worlds and worlds of legal troubles rain down on a lode owner when word gets out about his find, with droves of idlers rushing in to stake adjacent claims just to make it harder for him to extract his wealth without paying them off. So I next suggested that, since Johnny and I were two men, we could certainly make two separate claims. He could stake the spot on the river, and I would stake the apex. This felt generous in the moment, for I was letting him have his way, and he of course believed he was getting the far better end of the deal. But I worried that he would feel betrayed once he learned the value of the apex claim.

I'd been well aware that the newcomers, too, would find it strange that I'd while away my time on a hilltop when there was gold to be plucked directly from the stream. And so on the very first day, I'd confessed to some of the old-timers that, in the years since I'd seen them last, I'd caught the dreaded, often fatal, *pocket-mining* bug.

Pocket-mining is a rarified practice, only feasible in areas in which a quite specific set of geologic forces has been at play such that the gold has become scattered all down a hillside in a fan-shaped pattern, with the imaginary fan handle pointed upward toward the top of the hill. At the tip of that handle, at one depth or another, lies concealed in the earth a pocket of gold, sometimes of considerable value. So far as I or anyone else knew, pocket mining was, as dictated by geologic circumstance, limited to one or two counties in California; but this country still held mystery, and anything could have been possible. So I'd told the men that I'd been at pocket mining and believed a robust pocket to lie within my claim.

They'd taken this to heart, and when I'd turned up no jackpot after several days of what looked to them to be a lot of unbearable labor, they'd come to view me as just another broken prophet lucklessly pursuing his Lorelei.

For nigh unto three weeks, I'd continued "working my claim," both to hold it legally and for the benefit of appearances, knowing full well that there is precious little that a man with a pickaxe can do to wring wealth from an underground seam of gold bound up in quartz and other base minerals, as this one was. Without capital, without machinery, without vast resources of labor, for me to have imagined producing gold enough to live high on would have been folly indeed, for it would have been more profitable to dig ditches for hire in town than to scratch at that quartz in hopes of prying free a decent hourly wage.

No, what I needed was to sell my claim to an established mining company. But first the ore would need to be assayed and the claim inspected, and I did not wish to draw attention to myself by disappearing across the mountains and then showing up with a host of engineers and executives in tow. So I'd been playing a waiting game, hoping the miners would deplete the riverbank and move on, as they always do when the easy placer pickings dry up. But my ample vein had been generous over the millennia, coloring the stream with promiscuously disseminated nuggets and flecks, transported hydrologically and wallowed into the alluvial soil. And so the men had plucked and plucked, and as the days wore on, I had grown sorely impatient with that interminable plucking.

So, when Peter the Great was murdered, I'd seen my chance. The miners had flailed with their predictable stupidity, and I had nominated myself to cross the Sierra in search of a judge. But I'd be bringing back more than a judge and, if things fell into place as I wanted them to, would be leaving these mountains as a very rich man indeed.

I soon confirmed what I'd somewhat suspected on leaving camp: this was no country for crevicing, nor for any other form of removing gold from the earth, for the very good reason that there was no gold here, so far as I could tell. We had left the quartz behind us in the lower foothills and were now treading upon secondary strata, land that looked to me like coal country.

I have known many miners who cannot find beauty in a piece of land if they know it to be destitute of precious ore, but my fever has always run just slightly cooler. This was harsh country, hands-and-knees country in places, and lonesome worse than a boneyard, and bereft of gold, but still I found it lovely in its way, with the intersecting valleys gathering up dry shadow and the late light plying the low summits, haycock-hued in the twilight, before that iron wall of the Sierra.

As I stood admiring the view, though, I came to notice an almighty curious thing: the neighboring peak, just to the north of where I stood, differed from its close fellows in both texture and tint. It lay washed along its top and partway down its southern flank in a blue-black shroud formed neither by shadow of mountain nor shade of cloud. I stood for a moment puzzling over it, searching my meager understanding of the rudiments of geology for an explanation.

I could find none, and so, with nothing better to do, I set off to inspect the peak up close. Ten minutes later I was standing on its summit.

I stooped there and swung my tack hammer, readily dislodging a hunk of blue-gray material the size of a child's foot. This I held in my palm and tapped at with the hammer, finding that it split rather easily into cubic crystals. At this development my heart bolted from its stable and leaped the paddock fence. Almost gasping for air, I moved down the mountain a little, prized free another hunk of the stuff, tapped at it: same result. Lord Almighty; for the second time in a month, my stomach dropped through the soles of my boots and kept on going; for the second time in a month, unless I was badly mistaken, Providence had blessed me with a discovery whose implications surpassed my ability to fathom.

The hill on which I stood was shot through with galena: lead sulfide! Oh, this would do all right, wouldn't it? At the very least, I had here a handsome lead mine, which would make a fine side business to my gold operation downriver. Ah, but only the most luckless wretch of a galena striker is condemned to smelt lead and call it a day, for galena's true value generally lies in another element bound up within the ore: silver!

Once again, without the correct tools and equipment, I had no way of assessing the richness of the silver content, if indeed there was any, but I had just enough knowledge to fuel a mighty strong feeling about this hill. I would certainly be carrying some samples with me down to Placerville to have assayed alongside my gold-bearing quartz. And, unless I was absurdly off the mark, I had just become incomprehensibly rich. Riches upon riches!

My heart was a bullet rattling around in my chest. Good fortune? Maybe just a little! Blessed beyond measure, not once but twice! Why, only to think of it: these western mountains teemed with men quite literally driven to distraction by dreams of easy riches, men who, to tramp after gold, had quit their livelihoods, farewelled their wives, left their children to shift for themselves, cut ties with their kinfolk. These were men who knew gold to be lurking under every stone, lodged in the crooks of trees, hiding in hollow logs, biding its patient time and waiting for them.

A prospector had once confessed to me that any time he slit open a fish's belly, he could not stop himself hoping to find a fat nugget smiling there in its innards. These men dreamed fatuous, preposterous dreams, dreams unattainable in a thousand lifetimes, and dared to dream them brazenly, with a fervor that verged on expectation. And here I, Stern Whitman, was now living a fantasy that the modesty of their scant, unpracticed restraint forbade them to envision, being altogether too outlandish for even their most strenuous mooning. To be the sole proprietor of the apex of a rich vein—*and* standing on my very own mountain of silver!

I have said that my gold fever was never an outstanding case, but that is not to say that I have ever been immune. Certainly my locating the gold lode had prompted several sleepless nights of excited imagining in which I had carefully laid out in my mind's eye the lavish lifestyle of my near future. Now, with the addition of this silver mine, I would need to revise my schemes upward, I could see that. The paltry mansion I had been counting on must be replaced by a sumptuously appointed palace. The primitive coach and footmen must become private gilded railway cars. And I would get to all the rest of it later, when I was lying on my back looking up at the stars, the silver stars.

I filled my pockets with galena, and then, with an overabundance of energy, I cut a joyous little dance there on the hillside. Nothing very extravagant, just a caper or two to burn off some of the excess of feeling. No, just three or four bouncing gambols, and a whirl—and there I beheld Philemon Gray, standing not thirty feet away and watching me with a strange new hunger in his eyes.

Chapter Five

A new contract—The problem of disarmament—Honey in the wickiup—Ford behaves rashly—An astonishing gift for profanity—Rain at last—Gray quizzes Ford—The secret is out.

Well, if I was a burning Lucifer match, Gray was a whole cistern full of water. You never saw anybody lop a dance off at the knees the way I did just then. He'd caught me by such total surprise that I just stood there and gaped at him for a pretty respectable stretch, and then he closes the distance, smirking something awful, and when he gets up to me he says, "I hate to have interrupted your fandango, Mr. Whitman. Please continue."

That was just what I needed to thaw me out, actually. A word from his perpetually grating tongue was sufficient to bring me back to my senses and stir up my fight.

"Gray," I said, "maybe you can explain why it is you're following me around in these hills."

"Quite simply, Mr. Whitman, it's that I don't trust you."

"Don't trust *me*? And yet you trust Stormy Isaac Ford back there with your injured wife?"

He waved his hand. Or waved his rifle, I should say, for he held it in his hands, and it appeared set to remain there, pointed at me. "She's safe with your Indian consort, especially since Ford is hard asleep. But when I see a man, after traveling for the better part of a day, develop a sudden energy and disappear mysteriously into the hills, it arouses certain suspicions in me.

Particularly when my lot is bound up with his, however briefly or unfortunately."

That was him all the way. He could talk like someone had written it down for him in advance and keep it up the whole day through if he wanted to. He was leering at me now with a new odiousness, supplemental to the underlying ugliness that was his by natural right and was so envied by bats, stinkbugs, and piles.

"What I do outside of camp, or in it for that matter, is none of your affair, feller," I said.

He was not to be intimidated. "And suppose I disagree, *feller*?" he said. "Suppose you tell me what you were dancing about before I so rudely interrupted? And with what mysterious substance you've just lined your pockets?"

My, but wasn't he all alone in his class when it came to cheek. It was time to knock him down where he belonged. I cleared my throat and let him have a taste of his own grandiloquent medicine. "Gray," says I, "you've been the fortunate recipient of a whole streak of mercy over this last day or two, owing to the purgatives of your profession. By all rights, you ought to be dead already. Howbeit, you've now played your very last card, and I'm going to offer you this final piece of wise counsel, *gratis*, after which you'll be held to full account for your words and deeds: When a man is in the mountains, he expects a little privacy, and it's awfully bad form to go spying around on folks, and not just bad for your manners but for your health, too. Now, then. You just turn yourself around and stroll back into camp unharmed for this one last time, and be thankful for it. And if you breathe so much as a syllable to a living soul about what you've seen out here, you'll rue it awful terrible."

It was a fine speech, I thought, and even now as I set it down in writing, I cannot help but admire it, despite my natural modesty. But in its delivery I must somehow have misjudged windage or elevation, for it whistled past him and on into the empty foothills just as innocuous as a compliment.

"Whitman," he said, and I really didn't like the look come over his eye. "Whitman, you've just filled your pockets with precious stone of one kind or another. Tell me what it is."

"Why would I do a thing like that, I wonder?"

Now he smiled, which I could just as well have done without. "Because you and I are going partners, that's why," he said.

This was too many, this was. Attempted robbery, of all things known! It called for special measures. So I cleared my throat again and plundered around in my sack of religious learning. "Matthew 6:19," I said. "Lay not up for yourself treasure upon the earth—"

"Oh, it wouldn't be for myself," he said. "It will be to bring forth the work of God."

Well, there was another punch to the liver, even though I was a little relieved that he'd interrupted my recital (for while I'd made a good start at the verse, I couldn't have brought the whole thing off even if he'd had two or three more guns pointed at my head). What I needed was a minute to think, to calculate a suitable response.

Fact: I already possessed a gold mine and didn't need additional wealth. Fact: Gray was sufficiently fanatical to take a silver mine at gunpoint and then piously devote its profits to his religion. Fact: Gray was sufficiently insane to shoot me if I didn't placate him in a hurry.

"All right, Gray," I said. "Since you were so nigh during the discovery, I'll grant you a quarter ownership in the claim."

He smiled again, and though I've had dozens and dozens of smiles aimed at me, from politicians and gamblers and lechers and undertakers and alligators, this one was the very beatenest for gall. I'd rather find a smiling cottonmouth in my bedroll than look on that awful grin of his. "One half," he said simply.

Oh, a man like that ought to be killed three or four times a day, just for maintenance. "One third," I said, feeling all slushy inside to hear myself say it.

Then he laughed, and if I'd thought the smile was bad, why, the sound of that laugh made me go so cold and bloodless as to wish I could swallow lye instead of hearing it any more. "One half," he said, "or I take it all." His damn fool finger was on the trigger, which sort of clinched it for me.

"Half of it's yours," I said.

"Thank you. Partner. Half of what, by the way?"

"Lead. Half the lead on this mountain."

"I'll want that in writing when we get back to camp."

"And you'll get it, too. But not a word to Ford."

Isaac was snoring blissfully next to the cookfire, one hand grasping the forestock of his rifle and the other cupped over his crotch. Clarissa Gray lay stretched out sleeping opposite him, and it was a measure of my lovesick devotion to Honey that my eye passed only briefly over Clarissa's figure, for her bare legs were exposed above the knees, and the swell of her alabaster bosom was visible at the top of her torn dress. Honey was dragging a section of tree fall into camp for firewood. Her face lit up when she saw me. Through signs she inquired as to the vigor of my appetite, and through signs I gave her to know that a little bacon and dough would not come amiss.

While she was cooking, I wrote up two copies of the contract with Gray and silently handed one to him. He pocketed it away with a complacent, fevered grin and sat down to eat our food.

Over supper an idea came to me for getting Gray's rifle away from him without struggle. "Gray," I said, "we are not rich in provisions. I left my only rifle with my brother back in camp; how are you in the direction of hunting?"

But the clever old chilblain had already scented me, I could tell. "I am nowhere close to incompetent," he said.

"Then perhaps you'd contribute by bringing in some game one of these evenings?"

"If there were any game, perhaps. But I haven't seen a sign of any."

"I have. Say, maybe *I* could take your rifle for a few hours."

"Oh, that's quite generous of you to offer," he said with that sticky smile of his that outdid all other sticky smiles, "but it may be that I have some need for it. Perhaps Mr. Ford there would have no objection to your taking his."

"Perhaps not," I said, irritated. "I'll have to ask him once he comes awake."

When night gained our side of the mountains, I told Gray to get some sleep. I'd sit the first watch, I said, if he would but lend me his rifle.

No, he reckoned. After the events of the previous night, he'd just as soon keep his own gun by his side. Surely I could understand, given what he'd been through, if he was just a little bit particular, now, about holding onto his weapon. Say, why didn't I wake Ford and ask to borrow his?

I do hate a clever man.

"Come to think of it," I said, "Ford's been sleeping long enough now. If we're going to roust him anyhow, no reason why *he* shouldn't stand watch. You're closer; give him a shove, there, and let him get up."

Gray looked with those glittering eyes at Ford's bulky form and then back at me.

"Normally, of course, I would not shrink from such a minor chore," he said. "But you witnessed the animosity between Mr. Ford and me this morning. It is only in these recent past few hours that our enmity has got smoothed over somewhat, enough at least for a quiet civility to obtain. It would be a grave disappointment if my awakening him were to re-arouse any of his ill feeling and interrupt the blessed tranquility that has come down upon our little encampment."

He was just that chalky, too. So help me if I've changed a word.

And so without approaching Ford I attempted to awaken him. "Psst. Ford. Ford. Psst. Your watch, Ford." He droned on in his slumber completely oblivious to my importuning. "I say, Ford," I said a little louder. "Wake up, Ford!"

No result.

I picked up a twig and tossed it gingerly at his chest. It landed there, rising and falling with his breathing in the firelight. A pinecone lay nearby; this I threw a little harder. It bounced off his belly and rolled into the darkness, and his breathing continued unabated.

Honey sat watching all this with a strange smile. Silently she rose and stepped up to Ford's sleeping form, and before I could warn her she fetched him a kick in the ribs that would have been good enough to lift a yearling buffalo clear of the ground. And, almost as abruptly, she vanished into the night.

Ford sat up slowly, looked around him rather dazedly, spat once, and rubbed at his face. His eye fell on me. "You roust me?" he said.

"Yes," I said. "It's time to stand your watch."

"Oh," he said thoughtfully, still rubbing at his jaw. "That right there's where you run foul, see. Stormy Isaac don't stand no watch."

"Nonsense, Ford," I said. "Every man stands a watch."

He shook his head a little sadly, as if I were to be pitied for missing an academic point far beyond his ability to influence. "No, no," he said. "There's certain things is beneath the dignity of a Forty-Eighter. Guard duty's one of 'em. No, that's the kind of chore that's left to such pups as you two fellers. I'd help you if I could, of course I would; but it runs contrary to decency, and it wouldn't be right if people was to hear about it. A thing like that would embarrass this whole camp. We're better than that—ain't we?"

The old fool had forgotten all about our plan to disarm Gray.

"Why, look here, Isaac," I said. "I haven't got a rifle, and Gray here is too shook up from last night to *give up his.* So you'll either need to stand watch or lend me your gun, or *something else.*"

With all due apologies, Ford explained that it was the hard lot of the Forty-Eighter to be even more constrained in the matter of lending rifles than he was on the question of standing watch. For there were titles of significantly lesser grandeur—scout, trapper, *coureur de bois,* postmaster—for whose bearers the practice of going unarmed was viewed as base and indecorous. If the dignity of those low offices prohibited the lending of firearms, imagine the insult to the fraternity should a figure of Ford's eminence lend out his gun to the likes of me.

"Well," I said, trying to control my impatience at his thickheadedness, "I can see I'm in a bind here, that's one thing certain sure. I'd like to do my duty and stand watch over the camp. Only I haven't got a rifle. On the one hand, there's you: perfectly good rifle, but regulations forbid your lending it out or standing watch yourself. On the other hand, there's Gray: perfectly good rifle, but I can see the only way we'd get it from him was if we were to *take it away from him bodily.* And that wouldn't be right to do to a man who's been through what he has recently."

At last the light came on in Ford's eyes, and while that was a relief, I feared that I'd had to be too obvious and that his imbecilic grinning would elicit Gray's suspicions.

And sure enough, already Gray was saying with an iron coldness in his voice, "Well, as far as that goes, gentlemen, anyone thinking to relieve me of my rifle should accept this as fair warning: I will kill the man—" he looked around for Honey—"or woman—who lays one finger on it."

It was quiet for a good long while after that, just the crackle and hiss of the fire, and a distant band of coyotes singing a mournful song about hunger and how they could never be quit of it. After a while, the Forty-Eighter said, "Well. Isaac Ford don't stand no watch. But I mean to sit up for a spell tonight and do me some thinking. So you two pups can close your eyes, and I'll wake you by an' by."

"Come to think of it," Gray says, "I believe I'll sit up a while, too."

Honey still hadn't returned since kicking Ford and fleeing into the night, and I'd begun to worry a little about her. I stood and softly called her name.

"Louder, Whitman," Ford said from his seat by the fire. "Paiutes can't quite hear you."

Silently I stepped into the woods a few feet past the ring of firelight and stood waiting for my eyes to adjust after the glare of the coals. It was darker than I'd known. Although the sky had been cloudless at sundown, now only a few hazy stars shone between the treetops. I took four blind, shuffling steps more, whispering Honey's name, stopped, listened. She answered me in an almost imperceptible whisper: "Stern Whitman."

Her voice had come from nearby. A moment later I felt her reach out of the darkness and grasp my hand, her touch running through me like a lightning bolt. I clutched that little hand in mine. I smelled her hair and felt her other hand slipping around my beltline and sliding up my back, drawing me toward her, and then the exquisitely urgent push of her body against mine.

In the darkness she found my face with hers, and we were

laughing silently with lips brushing together and our breath intermingling. She backed away, still holding my hand, and led me a few steps further on, then guided me to the ground. In this new place of stillness I knelt and reached out my palms to discover the little wickiup she had made for us of willow stems, pine boughs, leaves, needles—and our bedrolls. I followed her inside, and when I got there she had already wriggled out of her tunic and was waiting for me to take her.

I had hoped that to lie with Honey would be to purge myself of the shameful feelings of love that had been plaguing me, but what I found was that it only sped me along in the direction of my ruin.

Under the right and decent order of things, by lying down with a squaw a white man innocently consummates his lust and turns to slumber in good conscience. But in that brush hut in the Sierra foothills with the coyotes calling, we were like two young lovers newly wed: giggling, sighing, exploring, nuzzling, whispering our mutually incomprehensible declarations of affection.

An enthralled couple cannot sleep. They lie still for spells, each respectfully silent in case the other has at last succumbed, and then one tentatively budges a foot or a knee, lightly brushing against the other. The other responds with the subtlest little movement in testing reply, and then they have rediscovered each other and are laughing and rolling together anew. And in this way a whole night passes without sleep.

So this night would have passed in heavenly congress, had we not both heard the awful smack of Isaac Ford's rifle butt connecting with Philemon Gray's head. Somehow we knew in a twinkling what it was, and I immediately hollered out, "Stop that, Ford!"

In less than an instant I was there in the clearing beside the blazing fire Ford had built, waterfalls tumbling down my limbs. Gray lay still on the ground, and Ford stood immense above him, his back humped like a buffalo's. In his hands he held two rifles, one of which he silently thrust out toward me.

"Here, take it, damn you."

"Goddamn it, Ford, what in blazes did you have to kill him for?"

Ford peered down through his narrow pig eyes, mildly perplexed. "*Did* I kill him, you reckon? Why, I only fetched him one lick." He reached out one foot and nudged Gray over onto his side. "Nah," he said. "He's still breathing."

He turned then and looked at me for the first time. "Go put some clothes on, ya heathen," he said.

I groped my way back to the wickiup. Honey had pulled on her tunic, and she handed me my trousers. When I returned to the fire, Ford was squatting over Gray's prostrate form fumbling with some pack string. I'd seen him try to use rope before and knew that it wasn't quite in his line.

"Here, Ford," I said. "That isn't anything a Forty-Eighter should have to stoop to. Let me take care of it."

I bound Gray's hands behind his back, propped him up against a tree, and threw another pine bough on the fire to get some better light to see by. His skull was not broken; the skin was just torn slightly at the temple and bleeding but slightly. "Christ Jesus the Almighty Lord and Savior of Us All, Ford," I said. "We agreed to overpower him, together, not for one of us to dash his brains out."

"Wahl," he said. "I'd admire to see the day when Stormy Isaac Ford needs help with subduing a goddamned limp-wristed missionary."

"But you couldn't have subdued him without trying to crush his skull?"

" 'Twas the expedient thing," Ford said. "You heard him

your own live self say he'd kill the man tried to take his gun out of his hands."

"Well. I reckon he'll live, and we're all safer for having got it from him."

But Honey was gesturing rather urgently, and in a moment I saw she'd thought of the one thing neither of us others had: Clarissa, too, would need to be bound. Otherwise she would insist on freeing her husband. The time to do it was now, while she was asleep, rather than waiting for an unlikelier moment. How Honey could get us to understand all that, and so quickly, I can't explain, but I mention it as testament to her unending cleverness.

I cut a couple more lengths of twine and stood over Clarissa, straddling her where she lay on her back. Gingerly I reached down and grasped one wrist—and she sat up so hard and fast as to bring her forehead crashing into my right eye socket with such destroying force that white stars burst before me, and I reeled backward onto my seat. I rolled there in the dirt for a while, clutching at my eye, and when I sat up and could see again, Honey and Isaac Ford were standing opposite a most cognizant and irate Clarissa.

"What is the meaning of this?" Clarissa sputtered.

Me, I was too flummoxed and hurt to answer. Over the years, I've received blows from fists, feet, marble-topped walking canes, blocks of cordwood, stones, bones, canoe paddles, the handle of a bullwhip, and two separate ballpeen hammers on two separate occasions—that's two each time, for a total of four strikes with ballpeen hammers—but I can't recall anything quite equal to Clarissa Gray's forehead for leaving a man confused and headache-y all over.

Ford spoke in my seeming absence. "We're fixin' to tie you up on account of you'll most likely fight us over your husband, ma'am," he said, pointing.

You should have seen the look of her when she spied old Philemon slumped there against the tree with his hands tied behind him and the blood drying beside his ear. You never saw a more stirring picture of injured nobility, of dignified fury: those nostrils flexing like a bellows, that contemptuous brow plunging and rising and plunging again, and the twin mounds of her stately bust swelling so proud and majestic just like a pair of noble flagships on a boundless windswept sea, colors snapping, spume scattering in the gale, masts swaying, crew racing about the deck like ants. I don't care what museums you've been to, you haven't seen the likes of Clarissa Gray when riled. Her injured eye was all swollen shut now, but her mind was back, and all her sand along with it. She allowed that no person would ever touch *her* with a rope; and while any of the three of us might well have managed it, we didn't feel inspired to try right then, somehow.

And, oh, the language she used in damning us! Had I the perception of Zeus, I'd never have dreamed she'd been hoarding such a cache, just waiting on the right occasion to discharge it. I was glad Honey couldn't understand her, for that missionary woman tore through the entire catalogue, cover to cover, twice, and then chewed up the pages and spat the pieces at us. This altered Clarissa Gray in my esteem, and considerably for the better. She'd always shown brass enough, and I've said so more than once now, but this new thing told me there was a mighty hot furnace glowing inside her. I saw now that she must have taken a nibble or two of the fruit of the garden, to have got that thorough an education. I confess to feeling a pang of regret at never having tried my luck with her back at camp, for now it appeared that such hopes may not have been unreasonable.

I won't print what she said; I'll not even try. But speed of delivery? Why, that invective couldn't have flown thicker or more steady if she'd had a whole brigade of swearers at her command, yet she was just one woman, working alone. I could see that with my own eyes, so I had to believe it. She struck us enfilade, oblique, direct, slant, and plunging, so relentless I feared she might melt the tubes.

Even she was but mortal, though, and in time the fusillades seemed to come spaced just a little bit farther apart from each other, leaving the suggestion of a pause here and there. And by and by I found myself able to poke my own rhetorical barrel through a loophole and squeeze off a shot, as it were. This in itself seemed a feeble thing, but then a while later I managed another, and another, until with pains I made her understand that it was owing to concerns for the safety of all, including her husband, that we'd had to tie him up, for he had been acting erratically since the night before when they had been attacked by Indians.

Well, you never saw a woman change so suddenly, without marrying her. At the merest mention of the Indian attack, the maledictions ceased, and Clarissa fell stone silent, cocking her head like a bird plagued by honest curiosity, and took to scanning the campsite earnestly with her good eye.

At last her gaze came to rest upon the ground just before her feet, and she stared at that barren spot as if there laid some object of profoundest interest. And that was that. She had found whatever mystery she'd sought, and there her gaze would remain. For she had gone dumb again, gone blank, in an utter flash.

In California once I watched a heedless sot name of Hayward step unawares down an eighty-foot mineshaft. He'd been walking along whistling "The Blue Juniata," and doing a good job of it, too, to my untutored ear, hands in pockets, and then he'd suddenly been no longer there. *Swift goes my light canoe a-down the rapid riv*—Well, to behold this thing with Clarissa gave me the same sort of gummy feeling about the pit of the stomach.

Anyway, she wasn't fussing now. It was easy enough to tie her. At least Honey made it look easy. My head hurt too much to try.

But though I needed rest, I was not to have it, for it was one damned thing after another that night, and each one abrupter than the preceding. Just as Honey finished binding Clarissa at the wrists, the long-predicted rain began. No polite warning, no fat sentinel drop slapping into the dust or splattering onto your forearm. No, just a downward explosion of water, everything dry one moment and sopping the next. All told, it was enough to jangle up your nerves considerably, and enough to bring Philemon Gray back to consciousness, which was no blessing. Before the fire was doused by the storm, he had time for a good look around the clearing and had gathered the outlines of his predicament. And he wasn't any happier about the state of things than his wife had been.

"Ford! Whitman! Release me at once! Release me, I tell you."

I never could understand why a person who's been bound up feels compelled to order his captors to release him. Tying a person securely requires forethought and some application of effort, and therefore some commitment to the course, so it seems to me that if a captor was inclined to release a prisoner at the first casual demand, he'd likely never have gone to such pains. Now, I'm not familiar with every single instance in the literature, of course, but I don't believe there's ever been a time when simply demanding freedom secured a prisoner's release. People are funny that way, though. They get in that situation, and it's the first thing out of their mouth, just as if they have a script they must follow. I guess that, in a general way, a human loathes to thwart convention.

So we let old Gray fulminate some, and he tried to make a good show of it, but I felt embarrassed for him at being so plainly outclassed in that discipline by his wife. Ford said so later, too, said Gray "warn't shucks compared to that pelt of his." Oh, he was the greater snake, I'll give him that, and in haughtiness of everyday speech he was without peer. But he couldn't hold a candle to Clarissa when it came to sheer talent for profanity. Anyway it was hard to make him out with all that rain slamming to ground, and after a while we quit listening, and he quit trying, which we supposed was better for his dignity.

Honey and I led Clarissa to the wickiup, where she settled in without quarrel, and then the two of us spread our manty over our heads and over Gray where he hunkered next to the washed-out remains of the fire. It wasn't any pitter-patter on that canvas, by the way. It was a thunderous pounding that went on and on, and we were already soaked through before we ever got under there. But we thought it inhumane to leave even such a manger-dog as Philemon fully exposed to the weather, so we held up that manty and waited for the rain to quit.

I can't say how many hours it lasted, because time always chooses such moments to show off its remarkable elasticity. But I know that my arms and neck were godawful cricked up and sore, and my Clarissa-wrecked eye swollen shut, by the time that rain finally began to taper to a more reasonable cadence and we shuffled out from under the manty and stretched. It was still dark as the bottom of a well, and still raining, but I guess we reckoned Gray could survive now without drowning.

We built back up the fire and sat there itching and shivering in our wet clothes waiting anxiously for sleep or morning or kingdom come, we weren't particular about which, just so long as it came.

But after a while Gray sets in again, and now that the rain has slackened so, he's easier to hear. This time, too, he isn't spewing it out, or trying to. He's got his highfalutin diction back, and his superciliousness has made a full cure, and I can hear him working back into that same guile he'd shown on the galena mountain. By and by he lets on to have calmed down completely and come around to an understanding of our point of view. Not that he *approves* of having been tied up, he suggests, but he can see why we might have felt we had to do it. And then after a few minutes of this kind of talk he says, subtle as a bugler on a donkey: "Say, Ford, you're an accomplished miner; let me ask you a question."

Ford grunted.

"What does pure lead look like? In the ground, I mean."

Ford grimaced with the effort of thought. "Pure lead?" says he. "Now let me think about that one. You've sort of caught me with my pants down and my pecker in my fist, Reverend."

"Ford," I said, "don't answer him. Can't you see he's trying to trick you into something?"

This befuddled him even more. "Into what, though?" he said.

"I don't know. But don't you think it mighty strange that a man tied up in the rain and dark would decide to ask you such a peculiar question as that?"

Ford sat hunched there for a long moment, chewing his fat tongue.

Gray said, "Why, stop sowing suspicions around, Whitman. A man has to occupy his mind with one thing or another when he finds himself in such circumstances. Why isn't this topic just as good as any other? Ford, can you answer the question?"

"Wahl," Ford drawled, about as slowly as he could, "I reckon it's sort of a grayish look. Sort of lumpy. Heavy, too. Heavier than most rock."

"Not shiny and black?"

Ford scratched at his jaw. "Maybe," he said. "Sometimes."

I thought I was in the clear. But then, thinking better of it, the old jackass corrected himself: "But you said *pure,* didn't you? Nah, I don't reckon it would have much of a blackness to it when pure. Now, *galena*—"

"I have a question for you, too, Ford," I said, "since we're just making idle conversation here. As a true Forty-Eighter, I'd like to know: was there very much religion to your upbringing?"

"Oh, some," Ford said. "Not a great deal, though Mammy she kept her a Bible. Good-size one, too. Kept the door from swinging shut all summer better than a river stone, and easier to snatch up when it rained heavy or there was a spider to kill."

"Well, were you ever in a church, for example?"

"Scarcely."

"Some, though, I reckon?"

"Some, sure."

"All right: and based on what you know about religion, what do you suppose would befall a preacher who succumbed to a love of gold and was willing to cheat and kill for it? What would become of him in the hereafter, I mean?"

"Oh, I reckon it would be all up for him. Parbly spend the ages with a red-hot poker up his ass." He squinted at me across the fire. "You talkin' about the parson here?"

"Oh, goodness no. Only making conversation, same as him."

Gray's turn: "What was that word you used a moment ago, Ford? I'm not familiar with it."

"Ass," Ford said, a little pityingly, mindful of Gray's poor showing earlier. "Refers to your shithole."

"Not that, Ford. When we were talking about lead just a minute ago. You said a word that started with *G*."

Ford stared blankly ahead.

Gray persisted. "You said lead wouldn't look black when pure, but something else would, something that sounded like *galoofa* or *galooga*."

"Galena," Ford said, and I felt all the wind go out of me. The old rapscallion had some surprises in him, I could see that.

"That was it!" Gray was saying. "Yes, sir. Now, tell me about galena, the better for me to pass these predawn hours."

"Oh," Ford said, blinking at the fire. "Ain't that much to tell, really."

"Shh," I said. "Did you all hear that?"

I made out to be listening for Indians, and it bought me a good half hour of silence, but that Gray was like a terrier got hold of your pants leg, for the instant Ford muttered, "*I* don't hear a single pison thing," he was right back on the topic.

"So you were about to tell me all about galena, Mr. Ford."

"Yes," Ford said professorially. "Galena is lead, you see, but there's other truck mixed up with it, and you've got to work it some to get the lead out."

"I see. So if you, for example, were to come upon a mountain of black stuff in the earth, would you be disappointed to find that it was galena and not pure lead?"

Ford looked at Gray as though the missionary had just taken off all his clothes. "Would I be *disappointed*? Man, there ain't hardly any such thing in all this world as pure lead laying around in the ground, which is why your first question stumped me some. So, no, I wouldn't be disappointed, for if I was going to find lead, that's just how I'd *expect* to find it. On top of which—"

"Shh," I said. "Paiutes."

"Paiutes the devil," Gray said. "Go on, Ford."

"On top of which, a good lot of what that lead's mixed up with could be *silver.*"

Well, there. It was out. I knew it, and I knew Gray knew it. I could see it crawling all up and down his person. Clap a set of horns to his head, and you couldn't have told him apart from Satan. Though I don't think Satan ever looked quite so sinister as when Gray leaned forward and rasped, "Mr. Ford, I know where sits a *mountain* of galena. Release me, give me back my rifle, and half of it is yours."

Chapter Six

Gray tempts Ford—Traveling with prisoners—Honey scouts—Consequential sheep—Isaac Ford's history.

Well, I guess Gray thought he had me fixed, but not yet he didn't. Not by a pretty far cry.

"Why, he's playing you for a damn fool, Isaac," I said. "Don't you listen to him."

Ford had gotten to his feet, which I took as no good sign, as it suggested he was entertaining Gray's offer, and he set in to pacing back and forth in the drizzle. He suddenly whirled on Gray. "Where's this mountain you're talking about?" he said.

"Hard by here. Just a few minutes' stroll."

"And it's galena, sure enough?"

"It certainly is. A fortune in silver."

This paused him, and I had to give him credit for hesitating. "What, it's been assayed already?" he said.

I laughed out loud at Gray's blunder, but Gray was too slippery to let a little nick like that slow him down. "Not yet," he said, "but I'm certain it's rich in silver."

"You see, Ford?" I said. "He *thinks* he's found galena, and he *thinks* it's rich in silver, and if you'd just be good enough but to let him go so he can kill you, he'll share with you half the spoils."

Gray smiled and addressed himself to Ford. "Whitman is nearly correct," he said. "If you'd be good enough to let me go so I can kill *him,* I'll share half the silver with you."

At least he was being direct now. I warned Ford: "First me, then you, Isaac. That's what he has in mind, mark me."

Ford ignored me. "Supposing it don't have no silver in it," he said to Gray. "Hell, supposing it ain't even galena."

"If it has no silver in it, then what you and I have together is a lead mine, which is more than either of us possesses at the moment. As for its being galena, rest assured. I have that on good authority."

He waited for Ford, and Ford obliged him with a low growl: "Whose authority?"

"Whitman's," Gray said. I never heard my name sound dirtier than Gray could make it sound. His words came faster now. "He found it, and he cut me in. But he wouldn't tell you about it because he didn't want to share with you. I wanted to include you, but he wouldn't hear of it. I own half of it now, and you can own the other half."

Ford stared down at Gray for a rather long moment, nodding his head the while. At last he said, "And so what you're propositioning at me is that we use him up and split the claim down the middle, is that it?"

"That's it. Nothing simpler."

I watched Ford closely, unable to predict his response. He was shaking and shaking his head, trying to process all this information. "What kind of trick is this?" he muttered. Then he turned to me. "Is that true, Whitman? Did you make that claim and share half with the parson?"

"Yes," I said, low so Gray couldn't hear. "We have a contract and everything. But you ought to know that Gray took his half at gunpoint. And what he has yet to understand is that what he owns half of is the *lead*, not the silver, which is how I laid it out in the document. How are you along the lines of reading, Stormy?"

"Middlin'. Show me that contract. I know 'silver' starts with *S*."

"Yes, it does. Then *I, L, V, E* and *R*."

I handed him the paper, and we squatted together over the fire. "You won't find the word anywhere in here," I said. "The only word you'll find in here starts with *S* is my first name. See?" I traced over every word with my index finger, to satisfy him completely. Then I concluded: "What Missionary Gray owns is a mountain of un-smelted lead. Or half of one, I should say."

Gray hadn't heard me, but he could see we were looking at the contract, and he was worried I might be turning Ford against him. "Pay him no mind, Mr. Ford!" he shouted. "With him out of the way, we'll make our own contract, between honest gentlemen, and we'll split everything down the middle!"

Ford folded the paper back up and handed it to me. He stepped over to Gray and stood hulking over him for a thoughtful moment. I could see him breathing. Suddenly he reared back and kicked Gray hard in the stomach. I don't believe it was the hardest kick he could have mustered, but still I was glad it was aimed at Gray and not me.

He squatted where Gray writhed, sucking in air, and said quietly, "You didn't know your man, see. Since Forty-Eight I been panning and sifting and traipsing through these mountains. You won't fetch a truer or bluer miner than Stormy Isaac. Us sourdoughs knows the rules and respects 'em. And as much as a Forty-Eighter hates to see a puffed-up little pup like Whitman here get rich, while a man like me goes on rockin' the cradle in ice-cold water up to his shins, well, that's just the way things be, and a Forty-Eighter wouldn't for the very life of him dream of taking at the point of a gun what was come by honestly. You ought to be first horsewhipped and then strung up, that's the fittinest thing for the likes of you."

One thing I learned over the next few days as we crested the Sierra is that traveling in company of prisoners is about the most unpleasant pastime I'd ever hit upon. Whatever future straits I might find myself in, I vowed, I should never turn my hand to the law, nor to kidnapping, nor bounty hunting, nor slave trading, nor to any other occupation that requires crossing country with people who must be kept in bonds. For you do ever so much nursemaiding. If your prisoner cares for a bite to eat, you must provide it or suffer the pangs of conscience. If the pitch is steep, you must lend a hand or risk seeing your prisoner topple to his death. Logs, bogs, mosquitoes—oh, it makes for slow going. More than once I was tempted to cut Gray free, just so he wouldn't be such a burden, or to put a bullet in his brain and be done with it. For it was as Ford had said: Gray had earned it, and I'd have been within my rights.

Gray didn't say very much for the remainder of the journey. Not that he'd been humbled, though. He was sullen and surly, stewing, and I reckoned he was quietly calculating some way of securing that galena claim for himself after all, once he'd reached Placerville.

As for Ford, he had acquitted himself well in the moment, but I'd seen his eyes light up with the fever when Gray had described the galena find, and an idea of Stormy Isaac as a paragon of virtue just didn't square with what I'd known about the man. I'd heard convincing rumors of his having jumped claims both in California and Colorado, his noble harangue about the sacred miners' code notwithstanding. So he, too, would have to be guarded against, and he appeared to be craftier than I'd been prepared to give him credit for.

It did little to allay my suspicions about Ford when Honey

confided to me that she'd seen him mark our campsite with his knife on a tree. It was clear enough that he had it in mind to return to the site and scour the neighboring hills for the monument I'd erected to stake my claim, on some future date subsequent to my untimely demise, no doubt.

But for now, we were traveling with the understanding that the galena belonged to me and to me alone, Gray's contract having been rendered null and void by his admission that it had been entered into by force.

Clarissa had got her voice back after another day, though she was slow in recovering her senses. Honey had mothered her something fierce, and when Clarissa pleaded to have her bonds removed, just for a little while, Honey petitioned me on her behalf. To this I easily relented, it was so poison difficult keeping her moving with her hands bound, especially given that she could only see out of one eye. So we released her but kept her away from her husband and only allowed her to have her hands free during daylight, while we were on the move.

She didn't give us a moment's trouble, acted more sad than angry, but voiced repeatedly that she couldn't understand why she'd been made a prisoner. Well, I knew she was in a fragile enough state, so I didn't tell her why, just let her think the worst of us if that was what she wanted to do.

As for Honey, she was the most delightsome little helpmate any man ever wanted. Handy with tools, unflagging, brave, always cheerful, last to sleep and first to awake, constantly on the lookout and never missing a thing. And, oh, our moments alone! Three or four hours without a touch from her were like crossing a waterless tract, and when we two crept off under a bower to snatch a few moments of bliss, that was stumbling into an oasis resplendent with pools and gardens and sweetmeats. The scent of her, the taste of her, how her little body felt up against mine . . . I had been with women before, and I had even been in love, and though I racked my brain for anything like it in my history, I could find no parallel. I told myself that I would get my fill and must be patient for the time when my ardor would have expended itself, perhaps when we reached Placerville, perhaps later. But by and by I must come to my senses and discard this infatuation, and the squaw with it.

Alas, I was to be denied the better part of my oases, for when we encountered an express rider hauling mails up over the mountains to the mining camps, Gray hailed him and began pouring earful after earful of woe about his and Clarissa's being missionaries robbed and kidnapped by us brigands and outlaws, who meant to spirit the good Christians all the way to San Francisco, whence they would be shipped as slaves to China should their families lose any time about ransoming them. It spilled out of him so smooth and fast that I knew he'd been silently rehearsing it for some time.

Well, an express rider stops for nothing, not even the plots of cheap novels, and there was no law for the stranger to alert back down the trail the way we'd just come, so we weren't awfully worried on this count. But we knew it looked pretty sinister to be traveling along with Gray all tied up like that, so I deemed it prudent to send Honey on ahead of us half a mile or so as a scout, with orders to run back to us if she spied anyone approaching, to give us sufficient time to hide ourselves and Gray. So now I saw her mostly at night. But I made the best of that, I assure you.

We topped out in the high Sierra, that rarified world of green and blue and white, and descended those beautiful steep slopes that were draped in all the loveliness of late spring, breathing the very freshest air to be found on earth, reveling in the clearest and most becoming light. We picked our way around the worst canyons, skirted the shores of majestic Lake Tahoe, which stood gleaming royal blue and compassed about by its rich forests of pine, and dropped down to lower country where chaparral gave way to sweet grasses and where we began to encounter cattle ranging far from their ranches.

Once at noon, with the group resting alongside the trail that snaked its way down the canyons, I lifted Gray's rifle and fired idly at a bighorn sheep that was grazing high above us in a small flock. It was nearly an impossible shot, at least for me, an indifferent marksman, and when the ewe fell over I actually gasped in astonishment. In my lovesickness I credited to Honey that stroke of good fortune, which had befallen us just in time to stave off serious hunger, for our food stores had become nearly depleted. But when I turned to her and grinned I saw in her features neither delight nor gratitude, but unmitigated anguish. She was gazing up the hillside through eyes that were but pots of bitter tears.

"Why, what is it, Honey?"

But she would not answer me. She looked and looked, with increasing sorrow, and then, scowling harshly, she turned her back and strode down the trail. Confused at this display, I climbed up to retrieve the animal, and before I was even close I could hear the lambs bawling. A pair of them, I soon saw, still standing knock-kneed and trembling on the ledge where their mother had been when I'd shot her, bleating their despair at being put alone in the world, too young to survive on anything but the milk from the mother I'd killed. Well, it made me feel awfully low, I can tell you that. I knew now why Honey had rebuked me so: she would rather have stumbled all the way to Placerville on an empty stomach than to have taken those lambs' mother away.

I stood there for a good long while studying those helpless little creatures. I knew that the merciful thing—shooting them both—was also the practical thing, for they would suffer starvation or predation if I left them, and we needed the meat. So I chose the bigger of the two, lifted the rifle—and lowered it. I couldn't bring myself to it. The woman had made me go soft in the head.

That night, Honey would not partake of the sheep, so I, too, abstained. I cooked a leg of it for the others and without any supper betook me to the open spot of ground at the edge of camp where Honey had made up our beds. She lay beside me rigid as an oar, her eyes wide open to the stars.

"Honey," I whispered, "I never knew she had little ones. If I'd have known that, I never in a million years would have shot her. It's true, Honey. You've got to believe that, Honey. I'm not that kind of a man."

Well, she just refused to answer me, and I confess that it got my dander up some. As a general thing, I'll apologize once, twice perhaps, but never will I grovel, especially when innocent. So I rolled onto my side with my back to her and my arms crossed, taking care not to brush against her. I'd been speaking the truth. It had been an innocent error on my part, and I saw no reason why I should be punished for it for the rest of my life. Besides which, I wondered, what self-respecting Blackfoot, facing real hunger, went all to mush over a couple of orphaned lambs? It didn't make a lick of sense. Honey could hang, for all I cared. It took me a good long while to fall asleep, but I managed it.

I woke up an hour later with her sitting on me and leaning to kiss at my neck, where I could feel her hot tears falling. I pulled her down against me and hugged her tenderly, chastely, to comfort her, but I felt her hips moving down below, which stirred up the animal in me. I took her ear in my teeth and wrapped my fist in her hair, and in a kind of desperate frenzy she worked up her tunic and fumbled with her hand until we were interlocked. We lay that way, perfectly still, breathing together like two beasts hiding from a common enemy, and when it got to be too much we began to move; and when we were finished I somehow knew that I'd put a baby inside of her this time, and that my days as a respectable citizen had drawn to a sudden and spectacular end.

Ford was more talkative than usual this night. We would be in Placerville in the morning, and I supposed he was feeling festive, his spirit exulting at the imminent prospect of quitting our prisoners. Besides, something about having sided with me in the claim dispute days ago had altered his estimation of me, a change which I took as evidence of a quirk of human nature with which I was not unfamiliar. I, of course, had not changed one iota as a result of his taking my side. But as he saw it, he had helped me when I was in a tight place, and so therefore I must have been worthy of his help, as evidenced by the fact that he had helped me. I point this out as no insult to Ford's intellect but rather to humans' general want of reason, for we all govern our affairs by similar illogic. Sometimes I marvel that we can even feed ourselves.

Yes, Ford now appeared to find my existence less offensive than previous. And tonight, with the lights of Placerville twinkling off in the distance and the prospect of ridding ourselves of the missionaries imminent, he took the occasion to unburden himself of several chapters of his personal history.

At fifteen, he said, he had been apprenticed to a chandler who was the head of a large family and the most prodigious drinker and philanderer the young Ford had ever encountered. In Ford the man had found not merely a student of chandlery but also an eager acolyte to the twin arts of tippling and womanizing. Like many a man of loose moral character and bawdy habits, the chandler kept rigid business hours. Forced himself to, lest he lose all to his passions. Thus he and Ford appeared in their shop by six o'clock sharp every morning, howsoever steep and ornate the debaucheries they had been up to in the previous hours, and worked with iron discipline until five every evening, with a dinner break at one, which was often enough spent in the company of ale wenches, *nymphs du pave,* or the wives of neighbors.

"We are set down here on earth to enjoy ourselves," the chandler often reminded his impressionable assistant. "We must earn our bread, of course, but only in order that we might continue in the pursuit of our pleasures." And: "Too many men enslave themselves to convention and to moral restraint, letting the good things of life pass them by. But the wise man knows that tobacco, drink, and women—*all* women—were put on earth for the enjoyment of men." This was their code, and they hewed to it with great honor.

Ford despised the chandlery with its drudgery and smells, the stooping and bending and the insufferable *taking care.* But he adored those other, extracurricular, aspects of his apprenticeship that I have just been describing, and he quickly developed a filial, even worshipful, regard toward his employer. One night they outpaced themselves with their carousing, slept not a wink, guzzled barrels of whiskey, and each of them took four women in succession.

When six o'clock came, they banished the women, slapped down their cups, and betook themselves to the shop as usual. But master and student were still reeling drunk and dog-tired, and so graceless and bungling were their efforts that soon the puncheon floor was coated with spilled wax. The chandler allowed that just this once he might do better with a little nip of something to shave off the edge and went home to fetch it from his cupboards. He returned to discover Ford standing asleep before a tub of wax boiling over into the fire. He clapped the boy smartly about the shoulders and pressed his flask to young Ford's lips, and they proceeded to make their condition worse.

Well, in a little while, it seems the blundering chandler plunged his bare right hand into a bubbling vat and brought it back out severely burned. He was not so far gone as to overlook the importance of returning home to see after his wound, and he was away on this errand a tolerably long time.

Unsupervised, Ford fell asleep again and let the fires go out. At half past one, the chandler's wife sent her daughters, seventeen and fifteen, to see why the young apprentice had made no appearance at dinner, and when the entire trio failed to return in good time, she dispatched her husband after them, burned hand or no. He discovered the three of them there in the shop in a most unholy state, Ford imparting to the girls an education unavailable in most institutions outside the church.

That old chandler seized an andiron from the stone-cold fireplace and would have put out Ford's brains with it but for his righthandedness and for the survival instinct that removed the astonished boy from harm's way just in time. The first blow landed on Ford's back hard enough to hurt like the very dickens, but not hard enough to stop him running for the door pulling up his britches as he went. He quickly outdistanced the chandler, who nevertheless made a second lucky throw that fetched the other andiron the very exact same place on the boy's upper back where he'd been struck a moment earlier.

Like a dog with his tail between his legs our young Ford gathered himself up and flew, flew clear out of that town never to return, though asking himself how in the deuce he had offended the chandler, who had always, right up till that moment, so heartily advocated for just such behavior.

It was a question of some lasting puzzlement to Ford, whether and how he had wronged his employer, and he at last concluded that only excessive drink could have made the chandler lose his mind so. And from the instant Ford arrived at that revelation (he would always remember the circumstances of his epiphany:

a rainy evening in a farmer's hayloft with the mists rising over the meadows, the farmer's wife dozing at his side), he resolved to abstain from strong drink for all the long remainder of his life.

And he did it, too, without wavering. So deeply ran his conviction for teetotalism that he took up with a temperance society, the better part of whose members were female, and he worked his way through that rather dowdy crowd, more or less getting his living by keeping those godly women occupied when their husbands weren't looking. But in time he was discovered and set naked astride a rail, and it was only the intervention of a free-thinker within the mob that saved him from being "doctored" for his sins, although the splinters of that weather-beaten old length of fencing almost accomplished the same end.

Well, he drifted to Illinois, where he happened to fall in with the Mormons, about whom he'd heard it whispered that their marital habits might be to his liking. And they were, though plural marriage was still an open secret at the time. He took a mere three "spiritual wives," which was a tasteful show of restraint. But when Joseph Smith was killed, Ford reckoned it was all up for the church, Brigham Young being coarse and blunt and monogamous where Smith had been refined and eloquent and promiscuous. So he quit the religion and took to high-seas piracy. (Of course time would prove him wrong about Young and about the future prospects of Mormonism, for the Saints would thrive in the Far West, with both the land of the Great Basin and the institution of polygamy greening to full flower under the firm hand of Brigham, who came around all right to the idea of having more than one wife, deciding at long last that he could possibly stand it as long as it was kept within reasonable bounds, and so established in his household a modest harem of seventy or so. Yes, Ford would have done all right staying with the church, but no matter: he'd learned enough during his brief affiliation that now he could slip into any Mormon encampment or city, "brother-and-sister" the residents, mouth the words to *The Spirit of God Like a Fire Is Burning,* and be fed and sheltered like any long-lost member of the flock.)

In the event, piracy disagreed with him altogether. He discovered, too late, that he had been deceived by the brochures, for despite the high promises of adventure and romance, life at sea was far worse drudgery than candle-making and completely destitute of those alluring consolations that had made bearable his chandlery apprenticeship. Having forsworn drinking, he had no use for the constant flow of rum shipboard, and one finds at a glance that a pirate ship is generally bereft of women, unless a prisoner is taken, a happy event that occurs with but regrettable infrequency.

No, nothing would answer but for Ford to do the practical thing and learn to content himself with sodomy, a thing he tried out but never quite took to the way some of the fellows did. Many of his swarthy, bloodthirsty comrades swore they had everything they wanted right on board that boat and wouldn't go ashore for all the vast riches and compliant virgins on earth. They called each other by pet names and forged amorous allegiances that weren't any different from marriages. Ford gamely tried his hand at it—he was conscientious in those days—but there was always something missing in it. "Three things, to be exact," he said with a wink, and I reckoned I could guess those three things but doubted that Gray, who I saw was listening despite himself, had the imagination to name them.

When his ship, the *Cock and Bull,* overran a French vessel in the shallow waters off Jamaica, putting its surviving crewmen overboard, Ford went below decks of the captured ship and discovered a scullery maid cowering in a cabinet amongst her pots and pans. Under the rigid ethical code of the pirates, Ford was obliged to report his find to his superiors, and in the natural course of things his captain would have demanded the damsel for himself. But Ford was not in the sharing mood.

He hid with the maid there in the galley of the French ship until nightfall when, his companions presuming him lost in the skirmish, he stole a skiff, spirited the maiden aboard, and rowed off, directionless, in the moonlight. They honeymooned in that open boat as it drifted for days upon days and then weeks upon weeks, never coming in sight of land for the space of five months.

They subsisted on rainwater and flying fish, which Ford caught in his hat like a naturalist netting butterflies, as mysterious currents pulled them along in a firmly northeast direction, finally depositing them smack on a beach in Normandy within view of the girl's ancestral home! For she had begun life as an heiress, one understands, and it was only through treachery and kidnapping, etc., that she had fallen to her low estate. Now all would be restored.

The charming young couple strolled up to the mansion in fine fettle, for the rains had been plentiful, and they'd never wanted for flying fish during their voyage. But alas, Ford's ardent ministrations on board the rocking skiff had not been without effect, for at the time they made landfall the wench was big with child, which infuriated her parents, who incidentally had long ago made up their minds on the Mormon Question, making things even hotter for Ford.

In that family they had a fine dungeon and a guillotine so fetching as to be the envy of all their neighbors, and Ford found himself reflecting that while the heiress was interesting to him, so was the idea of keeping his head attached to his body. Once again he fled for his life out into the cold world alone.

He drifted eastward, ever eastward, and had equally astonishing adventures in Italy and Greece and the Holy Land. He broke the heart of an Ethiopic princess who wore a gilded whalebone nose piercing and fashionable wooden clogs imported all the way down there from Holland.

He crossed the mighty Himalaya by llama, which he assured us was the commonest conveyance in those parts. ("If they haven't got an errand across town, they'll invent one, just so's to clap a saddle on one of them llamas same as you or I would any plug; and skill? Why, our plains tribes should blush to call themselves riders! These fellers—and I've seen it more than once, mind—can stoop to pluck a hairpin off the grass at full gallop—*with their teeth.*")

He distinguished himself as a soldier of fortune in some of the "famousest" battles of the "Ming Dynasty of Japan."

He sampled a hundred nationalities of women ("Persian are the freshest, Russian the most technical") but had at last grown lonesome for the sights and sounds of America and, swallowing down his aversion to shipboard life, had boarded a sealer in the Commander Islands bound for San Francisco.

Having fetched up in California, he resolved to make his way over the Sierra to look in on his brethren the Saints, who were at that historical moment streaming into Deseret in a mighty caravan stretching from Missouri to Utah. But some of his fellow Mormons working in Sacramento had breathed a single word to him that had changed his life forever: *gold*!

On hearing the word, he had taken to the hills and never looked back. Oh, he had seen the whole world and tried his hand at a thousand occupations, but none suited him like the life of a miner. Bend and help yourself to a little wealth from the ground, a little float from the brook—the Creator had just left it lying about!—and then go on a spree until your pockets are empty again and then collect some more.

"Still," he said, "sometimes I do fall to thinking about how things might have gone different for me and that French gal. Maybe if I hadn't of ever joined the church, her parents might have had me."

He sighed heavily and poked at the fire. "Alas, to think of my little boy the marky—"

"Marky?" Gray said, scowling (for he had leaned forward now to listen in earnest).

"You might pronounce it *marquis,*" I said.

Ford shot Gray a thunderous look and continued. "Yes, just to think of my boy, the marky, livin' it up over there in France all right but still all the time wondering where his rightful Daddy be. Oh, gentlemen, I sometimes take a notion to give up the miner's life and hie me right back over there to Europe, take that boy in my arms and do my honest part towards his rearing. To think of me, the father of a marky, out in these hills around a wood fire, eatin' half-spoiled mountain sheep with such a set of swindlers and Injuns as the lot of you." He shed a fat tear at the shame of it all, which was admirable histrionics for someone without any training.

"But Ford," I said after a respectful pause, "if you're his father, then he hasn't got any claim to title, has he, being the bastard line?"

"There's your ignorance showing, right there," Ford said. "What he's got is uterus nobility, which comes straight out the hole with him at birth and can't be shook off him or stole from him for nothing. There's every different kind of nobility over there, you know. Uterus, clock, military, horseback, gradual. His is the uterus type, which is the one that *sticks.* Got it straight from his mother."

"Interesting," I said. "I wonder how do you get the gradual type?"

He shrugged. "Little at a time, I reckon."

"And the clock?"

"Rile my picture, *I* don't know. There's every kind of nobility there, and all kinds of ways to come by it. But I only ever was in

France for a short spell and hadn't time to memorize it all."

Gray couldn't help himself. "But all that time during your sea voyage with the maiden, you must have learned a great deal of the language from her, one imagines," he said.

"Oh, yes," Ford said without hesitation. "Every last word of it."

"Alors, dis-moi, s'il te plaît: quel était le nom de cette fille, la mère de ton fils le marquis?"

"Wahl," Ford says. "That won't work on me, I'm afeared. I forgot to mention this gal fell off a wagon when she was small and bit half her tongue off. Left her speaking a Francis all her own, you might say. 'Twas that she taught me, for hers was the only kind she had available. She was my main teacher, so when I speak the Francis, I sound exactly like her, more less. You parbly wouldn't understand me, even with all that education of yours. But we can try, since it means so much to you. *Swampfish spillgravy shoofly dungmound?*"

"Impressive," I said. "What exactly did you say to him there, Stormy?"

"Just asked after his kinfolk."

"Low humor, befitting the base," says Gray.

"Gray," I said, "It isn't very good form to go aspersioning another man's upbringing, and if you'd spent any amount of time in the mountains you'd know that. You ought to be ashamed of yourself."

"Ah, leave him be," Ford growled. "He's just embarrassed to see I can do the gibberish just as good as he can."

I went to bed that night alone, as I had for the past two nights. Although Honey and I had seemed to have put the incident of the ewe pleasantly behind us, the way in which we did so had had its own regrettable sequel. To put it plainly, in the very next moments after I'd got Honey with child, I'd felt the onset of creeping remorse, with the regrets washing over me so heavy and thick that I near to have drowned in them. Couldn't sleep at all and found myself gnashing in the darkness and pleading to a God in whose existence I disbelieved to undo my sin. I bargained that I'd do most anything, up to and including leaving off harassing his missionaries, if he could only but see his way clear to wipe clean my blunder.

Well, I guess maybe Honey saw the chagrin all over my face the next morning, and I'm sure that I failed completely in disguising the cold contempt that had sprung up in me overnight. Now all that tender passion she'd shown there in those few moments after she'd awakened me had vanished away completely, and no woman ever looked more like a mile of stone wall than she did.

I don't know but what maybe she was just as proud and stubborn as I was, and that she had reasoned that if she couldn't have me then she refused to *want* me. And so where once we'd made every noon and night and chance interaction crackle with mutual desire, now it was just all business on the trail. If I needed a thing done, I asked her in the same way one asks a servant or a clerk. And as our party's scout, if she had information to impart, she did so dutifully, without the slightest trace of affection to disturb her countenance. After only a day of this it was easy to believe that the love-warmth that had once existed between us had been nothing more than a moment's dream, now past and over.

All this was happening just as Clarissa Gray was becoming more talkative. At first it had been just a little request here and there. *A mouthful of water, please,* or, *I would like to rest now,* most such utterances being directed at Honey but a few aimed my way, and I took them with pleasure. Over time Clarissa began commenting on the weather, on the scenery. By and by she began helping Honey tend the fire and do the cooking. And as the days went on, an understanding dawned on her that awful things had befallen her recently. By that last night, above Placerville, when Stormy told us his life's tale, she'd waxed just loquacious enough to draw me aside and ask me outright what her husband had done to deserve his bonds.

There might have been a loaded cannon pointed at me instead of that question, but nothing came of my wishing. "Well, ma'am," I said sort of slowly, "I'm not so certain I should tell you. You're in a fragile way yet, and I'd surely hate to see you come to further distress."

"I'm a stronger woman than that, Mr. Whitman," she said. And while there was once a time when I'd have believed her, I took her silence over the last several days as pretty sufficient proof to the contrary. She also said, "I know you for a good man, and doubt that you would bind my husband without some cause. What is it that he's done?"

Well, hell. I could see she was going to be persistent, and I decided I'd rather have her know all that had transpired before we reached Placerville instead of letting everything fall on her at once. So I said, "I'll put it to you straight, then, Mrs. Gray. Your husband raised his rifle three times. Once at a miner, once at Mr. Ford, and once at myself, finger on the trigger all three times, all in the space of a few quick hours. Something in him got knocked loose, I'm afraid, and Mr. Ford and I don't feel he's to be trusted with weaponry until he gets down out of the hills and takes his rest in Placerville a while."

She listened closely, nodding and looking at the ground. Then she lifted her head and met my gaze, and my heart melted a little bit; I couldn't help it. "And what happened to my eye and mouth, Mr. Whitman?"

"Indians, ma'am," I said just above a whisper. "You all were attacked, and 'twas that which set loose the demons in your husband."

She looked on me and looked on me, and I set in to squirming and blushing. I could feel her opinion of me improving as she looked, and that made me awful bashful. Besides, she was about the handsomest woman I'd ever laid eyes on, other than Honey. "You saved us, didn't you, Mr. Whitman? From the Indians?"

"No, ma'am, I most assuredly did not," I said. "We got there too late."

"But then you helped us. You came to our aid and saw to our injuries."

I shrugged. There was no great honor in what we had done. Anyone who roamed the prairies knew that it was unconscionable to ignore a party in distress. That woman just kept on looking at me, though, and it surely made me feel a way, kind of like I'd just been born and died and born and died.

"Mr. Whitman," she said at last. "I know that you're telling the truth to me. Thank you for doing the humane thing in binding my husband instead of choosing a more aggressive course. I'm well aware that many men would have been considerably less forbearing."

I felt my innards all go to liquid and pool up in my boots. "Shucks, Mrs. Gray," I said through my swollen tongue. "It isn't any kind of a thing at all."

Then she reached out and grasped my hand, and I about leaped clean out of my shirt. "Please," she said softly, "you may call me Clarissa."

I cleared my throat and stamped my foot like a stutterer. "I reckon I hadn't better," I said, "although I appreciate the opportunity to do so."

So that was where things stood the night before we were to descend upon Placerville: Honey become bitterly estranged, carrying my child, and Clarissa Gray purring her thanks to me *for keeping her husband tied up*! Well, tomorrow all this madness would end, all but my dealings with Stormy Isaac Ford. And the miracle of it was that the old cob was beginning to grow on me. He'd even honored me by trying his hand at a campfire "quaint." Oh, that tale of his was rather pale and sickly next to a lot of them that you and I have heard. Too much truth in it, to my ear, which spoils the savor. But he'd exerted himself in the telling of it, and I've always believed a man should be given credit for making an honest effort of a thing like that.

Don't you?

Chapter Seven

Honey walks on—How trifles can spoil attachments—We meet Judge Cutler—Clarissa impresses—Heartbreak—Provisioning up—My friend the assayer–Clarissa surprises—An alarming revelation.

Our first order of business on arriving in Placerville was to look up a judge. Under easier circumstances, we might have seen to a bath or a meal first, but the fact was that we sort of had a boar hog by the legs and needed somebody to hand him off to. That is, we'd bound Gray and led him into town like he was a convict, which of course he wasn't. But if we set him free, he'd quite likely try to kill us there on the street, which would have been a hassle. So now we had dual purposes in seeking out legal counsel.

I stopped in the middle of Main Street to ask the first man I met where we might locate a judge. He pointed us up the way just a short piece, and we continued, with Honey in the lead as usual. But when she reached the judge's office, that woman never stopped, just continued all straight backed and proud clear on up the street. I hollered after her, thinking at first that she'd missed her turn, but she gave no notice of having heard me (despite being equipped to hear ants crawling half a league away), and in another moment she'd disappeared around the bend without so much as a fare-thee-well.

Another man might have been stumped by this behavior, but

I didn't have to study over it too hard. I knew in my heart she'd taken permanent leave of me. Lord, to think of it! Just one little misunderstanding involving a sheep, and what you believed was true love forever is flown out the window, spoiled eternally and finally. It just goes to show you that our universe is capricious and that humans are built for sorrow and solitude, constructed to be so feeble of mind as to let any little thing destroy their happiness.

The sudden and haphazard dissolution of my bond with Honey put me somewhat in mind of my once-dear friend Joe Bash. When the two of us met for the very first time, we'd felt an instant mutual affinity born of similitude of spirit, commonality of values, intellectual kinship. Blood brothers, we became, on the very spot. So amenable was our comradeship that we passed, pleasurably, an entire winter crammed into a tiny cabin in the Rocky Mountains, snow to the very eaves and so cold up there we slept with our potatoes; no other human company but just each other. But that was enough, for our conversations were endlessly diverting.

"Joe," I'd say, "is there life on other planets, do you suppose?"

Or, "Joe," I'd say, "share with me your closest-held dreams for the future."

And oh, the discussions that would follow!

By and by spring peeked its head out, and we wandered down out of the mountains and into town, resolved to treat ourselves to a hotel bed. And there in the lobby when I looked over his shoulder at Joe signing the ledger, I had to blink two or three times to be sure I was seeing aright.

"Joe," says I, "you're legally obliged to use your correct name, you understand. No comedy."

Pretty coldly Joe answers, "I did write my own name."

"See here," I said. "You've written *Job Ashe.*"

"Which is what my father named me."

Why, for nine months that callous, uncaring bastard had let me go on calling him Joe Bash! Joe this and Joe that and Joe please pass the salt. I never felt more of a jackass in all my life. I couldn't forgive him for it, yet he wouldn't brook a stitch of displeasure on my part, since he'd been the one to have to endure answering to a faulty name for all those months. And so it was all up, forever and ever, between me and Joe Bash. I can laugh about it now—a little—maybe—but where he is in the world today concerns me not one jot. And I suspect his most closely held dream now is that I'm rotting in hell. You see? A little thing like that, if it gets both parties rankled sufficiently, can undo even the solidest human relations.

Anyhow, this judge's name was Cutler, and his assistant—a beady eyed, beleaguered little fellow name of Alexander—informed us that Cutler was altogether too pressed with any number of matters and could not hear our troubles for just days and days. Then I started depositing gold dust on Alexander's desk and saw the urgency of Cutler's other obligations begin to slacken off some; more gold dust, a little more, and—there! Turned out Alexander had been misreading the docket, and Judge Cutler had a few minutes right now if we were ready. I told him we were.

We stepped into the judge's office, the four of us, feeling rather ragged and rank, considering where we'd come from and how hard we'd traveled, and how fine and sumptuous the judge's diggings were appointed. But he was gracious enough not to have appeared to notice. "Alexander!" he shouts. "Bring this young lady some water. She looks just about fit to swoon into my waiting arms!"

He helped Clarissa into a chair, then stood stroking her hair in a fatherly way, gazing down on her with all the tender regard that late middle age directs upon youthful beauty, murmuring to her that all would be well. And then he chanced to notice us other three.

"Well?" he says, "what the devil do you all want of me?"

I cleared my throat. He did have a brusque, learned way about him.

"Well, sir, your judgeship," I said, "it's a funny couple of matters not fully intertwined though not entirely independent one from another, neither. That is, the one stems from the other, but only in a sort of offhanded kind of a way." I was picking around for the word "tangential," but the blamed thing just would not show. "That is, sir—"

"He's an imbecile," Judge Cutler pronounced, turning to Ford. "You explain it."

Ford drew in a deep breath, studying the ceiling as he gathered his thoughts, but the gathering went on and on without issue, and the judge lost patience with him, too.

"You there," he said to Gray. "Your hands are bound up. Perhaps you can tell me why that would be."

"Certainly, your honor," Gray said, just as cool as if it was old times between him and this judge. "My wife and I are humble missionaries to the tribes and camps. Quite incidentally we discovered a silver mine. These vulgar men bound us up, meaning to cheat us of our claim, and to rid themselves of us by some nefarious means that is not yet clear to me. They are frauds and brutes. They must be arrested at once."

The judge appeared to have heard about one third of Gray's speech, tenderly stroking Clarissa's fair hand and looking fondly down upon her. "Tell me, dear," he said, "of the crimes of these men. Leave nothing out. I am only too familiar with the ways of such malefactors and suffer no illusions but that when they had you bound up, lovely and helpless, they unleashed their appalling animal urges; they always do. No, no, you needn't blush. You are in safe hands now, and I will see the brutes hang for their outrages or die myself. Impossible, though, without your testimony, which must be as complete as you can make it. Go on, in detail. Begin with the ravishment, and we shall hear the remainder later on."

"Your honor, you are very kind," Clarissa Gray said. "And yet you are mistaken, I'm afraid. These two gentlemen never laid a finger upon me. And, in fact, it is my husband who—"

"I see! I see! Now it becomes clear. It is *he* who ravished you, and these good men are your deliverers." To Gray: "You, sir, are both a liar and a scoundrel eternally undeserving of such a bride." Back to Clarissa, softly: "The case becomes more difficult, dear heart. As you are no doubt aware, a man does possess certain rights *vis à vis* his lawfully wedded wife, and I am not off the top of my head aware of precedent for bringing charges against a married man for the crime to which you allude. And yet I cannot but believe that a careful study of the case law, subsequent to your most thorough description of the specific acts, leaving out no details, however trifling you might judge them, should yield a result favorable to your cause. Begin now, taking care to omit nothing."

"No, your honor," Clarissa said patiently. "No crime of ravishment occurred."

"Well, the criminality of the act is for me to determine, based upon the evidence, lamb. I must hear the evidence. You may begin."

"But no ravishment occurred, your honor, be it criminal or be it sanctioned by matrimony."

"No ravishment? Blast! Then why the deuce have you come?"

"Your honor, there is a small mining camp situated along the Carson River on the eastern slope of the Sierra," she answered. "We come from there. A murder occurred, the sequel to which is this: two factions contend in mutual accusation, a loggerheads that appears as dangerous as it is intractable. These two men, nominated by their fellows, each representative of one of the two factions, have traveled here to secure your aid in resolving the conflict, which threatens the lives and fortunes of some forty miners. Their party rescued my husband and me after an Indian raid, the trauma of which appears to have undone my spouse's reason, for he became so belligerent and threatening that these men were obliged to restrain him for the remainder of the journey. Thus they wish to dispose of these two distinct, yet tangentially related, matters."

Tangentially! Why, she made it look so easy.

I wasn't the only one to think so. "Good heavens, woman," Judge Cutler exclaimed. "How you wield the gift of talk! Would that a single solitary lawyer ever standing before my bench could speak with even half your cogency, mellifluousness, and charm!" By now he was petting her bare arm and pressing his cheek against hers. "Of course I'll jail your husband for you, just as you ask . . ." Then he turned to us. "But as for you and your mining camp, you can all go hang!"

He stepped to his desk and tapped at a little brass bell, but the clapper must have been broken, for it plinked once, muffled and truncated, and the sound did not carry. "Alexander!" he shouted. "Get Fuller in here to tote this rapist over to the jail!"

"But your honor," Clarissa said, "I never said to jail him! And—"

"Of course you did, dear." He looked at us again. "Why are you two still standing in my office?" he said.

"Well, sir," I said, "there's one other thing more."

"Sir?" he said. "*I'll* call *you* 'sir.' You'd best go in for 'your honor'."

"Yes, sir," I said. "Yes, your honor. See, this rifle belongs to Mr. Gray here."

Cutler flapped his hand. "Lean it there behind the door, and I'll see he gets it on his release."

"And sir, your honor?" I said. "I wish to impress upon you the grave urgency of your visiting our camp and resolving this dispute. I mean, your honor sir, that it is imperative you come out there with us and hear the evidence."

Cutler had moved to his desk, where he lit a clay churchwarden pipe and sat puffing it, staring at Clarissa. "Out where?" he said rather distractedly.

"To our camp, your honor sir."

"I know *that,* confound you." Reluctantly looking away from Clarissa, he stepped to the enormous bookcase behind his desk and pulled forth a volume, and I noticed that most of what he had back there were mining, not legal, texts. "Here's a map of the Carson," he said, opening the book. "Show me the place of your camp."

"More or less in through here," I said, pointing.

"Why, that stretch of river was picked over years ago," the judge said. "There isn't anything in there."

"We're finding the color all right," I said.

"The hell you say." He closed the book. "Language; sorry, ma'am."

Clarissa nodded demurely, but Ford said, "Oh, you needn't trouble yourself on her account, judge. She can serve it up thicker'n any hostler."

Cutler gazed upon the blushing Clarissa with increased fascination. After a moment he seemed to remember something. "Ma'am," he said, "what's all this about silver?"

"Your honor, I know nothing at all about any silver."

He turned to the sulking Philemon Gray and clucked his tongue. "Another filthy lie. You coward."

Now that Ford had opened his mouth, he appeared reluctant to close it again. "Oh, no, sir, your honor," he said hastily. "That part ain't a lie. Whitman here found him a galena deposit, and Gray tried to smouch it from him at the point of a gun. Didn't tell his wife about it, likely on account of not wanting to share with her. But thunder and lightnin', the galena's there. That part's true. Just that it belongs to Whitman alone."

I could see that during the talk of galena, the judge's cheeks had gotten quite a bit ruddier under his gray side whiskers. When Ford was done talking, Cutler turned toward me, his eyes glittering. "You're Whitling?" he said.

"Yes, your honor sir. Whitman."

"And you know galena when you see it?"

"I believe I do, your honor sir." He was leaning in now, same way a heron hunches over a minnow, so I reckoned it was time to prick him to his trade. From my pocket I produced a specimen, a hunk no bigger than a church mouse, and handed it to him without a word.

The judge turned the galena over in his hands, tapping at it, scratching it with his thumbnail. "Hmm," he muttered. "Looks to me like the article." He fetched another volume from his shelf and bent over his desk with the specimen and the text as if he were alone in his office.

In the stillness a quartz wagon labored by in the street, churning and creaking, and then faded off until the only sound in the room was the echoing rumble of Stormy Isaac's belly. By and by the judge seems to have satisfied himself, and he says, "You'll want to have Billy Moore look at that. Did you bring others?"

"Yessir. I aimed to see Moore immediately we were finished here with you."

"Do that."

I knew I had him hooked now, and I wasn't about to let out any slack. "Sir, your honor sir," I said, "I hope you might think again about coming out there and resolving our trouble, your honor sir."

The judge scowled hard at me, but I'd already satisfied myself about him. "And why in the ever-living hell would I ever take it upon myself to do such a foolish thing as that?" he said. "Pardon me, ma'am."

Clarissa shrugged.

"Gold," I said. "And plenty of it. I'll pay you a hundred dollars right now and another hundred-fifty once you've settled the case. And I'll see to it that the boys chip in another two-fifty to see you home on."

The judge stopped smoking for a moment, and now his bewhiskered cheeks and sweeping forehead turned downright pink. "Five hundred?" he said. He held out the fingers of his hands and made as if to be figuring. "Expenses," he muttered. "Time away. Three. Seven. Yes, I see. No, no; I'm afraid it cannot be brought off for anything less than eight hundred."

"Eight hundred, to take a brief journey and spend an afternoon hearing a case?" I said. "Too bad. Well, I reckon there's another judge or two here in town that could be more reasonable."

"Mind your cheek, boy. Seven hundred."

"Six," I said.

"Half now."

"I don't have half now," I lied. "I have two. That doesn't leave me with enough for a bath and a drink."

"Give me the two," the judge said, "and I'll see to your bath and your drink."

I was setting the gold on his scales when the big brute Fuller came in to escort Gray to the jail. At the sight of that lummox, who was armed with a fat cudgel, Gray began sputtering and spitting like a treed cat. "Deceived! She's lied to you, judge! Haven't you eyes to see? Stabbed in the back by one's own helpmate! O, treachery! Betrayal! Diabolical conspiracy! Unholy combination! She has sold herself to these men like any cheap harlot!"

"Hold still, dammit," Fuller grumbled.

But Gray was beside himself. "Delilah! Gomer!" he ranted. "Whore of Babylon! Jezebel! Foul—"

With the speed of a panther, Ford lunged forward and swung his open hand hard into Gray's face, stunning him into silence and damn near knocking him unconscious.

"Good God, man!" Judge Cutler cried. "What in hell did you do that for?"

"Sorry, Judge," Ford muttered. "But he had no call bringing my mule into it."

An hour later I was soaking in a washtub upstairs at the Spangled Agnes, blinking hard to keep my own damn fool tears from fouling up my bathwater. Well, it was just about the damnedest thing. I'd watched Honey go on up the street without me and disappear out of my life forever, likely carrying off my son in her womb, and it hadn't hardly fazed me in the moment. I'd been too preoccupied with how to dispose of Philemon Gray and how I'd convince a judge to come out with us to Whitman's Gulch. It wasn't until I was alone in that room, with all that good clean-smelling soap rising and hissing about me, that I began to feel it. And Lord, I felt it hard.

It was a puzzle to me why it should gut punch me so, for Honey was scarcely the first woman ever to have walked away from me—I'd seen a good deal more backs than fronts over the years—and I had never shed a tear over a woman before now. So why was Honey any different from all those others? It wasn't the baby, if there even was one, because when I canceled him out of the picture, my heart still yearned for Honey. Yet by the natural order of things, she should have been the last woman whose leave-taking I would mourn. I turned it over and over in my mind and came up with the only answer that made sense, except it didn't make any sense at all. The answer was: *Because she was Honey.* With reasoning like that, I guessed maybe the judge was right: I *was* an imbecile.

Sitting there in that water ciphering it all out, the certainty of my destiny with Honey hit me so hard and sudden that I stood straight up in the tub, resolved to bolt off after her right there and then, streaming suds behind me as I went. But just as fast, I checked myself and slumped back down into the bubbles. She was likely long gone, and, besides, she didn't want me, so what was the use?

I lingered for a long time there in my room, licking my wounds and wasting time, then finally dressed and went down to the street to buy up some stores. Not too much, because I didn't reckon on staying very long in those mountains anymore. Johnny and I were wealthy as old Midas, twice over, so as soon as we'd sold out we'd ride our riches back to Missouri and set about establishing ourselves as kings. The placer claim alone had furnished me with enough gold to buy just about whatever I wanted here in town, so, given the events of the past few days, the first thing I did was pick up a large-bore rifle, a twelve-gauge shotgun, and a pair of Navy revolvers.

I locked the long guns in my room, under my mattress, then loaded the revolvers, placed them in the beautiful black, tooled gunbelt I'd just bought, and buckled the outfit around my waist. Feeling like a dashing lawman, I stood before the little cracked mirror in my room and saw that, with my closely shaved face and newly cropped hair and all that freshly exposed skin pale as a snowbank, I resembled nothing more than a child idiot who has found his father's sidearms and is about to injure himself. Well, that couldn't be helped. A man of my means could not afford to go about empty handed.

Next, I purchased a hundred pounds of bacon, coffee, flour, sugar, salt, candy, and all the jerked beef that I could find. I shuttled all this back to my room, grinning like a hyena at the desk man each time I passed through the lobby, and stacked it in a corner. I retrieved the bags containing all my samples and set out for Billy Moore's office.

Moore kept his daytime hours at the near end of the bar called The Gilded Virgin. The place was crowded, but I ordered a glass of rum and managed to wedge myself in right beside Billy. I clapped him on the shoulder.

"Stern Whitman," Billy said.

"Hello, Billy. What, you haven't fled east yet?"

Billy grinned and shook my hand warmly. "No," he said. "There's still enough gold coming down out of those hills to keep me flush. Not a lot of new strikes anymore, but where there's gold there's gold-seekers, and gold-seekers need a bastard like me to break their hearts."

"Well, today I'm one of them damn fool gold-seekers who needs you," I said, tapping my bag furtively.

Billy didn't look too surprised. "Did you bring me enough to work with?" he said.

I nodded.

"What's it in? Quartz?"

I nodded again.

Billy leaned back and swallowed the last of his drink. Crushing his cigar on the bar, he said in a low voice, "I'm headed over to my office to wait for you. Don't come for another hour."

I stood there drinking my rum, which I shouldn't have done, for it darkens my mood every single time, and now it just put me straight back onto thoughts of Honey. By and by, I got to feeling pretty nearly as forsaken as I had up in my room, and I decided I'd better finish out the hour by stepping down into the eating room and getting something into my gut to soak up that rum and stop it doing me harm.

When I got down there and took my chair, I spied old Judge Cutler seated a few tables away with Clarissa Gray. She was wearing a new dress whose overall effect was to make that side of the room something like a flash of lightning, a big generalized one that fires fierce and white, and then stays lit. Never mind Cutler, or the other men, or the women, or the children or dogs; the very cockroaches in the corners were gaping at Clarissa Gray and how she looked in that dress. And her sitting there just laughing warmly and reaching for her teacup, nonchalant as a housecat, as if causing an earthquake were the very last thing on her mind.

She smiled when she saw me. Her bad eye was still black and yellow, but she could see out of it now, and I didn't mind one little bit about that broken tooth, nor did she or anyone else, apparently. I nodded my greeting and wished I'd sat where I couldn't see her. I did my best not to look up.

About halfway into my meal, though, she sort of floats over and hovers there next to my little table, so I jump up and skid the other chair out, and she thanks me and sits. I looked around for the judge, but he was gone. Lord, but she was beautiful. Stem to stern, complete.

"Mr. Whitman," she said, and just those two words had me agreeing all over again with Judge Cutler's assessment of her oratory. "Tomorrow I'm leaving for San Francisco, and then home to Baltimore."

" 'I,' you say. Without your husband, then?"

She smiled, but it was thin as a page of the Bible. "I'm a proud woman, Mr. Whitman. I shouldn't be, but I am."

"No, you should be, ma'am, if anybody's going to take that up."

"Anyway," she said, "I wish to thank you again for your humanity."

"Oh. Well, that isn't anything at all, ma'am."

"And could you also please thank your—thank the woman Honey for me?"

"Ma'am, if ever I set eyes on her again, I will do just that very self-same thing."

Clarissa Gray's eyebrows went up, and her cheeks flushed. Not all at once, but in delightful little patches. "How do you mean, Mr. Whitman?"

I looked down at my plate. "What I mean is that she's flown off, ma'am."

I looked up at her then and couldn't decide from her expression which way she felt hearing that. Maybe neither could she, for then she says, "Why, that's a pity . . . isn't it?"

"I believe it is, ma'am. For me, it is."

I had to say it quick and then take a sip of that awful California wine, to keep from making a complete ass of myself.

While I'm still drinking she says in a new clear voice, "It appears, then, that you and I are both suddenly alone."

Lord, hearing that kind of talk coming from her, I didn't even pause but gulped down the whole glass of wine and would have drunk down three more just to keep from having to answer. She leaned forward. Didn't she know every eye in the place was drawn to her every movement?

"Mr. Whitman," she said, "forgive me if I make you uncomfortable, but I find that candor often serves best. The truth is that as I sit here, it's hard work not to imagine how things might have been different for you and me. In other circumstances, I mean."

Well, no woman that beautiful ever said anything so brazen to me before, but plenty of less beautiful gals certainly had, enough that I knew perfectly well just how vulnerable and deceived she was at the moment to be spewing out that kind of rot. I gave her kind of a sickish smile.

"Well," I said, "fact of the matter is, that's *only* circumstances talking. In the normal course of affairs, a quality woman like you wouldn't have overmuch to do with a robustious, unread prospector such as myself."

The smile my comment produced in her was the saddest thing I'd seen in days. "Stranger things have happened, Mr. Whitman," she said.

"Like me and Honey?"

"Certainly, for one example."

"Come to naught, though, hasn't it? And like what else?"

She leaned even further forward, so I had to fight to keep my eyes up on her face, and she very fairly whispered, "Like me and Philemon Gray." She laughed a tiny, bitter laugh, and then, more to herself than to me, she scoffed, "Me! The wife of a missionary!"

Of course I'd never imagined her as anything else. To me, she might as well have sprung from the womb right along with old Gray, Bible in hand, which come to think of it would have been a killing shock to the mother and to anyone else present at the birth.

"What . . . what were you before?" I asked quietly.

Now she was the one looking down at my plate. "I was his convert," she said simply.

I studied her hand lying there on the table, still soft and pretty despite the hard outdoor life she'd been living, and some enormous portion of me grew just about desperate to reach for it. But instead I bit my lip and watched that hand sit there in its lonely, inviting solitude on the rough, water-stained tabletop and dropped my hands right into my lap where they could keep out of trouble. "He was in no position to be converting you," I said. "You're the one could have taught him about decency."

"You're very kind, Mr. Whitman." Tears were in her eyes now, and that's a mighty dangerous thing for me to be around.

She stood, and I was glad to see her do it, for I doubted of my continued restraint. "Go and find Honey," she said.

I waved my hand. "I think not," I said. "It isn't right for a white man to go chasing down a squaw." Damn me, I had to force the words past a giant lump in my throat.

She was standing there next to me with her hands folded in front of her and everybody in that place still drinking her in. "Mr. Whitman," she said, with those tears just blobbing up there in her eyes, immune to gravity, "many aspects of our religion are, for me, sources of struggle and doubt. But when we teach the Indians, we tell them something I believe unshakably, deep in my heart: that we are all the same in the eyes of God; that if each of us had sufficient understanding, we could see that there is no difference in spirit between the most educated nabob and the hungriest Digger."

I could barely squeeze words out, for the sentiment. "I wish more people believed that, ma'am," I more or less whispered.

"So do I. But you have better understanding of it than most, Mr. Whitman."

I cleared my throat. "Thank you for saying so."

"Goodbye, Mr. Whitman."

"Goodbye, Clarissa."

And with a swish of her lovely skirts, she was gone.

Did Clarissa Gray's kind words lift my spirits any? No, friend, they did not. I staggered over to Billy Moore's shop feeling more or less like I'd been gut shot, for I'd just declined the advances of the most all-around desirable woman I'd ever met. And why? Because of some misplaced attachment to an Indian who didn't care for my company. Oh, I was low, and feeling it, when I came through Billy's door.

"Ah," he says, looking up from his table. "Let's see what you've brought me."

I sighed to shrug out from under my mood and get down to business. "Thing is, Billy," I said, "I've brought you two sets of samples."

"Two? What for?"

"I found galena, and I found gold-bearing quartz both."

"The hell you did."

"The hell I didn't. Look here."

I handed him the galena first. He set it on his workbench and scratched at it with a tool that looked to me about like an icepick, then tapped it with a small hammer and watched a cube of it split free. "I'll have to run some chemical tests," he mumbled. "Fire assay."

"But it looks like galena, doesn't it?" I said.

He frowned and shrugged. "It does," he said, "but I have no way of assessing its content or its value without some rather complex analysis."

I nodded and set down one of the sacks I'd been carrying. "Is that enough for you to work with?"

"You know it is. Stern, where'd you take these samples from?"

"A hill between here and my gulch where the gold is."

"Yes, but how deep did you go for these?"

"Deep? I didn't go deep at all. Picked most of it straight up off the ground and tapped a few pieces off an outcropping."

"All surface samples, then?"

"Yeah. I didn't have time to do anything more."

"I see. Well, irrespective of what I say, an engineer will have to look at the site."

"Kind of figured on that."

"All right. How about the quartz?"

These samples I held in a larger bag, which I laid on the bench and pulled open. Moore lifted a hunk and turned it over in the light. "Good Lord," he said.

"I know it."

"Does it all look like this, or did you cherry pick?"

"I tried not to. These samples are from all over the mountain, surface down to about fifteen feet, which was all I could do by myself. It's a vein, Billy. I believe I've followed it for six hundred feet. Minimal thickness I measured was ten inches, and maximum was eighteen feet."

Moore stood there blinking at me. Finally he says, "Stern, if you've salted this goddamn thing . . ."

"You know me better than that, Billy. Hell."

"Well," he said, collecting himself, "let me get to work on these." I turned to walk out the door, but Billy was too excited to let me go. "You might just be the luckiest son of a bitch in all California," he said.

I nodded, but I was still feeling awfully blue about Honey. Ridiculous, of course, to be awash in wealth and pining over a squaw. But it couldn't be helped.

"Land," Billy said. "If I was you I'd be up there on the ceiling right now, but you nod at me like it was somebody else's gold, or as though your dog had just died."

I shook my head. "A woman," I said. "Busted every bone in my heart."

Billy had already reached under the counter and was pouring us out two little glasses of whiskey. "Why then, I suppose a little of the creature won't come amiss. Might even speed the mending of those heart bones of yours. I'd intended it for congratulations, but we'll swallow it for sorrows just the same."

"Thanks, Billy."

He had some tolerably good cigars there, too, and we smoked and drank, and I unspooled the whole sad yarn about Honey and how I'd gone and fallen in love with her like a first-class idiot. Billy Moore was hardly my closest friend, but Johnny and I had prospected a little with Billy when he was just an eastern college dropout on the ramble, and so it felt comfortable unburdening myself to him. Well, when I got through with my confession, Billy says in a solemn kind of voice, "Stern, I've got some news for you, and I doubt whether you'll find it one bit pleasing to your ear. But I've got to tell it to you or I'm no friend. Stern, that Honey of yours is Ward Carson's woman."

I gaped at him. "Ward Carson?"

Billy nodded his head.

"Ward Goddamn Carson?"

"Ward Goddamn Carson all right."

"Ward Goddamn Fucking Carson?"

"Yessir, the very one."

"Ward—? Hell."

It couldn't have hit me any harder if he'd told me she belonged to old Genghis Khan. I knew about Ward Carson—everybody did—and it taxed my drunken brain to conceive of the likes of Honey ever taking up with a murderous son of a bitch like him.

Ward Carson was a hard-bitten, rangy, lantern-jawed old villain with silver hair to his shoulders, flinty gray eyes, a steep bulletproof nose, and an incongruously weak mouth and chin; and if I had to name a crueler bastard than him or eat poison, I'd call for a little salt and pepper. Why, if you and Ward Carson ever moved at the same time to sit on a log, you made as if to be dusting off that seat for him, knowing he'd killed plenty of men for less serious offenses than out-maneuvering him for a chair. I should say, in fairness, that Ward Carson loved kittens. So much so that he would cross the street just for the chance to stomp one under his boot heel. And Honey had gone along with *him*?

"Why, the foolish girl," I said. "She's lucky he didn't kill her."

Billy only nodded. He was holding something back, and I rather wished he'd out with it, but I could see he wasn't about to volunteer. I looked at him closely.

"What?" I said.

He stuck his cigar in his mouth to free his hands and refilled my glass. "What?" he said through the cigar.

"Billy, don't play around. There's more. Come out with it."

He sighed heavily, and I swished down the whole fresh glass

of whiskey to brace myself for what he had to say. "Stern," he said. "I ought not to have to tell you this, and I can't understand why you don't see it yourself. When she left you this morning, she was headed out to *his* place."

That tumbler of whiskey hadn't burned going down, but it set to scorching me now like lamp oil.

Billy said, "She got clear of him once, and she's lucky she did. A man like Ward Carson tires of a thing, he can't see the point in casting it off clean when he could just as well enjoy torturing it and watching it struggle to die."

I was up and pacing now, my limbs all jerky and rigid.

In a voice almost too soft to carry, Billy says, "I'm sorry for you, old stump. But I believe the very best thing for you to do is to work on forgetting." He reached beneath his desk. "Let's begin that forgetting project now. I've got the very thing to help you along."

He produced an exotic looking black bottle and from it poured into my empty glass a laughably tiny splash of some viscous, green liquid that looked for all the world like pond scum.

"What in the nation is that, Billy?"

"It's French. It improves your dreams."

"Why, I don't need to be concerning myself with dreams right now. I've got to go after Honey."

"Go after her? And suppose you were to overtake her; what then?"

"Why, I'd explain things to her. Tell her about the kind of man Ward Carson is. Promise to love her."

"Explain to her in just which language, Stern?"

"Pff. She understands me every word."

"Well, suppose she does understand you. Don't you imagine she knows better than you what kind of man Ward Carson is, Stern? Drink your absinthe and forget all about her. There's my advice to you."

But in my mind I was already tearing down the road after her like a house afire. "She's got quite a start on me. How far off is his place?" I said. Then, to please Billy and show him I was agreeable, I gulped down the little thimbleful of the green stuff without really looking at it or tasting it.

Billy was watching me with his eyes wide, like I'd just busted into his office with a gun in my hand. "His place is a day's walk up the Sacramento road," he said quietly.

"And she's been gone about half the day. A horse is what I need. Lend me your horse!"

"So you can sprint him so hard he dies in this heat?"

"I'll buy him from you."

Billy sighed heavily. "Lord knows you have the means. You *won't* be reasonable, will you?"

"No, sir, I will not," I said.

"Then take the horse, blast you," Billy said. "We'll settle accounts if you should live."

Chapter Eight

Too drunk to ride—A temperance horse—Promise of reform—Rebuffed anew—A curious mourner.

Well, the years flew quickly by—No; no they didn't, either; I apologize; I'm writing two books at once, and I set that line down in the wrong one. Kindly ignore it, and let us continue.

There was too much liquor in my belly—and too much of that green stuff in my head, even if I'd had less than a swallow—for any such foolish extravagance as galloping a horse. I should have known that but didn't. But Billy Moore's horse did.

He was a stout, black fellow, shiny and fine, with a smart, supercilious eye. Moore's name for him was Grandee, and he warned me, all ahush and off to one side, that this animal had for years carried a temperance rider along the circuit and that the horse's opinions had not been immune from the zeal of his owner's fiery harangues. He had, that is to say, bought into some rather heady ideas concerning the manifold evils of strong drink.

I scoffed a little, inwardly, believing this to be granting just a little more credit than any horse deserved, howsoever fine and shiny his appearance. But I nodded solemnly, took my leave of Moore, and staggered up to the stall.

Upon my approach, old Grandee twisted his neck around and, whiffing my liquor-soaked breath, sort of looked at me as if to say, "You'll have to excuse *me*, but you appear to be in no kind of condition whatever. Now why don't you stagger on home or to the poorhouse or wherever it is you belong, and leave distinguished people to their work?"

Well, I wasn't having any of *that* truck. I was as good as any horse, and I'd show him as much. I led him from the stable with his ears laid back and his nostrils dilating something fierce, and I decided then that I might expect a little trouble after all.

But my doubts soon vanished away, for the horse evinced a world of patience, standing nicely as I poked around at his ribs with the toe of my boot, trying to penetrate the stirrup. At last I found purchase there and swung up into the saddle, and still he stood, straight-necked and attentive like a third-generation butler. I gathered in the reins and probed around for the other stirrup, knocking into two or three ribs in my search, attained it, sucked in a deep breath, and made ready to cluck my tongue to spur the horse into a gallop.

Well, just like any worthy butler, this Grandee could anticipate a man's requests, I saw, for I never got any show respecting the cluck. In a flash we were off. Or, rather, *he* was. I believe I was with him for no more than three or four feet, certainly no further than it took for me to somersault backwards over the cantle and slam to earth belly first like a flapjack dropped from a belfry, where I lay wishing I'd taken some wiser course of action—raping a wasp nest, maybe.

I lay quite still a while, contemplating grass—contemplating it in an immediate way with my eyeballs, nostrils, and tongue—eagerly awaiting the time when I should once again be able to draw breath. At last it came, and while it was a blessed relief, still I've enjoyed some other breaths more, for this one was a good deal shot through with twigs and soil and litter.

By and by I found that with some focused effort I could raise my head, and there but a few yards off stood Grandee, nibbling grass. Not munching it, mind you, the way a lot of horses will do when they know they're getting away with something and time is precious. No, he plucked a blade or two, here and there, deftly, disdainfully, as much as to say, "Well, the cuisine is tawdry, but there's only one item on the bill of fare, and I've got to be here, like it or no." Oh, he was a swell one; you never saw such a horse for all-fired, aching haughtiness.

I hauled myself up to my feet and staggered over to him, ready to lunge at the reins if he tried to elude me. But he was too high toned for that cheap brand of tomfoolery. Instead, he arched an eyebrow so as to say, "Back, are we, and willing to try again?"

"You're damn shtraight," I said. "An' thish time hold shtill."

"I held perfectly still last time, friend."

"Oh, that's what you call holdin' shtill, where you come from? Dump a fella clear out the shaddle?"

This new speech impediment was a bad sign. I never could pronounce an *S* once I'd had the drop too many, though the clods and pebbles wedged in my teeth weren't any great help in the matter, either.

"Why, you meant to gallop, did you not?"

"Sure—when I was ready to. I never even give you the command."

"Oh, well, pardon me for not waiting on paper orders. I had been under the impression you were in some sort of hurry."

"Oh, you pompush, vaunting thing! Cheek? I reckon not. Why, you beat the very Dutch for cutting a shwell. Of coursh I'm in a hurry, blasht you."

"Then remount, I invite you. We'll recover lost time, with interest."

"There. That's shenshible talk. Now, don't you flinch now."

"I? Never. Beneath me, you know."

"A lot of things musht be."

I scaled him anew and, once summited, wrapped my hand around that saddle horn like it was flotsam and I a man overboard. And it's a good thing I did, too, else I'd have once again *become* a man overboard, for that horse unbent his long body and shot forth like a well-fletched arrow flung from an elk-horn bow. Which is only a pale simile to give you the barest idea; I believe he would have beaten the arrow in any fair contest, for both speed and style. By some miracle I kept my seat, thankful I'd had him pointed in the right direction when he'd fired, and we flew along toward Sacramento with the trees and rail fences whizzing by so fast that three or four times I ventured to lean down alongside to see if Grandee's feet ever touched ground. They may have, for all I know.

Now, your average vainglorious horse will keep up that kind of pace just long enough to make his point. As soon as it begins to cost him his comfort, he'll slacken off, at least a little, reasoning that it won't do to put himself out overmuch merely for the sake of impressions. Not so this Grandee. I don't know how many minutes or how many leagues he ran before it occurred to me that he was like to injure himself, but it did dawn on me at last, and I gave the reins a middling tug. This operation brought about no change underneath me, but ahead of me Grandee's ears dropped, and he flung me a sideways look to say, "Bother you, what is it you want *now*?"

"I think you ought to eash up shum," I said.

"Oh, *you* think so, do you? And I guess that's because you're so good at running two-minute miles as a sort of everyday thing, yourself."

"It ishn't that. I jusht thought—"

"Oh, you *thought*! *You* thought. Well, pardon me if I doubt what a body like *you* might get to *thinking*."

"A body like me? Jusht what do you mean to shuggesht by that?"

"If you really don't know, I'll tell you. I mean to suggest by that: a habitual drinker!"

"Habitual—no! You read me wrong, I tell you. If I appear a touch impaired, why, it'sh for the very opposhite reashon. Drunkennesh is a unfamiliar vishe to me; I have no fashil—no facul—no talent for it."

These words seemed to weigh favorably on Grandee in some way, for on hearing them he slackened his pace. Not so much as to make me see the trees unblurred, or to feel anything like unthreatened, but somewhat, at least. He said sternly, "As a general proposition, I don't take soakers at their word. Yet say on."

"Why, Granjy, I don't know quite what elsh to shay. I'm journally shober as a dead Quaker, shee? Let the othersh rip their innardsh up with corn whishkey, but guard your own shobriety—that'sh me every time. For shobriety ish dignity; dignity, shobriety. If there'sh got to be only one shober man left around camp to doctor and father the othersh, let it be me. Yesshir. But I've had troublesh with a woman reshently, and wuzh blue thish mornin', and took a glash or two of rum, which made me but bluer. Then a friend heard out my trubbulsh and plied me with a thimbleful of a myshteriush French elickshur, which hash left me all ashkew."

Grandee slowed further, clicking his tongue pityingly even as he blazed on over the ground at a still-dizzying trot.

"And now do you see where the fleeting momentary pleasures of spiritous liquors may lead?" he scolded. "To what dissipation and ruin? An intoxicated man is a shame to his family, to his country, his religion, and race! More, an intoxicated man is a danger! A danger to himself and to others. Yes, you can see it in your own situation: why, you've landed squarely on your face this afternoon, a thing that might have killed you. May it have sobered you! May it have awakened you to the perils of the bottle! Swear to me you'll put an end to your filthy ways and walk, hereafter, upright like a man!"

This was no slouch of a speech, I thought, particularly for a Kentucky Saddler. "I shwear it," I said.

"Swear what?"

"To lay off the bottle."

"And to walk upright like a man?"

"And to walk upright like a man!"

"Good. Then walk, damn you!"

He couldn't have stopped more quickly if he'd run headlong into China's Great Wall. Me, I went soaring out over that temperance horse's head, over the road and the grove of elms at its edge, over the fields of freshly planted barley, over a brook where trout plashed and played, over three clapboard houses and a country church, over a boy running with a hoop past a farrier shoeing a cart pony, over a contentious session of Congress—and skidded to a halt face-downward in the dirt, in an attitude no different at all from the one in which I'd found Peter the Great that fateful morning. And if not quite all of that did happen to me, I'll excuse myself for thinking so, the way I did sail.

It hurt too much to lie in that position for any very long spell, so I resolved to get up; but it hurt too much to get up, so I resolved to remain lying in that position for a time longer yet, choking on dust and wondering about my spine. I might have lay there an hour, or it could have been only a minute or two, such was my bewilderment, when I felt a pair of hands at my shoulders, touching gingerly at my bones and joints to see if any of the pieces might fit back together. Slowly a suspicion came over me, and I strained through the pounding in my head to make out a sound. Why, yes. It was Honey's soothing voice!

She it was, cooing gentle assurances in that pretty heathen tongue of hers and petting me on the tender nape. Well, that was motivation enough for me to wrench my head around and have a look through the white stars that danced before my vision. There she squatted, just as handsome and likely a gal as ever. Oh, the relief to see her, the relief to think there was a person in the world who cared to help me—and that it was she! She!

Well, poor Honey was an awful long time getting me up on my feet, but she managed it, and then she urged me to take a few steps. That pained me something awful, but I knew as well as she did that idleness was the more dangerous course at present. As I staggered about with my arm across her shoulders I could smell that hair of hers—I believe she must have rubbed it with crushed sage as a regular thing—and that aroma sort of took me over. *Belonging* was what I felt when we touched, *destiny,* the answer to the mystery. This was my woman, for life, all settled, no more wondering how it might turn out. I limped in circles, smelling her, feeling how snug she fit beneath my arm, rejoicing.

It was a long time before I remembered to look around for that horse, and when I did I spied him just a short distance off, swishing at flies and dozing as if it were the Sabbath. My hand went down for my revolver, but just in time I remembered about the mountain sheep, and I reasoned that to have my vengeance on Grandee would likely cost me this my last chance with Honey. So I put away thoughts of murder, lurched over to where he stood, and grabbed at the reins. Old Grandee spoke not a word but stood as steady and innocent as ever.

"Honey," I said, holding out the stirrup, "let's you and me get us back to Placerville. We've got a future of riches to attend to." I was sober as a banker now.

She tilted her head and smiled faintly. But Lord, I didn't like that smile. Not that it was wanting for warmth—no, Honey was incapable of insincerity—but it held a pitying aspect that about froze up my blood. And now she was shaking her head side to side, gently as you'd rock a sick baby, seeming to tell me, "No, no, it's a shame, and yet it can't be helped."

"But, Honey," I said, all disbelief. "Won't you come along with me?"

She shook her head a bit more firmly this time.

"But I came all the way out here only just to fetch you."

Now she crossed her arms, no entry.

"Honey, you're my woman, and that's all there is to it, now."

"You go," she said.

"Well, I'll—English—first the horse and now—Hang it, Honey, I can't go and leave you here on the road. I can't do it. See, I understand it now, and you and me, why, we're meant to stay together. I'm not ashamed of a thing! I'll tell the whole world about you and me. Shout it through the hills. You and me *belong,* through and through. *I* can see it clear enough; why can't *you*? Honey, come along with me."

She stepped closer to me and slowly raised a hand, and for a moment I thought I'd won her at last, but she laid that palm against my cheek and sighed, withdrew it, turned on her dainty heel, and stalked off in the direction of Sacramento. Nothing ever hit me so hard.

I stood there helpless as an infant to stop her, watching her go, and when her little white figure crested the last hill and disappeared, an awful coldness spread over my spirit. Dying didn't seem like a very bad idea just then. I was busted clean in two, and the half I wanted most was gone forever. Big, fat, sloppy, embarrassing tears slipped down my face, and my throat felt like a tube of gravel.

I bawled for a good long while, alone there in the road. When I'd got the worst of it out of me I swung up into the saddle with my bones creaking and paining me like a railway crash, and that old Grandee behaved himself perfectly well all the way back into town.

Next morning we set out for Whitman's Gulch: me, Ford, Judge Cutler, and Billy Moore, who was burning all over to lay eyes on both of my mines. He'd stayed up all night mixing and amalgamating and firing my specimens in a retort, all those mysterious processes that all miners pretend to understand but only one in a thousand does.

When I'd called on him at six, I'd been surprised to see a loaded mule standing beside a saddled Grandee in front of his office.

"Stern," he'd said before I was even through the door, "you've got galena, sure enough, and it assays at *seven thousand dollars to the ton.*" His bleary eyes were wild with ill-suppressed excitement. "Now I'm going to ask you just one last time: did you give me honest samples?"

"Why, hang it, Billy, I already told you as much twice now."

"And you honest to God have got a mountain of the stuff all to yourself?"

"Well, I'm not in the business of lying about such things."

"Well, then, damn you, you're a surpassingly rich man. So rich it disgusts me quite a bit."

"I love you, too, Billy. What about the gold?"

"*Nine* thousand to the ton. Which disgusts me even worse, if such a thing is possible. But I need to see the site. If it's all as you say it is—"

"Of course it is."

"—then you're the richest damn skunk I've ever met. Sure as hell the *luckiest.*" He looked me over. "And still you skulk around no different than if someone had shot your uncle." He reached under the counter, shaking his head mournfully. "Have a drink," he said.

I waved my hand. "Promised your horse I wouldn't," I said. "Listen, Billy. Isaac Ford's traveling with me. He's fully unaware of that gold vein, and I'd just as soon keep it that way as long as I can."

"Understood."

That was all I needed to say. When it comes to professional secrecy, priests and lawyers and thieves haven't got anything on assayers.

Our little caravan put Placerville smack behind us in a goodly hurry, making eastward toward a still-rising sun that glowed yellow and cheerful as any old lemon. That roadway stretched wide and easy here, and the pastures and meadows lay damp and cool from the soothing night.

I heard my companions talking and laughing behind me, all of them in high spirits, and though my spirits should have been highest of all, they just weren't, somehow. Why, the Greeks themselves couldn't have concocted a richer irony: here I was, wealthier than old Croesus at last, but unable to enjoy it even a little. For Honey had ruined me. Ruined me for easy comradeship, ruined me for balmy meadows and lemony suns, ruined me for the thousand little consolations that fetch us along through these short lives of hardship and pain. I was forlorn now, solidly and irredeemably so, and forlorn forever would I be.

Yes, I could feel my new estate settling over me like a permanent mantle, mine to wear unto the grave. Darkness everywhere, even in daylight. Why smile at a quaint without my Honey nearby? Why taste of good food? Why marvel at vistas, or revel in one's health and strength of limb? Those things were empty hoaxes. The real light of the world had gone out.

I tried to shake those shabby feelings, but couldn't. I told myself that now that I was rich I could have my pick of women, could buy myself a harem and install it in Utah if I had a mind to. But I didn't want any harem. I didn't want anyone or anything besides Honey. I turned it over and over in my mind, and I couldn't understand what had made her sour on me so completely and so abruptly. Yes, I'd lost heart for a moment after that night of the sheep, and yes, I'd been ashamed at myself for loving her. But I had changed and told her so. I didn't care anymore who knew that I loved a squaw. I would stand before the multitudes and proudly hold her hand—if her hand was only there to hold. Which it wasn't, nor ever would it be.

She had gone on up the road, up the Road of Life, without me. And here is how I knew my love was true: wherever she was going—whoever she was leaving me for, even if it was that rattler Ward Carson—I wanted her to be happy.

Late that afternoon, amidst impossibly elongated shadows that reshaped the world into a dismal vale of sorrows, we found our way to where the Carson spills from the slopes, and there, along the wooded banks of that stream, we spied a stranger clad in blue woolen shirt and broadcloth pantaloons kneeling upon a freshly dug grave and tapping at a makeshift wooden cross with the flat of his spade. As we approached we could hear him muttering through choking sobs.

Moore dismounted from Grandee, and Judge Cutler swung down from his strapping Morgan, and the two of them approached the mourner with soft, reverent steps, hats clutched to their chests. Stormy and I followed, leading our mules. Gently interrupting the fellow's murmured lamentations, the judge said, "Soft, now, friend, and forgive us our intrusion; yours is a comfortless sorrow, and words no salve, that's easy enough for any man with eyes. And even yet do we feel compelled to proffer a hand in fellowship and serve up whatever meager inspiritment our humble fraternity might yield."

The stranger blew his nose into his sleeve and rubbed at his eyes. "What's that you say, now?" he said, blinking.

Moore cleared his throat. "Only that we wish to offer you whatever comfort a group of strangers can give to one bound up in unspeakable sorrow, as you so clearly are," he said.

I hadn't heard Billy talk that way very often. I guessed he was showing off for the judge a little maybe.

"Mighty kind of you," the mourner said and then plunged his face down into his hands, overcome by another wave of grief.

The judge laid a hand upon the poor fellow's quaking shoulder. "There, now, son," he said. "You've got to weep, so weep. The poet of Ecclesiastes knew all about hard times and urged us to go on and blubber when blubbering was the order of the day. Wail and faint like the frailest woman, for all we care; we'll not judge of you. Go on, whine and bawl like any maiden, we'll not question your sand. Put aside your manhood, that's it, and snivel like a tiny girl. Mewl out your vagitus, bleat—"

"Tell us, friend," Moore interrupted. "For what blessed soul do you pour out your noble tears?"

"Yes," said the judge. "Who was she? What comely young thing lies cold there 'neath the loam, so newly wrenched from our midst? Describe her to us, top to bottom, leaving nothing out: her symmetry, her lithesomeness, the supple contours, the swell and crest of—"

"It ain't a woman lies here a-tall," the man said, still shuddering with sorrow.

Judge Cutler clicked his tongue and shook his head sadly. "Your little boy," he murmured. "Oh, it's an awful thing when the young are taken! How can a man keep faith in a world where the candle of youth may be so cruelly snuffed out, and not a moment's notice either! He was your very image, wasn't he, glad and true-hearted and brimful of expectation. He—"

"Nosir," the stranger drawled. "T'warn't my boy, for I haven't ever had none."

"Well, then, who, confound it, so's I can direct my grievances proper?"

"My pard," the man said. "Mick."

"Mick," said the judge, crushing his hat against his chest anew. "Yes, *Mick.*" He dropped to one knee in the fresh dirt and a-hemmed loudly, motioning the rest of us down around the grave. The others knelt beside him, but I couldn't get there, quite, for Ahab had his ears laid back and his knees locked up, disliking the smell of things.

"Poor Mick," Judge Cutler began. "Poor, poor old Mick. No finer comrade did a working man ever boast. Strong? Oh, I reckon he was a little bit strong—if strength means carrying a keg of nails on each shoulder over half a mile, barefooted through the sleet. Loyal? True? Don't talk to me of such things, when Mick strode the earth. You never see a man whiter than Mick, quicker to sacrifice his own comforts for the good of his brethren. If there was chores to be done, Mick was there in a minute. He couldn't stand to see anybody else discommoded for an instant. There's Christians, and then there was Mick. How about the time he gave his boots to a wayfaring stranger who he judged to be a degree or two poorer than himself, and then caught a fever that laid him up six weeks? That was Mick all the way. Or when, hungry and destitute, he spent his only dime to feed a little pickpocket orphan and, thus depriving himself of sustenance, nearly succumbed to the Marasmus, and the urchin reformed so thorough that now he preaches to the cannibals along the Gold Coast? Children! That was his tenderest spot. If ever you spoiled for a fight with Mick, though I don't know why you'd want to, just disadvantage a child or two in his presence. Then you'd wish you'd sharpened down a stick and poked at a wolverine some. Did the *ladies* love Mick? Oh, I reckon *not.* They only slipped off their petticoats in helpless surrender the instant he hove into view. Mick knew how to *please* them, too, knew some techniques that were his and his alone, come by through hard experience. Why, he could—"

"Suppose," said Billy Moore, "we let this gentleman talk a while, since he alone among us was acquainted with the deceased? Tell us, friend: how ever did Mick come to grief?"

The mourner appeared to squirm a little at the question, as if he'd have preferred to hear the judge go on prattling, but all eyes were on him now, wide with curiosity, and so he drew himself up straight, brushed off his shirtfront, and said quietly, "Gentlemen, what y'all see standing before y'all is a broken man, busted sure as any stick of kindling." He sighed heavily and went on. "Mick and me, we was glued side b'side the better part of two year. I had me a brother back home in Tennessee and loved him—but not like I loved Mick. I had me a daddy, right up till I was eleven and he rolled off'n a bridge and drownded and died, and I loved *him*—but not like I loved Mick. I had me a woman, too, one time, and loved *her*—but not like I loved Mick. Had me a bluetick coonhound, fine animal, smart's a whip, tenacious, treer, hot-nosed, bawled on track, chopped on tree—"

"You loved him, I suppose," the judge said impatiently. "But not like Mick."

"Loved who?" said the stranger.

"Why, your blasted hound."

"Then why'd you say 'him'?"

"Thunder and lightnin'," Ford cut in. "Because you was just *talking* about the infernal blame dog."

"Well, I wouldn't have said 'him'," the stranger drawled, "for that hound was a bitch."

"I don't believe you ever did say 'him'," I said, with as much kindness as I could muster, which wasn't a heaping great amount. "I believe the judge presumed it."

The mourner nodded. "His mistake," he said. He turned to

Cutler. "Your mistake. Understandable, but still. Anyhow, as I's saying, I loved that coonhound—but not like I loved Mick."

Ford groaned.

"Mick, he and me just cottoned to each other straight from the git-go. He was a *stump,* a regular stump. We was hauling freight in the Reserve, is where we met, and then we had to run off on account of a bad occurrence in Cleveland, which was his fault as much's 'twas mine, or my fault as much as 'twas his, I should parbly say; and we cut heel and busted clear of the states, side b'side. Right side b'side. Skinned buffalo out in Kansas but didn't take to it, neither one of us. Too gutsy sort of. Guided some emigrants, though that was all bellyache and no profit, the way they fussed and squabbled. Loaned ourselves out to a sawmill, which was the drudgeriest thing either one of us ever put a hand to. And then come out to Californy to hunt the color. Right beside each other every step of the way, side b'side. And did we tire of one another, even one time? No, sir. Opposite thing happened. Why, I'd open my eyes in the mornin', and there would be Mick, and we'd grin like it'd been years and take up the thread of just whatsoever little old thing we'd been natterin' at the night before. Just side b'side, hear? Never got to know a man better, nor to have such feeling for one. Loved him better than my brother back in Tennessee, better than the father I had till I was eleven, bet—"

"Thunder and lightnin'," Ford said, "one single word about that goddamned dog of yours, and I'll put you right in there with Mick."

Some instinct for preservation told the stranger that Ford might mean what he said, and though I could see that it pained him to lop off his litany before he'd fetched clear through to the coonhound, he bore it manfully, lowered his head, and said softly, "And now, gentlemen, I come to the melancholiest thing that ever met men's ears. Mick was just as the preacher here described him—" he meant the judge "—affable, warmhearted, generous to a fault, kind to any and all, and all those in between. He and me we looked at the world through one set of eyes, you could say, agreed on everything, right down to the very most slightest. It was side b'side all the way for us. Why, me and Mick, we spoke of every single thing there was to talk about, and if there was an opinion to make, we'd make it up *together* and *share* it like brothers who's maybe only got one pair of britches between 'em. That warn't no stretch for the two of us, ever. Right side b'side. Well, anyway I *thought* we'd spoke about all there was to speak about, but somehow or other we'd missed a topic or two, it seems, and just this morning them topics sprang up, as things *will*, by and by. Well, make a long story short of it, this is it: Mick was . . . a Yankee!"

This revelation did not have its desired effect upon his audience, but he proceeded along just as if it had scandalized us all.

"Yessir, he told me so his very own self. Admitted to it like it warn't nothing at all, easy as you'd say your Mammy was a Jones or a Smith. Born and reared up in Massachusetts! *Massachu*setts! Now, I'd always known he talked a little funny, but I just thought he was a little different. Hell, I *loved* that slicked-up voice of his. But good heavens, this morning! Why, with a perfectly straight face he swore up and down that he'd vote Republican the first chance he got. *Republican!* That's exactly what he said, and if he didn't I wish I may never stir. Well, you can just imagine how it hit me, hearing this. Why, it spun me around so fast I couldn't tell t'other from which. A *Yankee*! All that time! And sleeping right shoulder to shoulder of me!"

None of us spoke; we were, at last, rather engrossed.

"How he kept that hid from me for so long *I'll* never come to fathom. But it must have been a strain on him, actin' so good for so long to fool me, with all that evil and hatred toward our way of life abiding there in the darkness of his heart. I tell you what stumps me most is how he ever come to be so handy with a rifle, for there ain't but one Yankee in a thousand, you know, ever touched one in his life. Or handy with other things, neither. Horses. Rope. Tools. Slept right on the hard ground, too, just as offhanded as a Santy Sioux. Put up with cold, and fleas, like a man! Yankees, you know, never goes outdoors, scarcely. Sure enough never *sleeps* out there, or *works* outdoors. But Mick? He did it all, without a moment's fuss, which is impossible for a Yankee, of course. But I ain't said the worst of it yet. Things got mighty warm mighty fast, conversationally, I mean, betwixt him and me, and pretty soon it come out that he warn't just any old Yankee. My Mick—*my* old Mick—was a true-blue, by-God abolitionist! *Abolitionist!* I know you won't believe me, but I swear it's true. He said so his very self this morning, and if he was still available I'd have him vouch for it, for Mick never was one to lie nor to make light."

We could not speak. We all could see now which direction this story was headed, and we were loath to hear its inevitably grim conclusion. In the awful silence, the stranger lowered his head and began muttering almost to himself in the same sorry tones we'd heard on our first approach, "I just can't under*stand* how a *Yankee abolitionist* could act so fine and manly, keeping up appearances for nigh unto two years. But Mick done it. Too many for me, I tell you."

"What did—what did you . . . *do*?" Billy Moore finally asked.

"Why, I did the only thing I *could* do. I brained him with my spade and buried him up, and here he lays, forever still."

He stared at us through hollow, red-rimmed eyes. "Oh, I warn't happy to do it. As I say, I'm busted up forever and ever. No good for life after this. But when a man bumps hard up against evil, he's got to *be* a man and stand up to it, or we're *all* lost. I did it for my country, for Jesus, for the sake of decency. Oh, I wish to the Lord I never had to. Why, if only he hadn't have *admitted* it, and so free and casual, too . . ."

"Why, you dimwitted cretin," Judge Cutler said. "You never had to murder the man!"

The stranger scowled bitterly. "Oh, *no,*" he said. "I reckon I could just as well have let him *roam around,* despising freedom and righteousness, maybe let him take a wife and raise up a whole *passel* of little old Yankees to ban the Bible and take away all that's good from us honest, God-fearing folks!"

This final outburst appeared to have expended him, for here at last the stranger gave over wholly to his grief, flung himself down on the grave, and with a great gnashing of teeth fell to cursing and bemoaning the departed Mick, to blaming heaven, and to petitioning the very stars for an understanding of how an abolitionist could have cloaked himself in feigned morality for so long.

We four crept back to our horses and mules and left him to his wild lament.

Chapter Nine

Two lazy travelers—A prodigious whore—Visit to the galena mine—Back to Whitman's Gulch—Catastrophe—Lone survivors—The hastiest of trials—Johnny's fate—Claim jumpers.

As we made our way back up over the spine of the Sierras, I recounted to Billy Moore the whole ridiculous tale of Peter the Great's murder and its aftermath. I took pains to avoid breathing a syllable of this within earshot of either Cutler or Stormy Isaac, wishing it never to be said that I'd tried to influence anybody toward a conclusion. Billy had little to say in response, but the look of concern in his eyes heightened my self-reproach for having left Johnny alone in that hornets' nest.

Isaac Ford was just as lazy and helpless on the trail as he'd ever been, refusing to lift a finger to feed or shelter himself or his mule. And it wasn't long before we saw that the judge was every bit as ornery regarding such practical matters. In fact, where Stormy's claim to aristocratic treatment arose from the solitary accident of his having arrived in the gold fields in the year 1848—a basis just tenuous enough as to require a constant slew of reminders in order to make it stick—Cutler's prestige was implicit. He was, after all, the undisputed possessor of an actual law degree, a real office with a bell of genuine brass, and a living assistant called Alexander. Besides, he was on our payroll. So he allowed us to understand, without stooping to ever saying so, that a cold day in hell would arrive long before anyone caught *him* squatting next to a fire and frying bacon.

Well, Billy and I put up with it all right. Billy almost had Johnny beat when it came to natural cheerfulness, and I was feeling so lowdown and bereft that I scarcely cared anymore whose errands I shouldered.

You never would have thought that two men like Ford and Cutler would take to each other, but life had been unrelenting lately in insisting to me that our world fairly seethes with surprises, and this absurd new comradeship only fit the pattern. A couple of days into the journey, the two of them had gotten onto the shared pet topic of women, and heaven save us, it was all livid talk and slavering fraternity from there on out.

It seems that during our stay in Placerville, Ford had lain with a soiled dove bearing the professional name of Dank Jenny, who as it turned out had for years been party to frequent exchanges with the judge, both in and out of the courtroom, sometimes in camera and sometimes elsewhere (no matter where, almost). They did it *mensa et throro, a latera,* sometimes even, when social, *inter alios.* Normally Dank Jenny's favors were offered *motu proprio,* sometimes even *ex gratia,* but occasionally, when the judge was feeling his keeping, he took her *a fortiori,* though he never failed to pay afterward, and she never took any offense.

Listening to him brag so, I came to suspect that his own offices were performed *brevimanu,* often as not, though of course he wouldn't have breathed of that to Ford. For that matter, I wondered whether either of them could stiffen the cord anymore at all, but if they couldn't, it sure was no obstacle to their boasting like men half their ages.

Despite my melancholy, I found myself taking a passing interest in their talk and soon came to regret not having gotten at least a glimpse of Dank Jenny back in town. This was an impulse born not of prurience but of basic human curiosity, same as I would have been eager for a gander at the pope if he'd been there, even though I was raised right. For, to hear Cutler and Ford describe her, Dank Jenny was a living marvel for the ages. As they sang her exploits, I began to feel a boastful pride at having not only been alive when she was alive but actually having *stayed in the same hotel where she did some of her work,* a thing I would tell my grandchildren about, years and years hence.

She was a remarkable specimen, Dank Jenny. Not beautiful, nor even comely, that I could gather, but an astonishing prodigy nonetheless. She had perfected a superhuman deed involving three champagne bottles and a cane-backed chair—a thing that would have killed a mortal—and performed it on a regular basis, private audiences only. I believe that one was called Milking the Elephant. Unless Milking the Elephant was the one with the ax handles, pine-knot torches, and bowl of walnuts.

Dank Jenny was such a font of fascination that once Stormy and the judge had got onto her as a topic, they lost themselves for two days in recitations of her extravagances, which were, in the end, so variegated and myriad as to defy all attempts at cataloguing, receding as they did into a hazy parade of broomsticks, tea saucers, blacksmith tongs, serving spoons, ship's hawsers, gunpowder, machetes, rocks, doorknockers, lances, and grapeshot. And I forget what all else.

Well, long about the third day, they more or less expended Dank Jenny and moved on to other things—other whores, that is—and while to my ear none of those others approached Dank Jenny for wild invention and sheer pluck, the two blood brothers were cozy and satisfied with the subject matter, and with their new bond.

I believe it was during our fifth afternoon of travel that we reached my mountain of galena. Ford and Cutler roved over it lustily, lifting up pieces of ore, licking their fingers, and testing it, rubbing the earth as if it were a woman's bosom, guffawing and cursing me for my good luck. In all their talk of women, they had temporarily forgotten about their other shared infatuation, but my galena pile had reminded them of it all right.

Still, it wasn't them but Billy Moore I was watching.

He tied Grandee to a chaparral bush at the foot of the hill, crossed his arms, and glared at the slope. There he stood for three long minutes, not saying a word. By and by he climbs a short distance and then begins traversing the hill, more or less following the contour at a certain elevation. Here and there he pauses and scoops up a handful of soil and drops it, watching it in the breeze. Sometimes he digs a little hole with his spade. I follow behind him, gulping back my apprehension.

Well, he corkscrews his way like this, as the sun is setting, all the way up to the top of the mountain, and there where I'd harvested my samples, he chips away a few hunks of ore, breaks them apart, holds up the shards to the fading light. At last he sits down and hugs his knees to his chest, facing west to watch the sun dipping below the horizon. I guess he wants me to sit beside him, but I'm too nervous for that.

"Well?" I said. "Have I got something here or not?"

"This was a hasty examination," Billy said.

"I know that."

"You'll have to have someone come out here with the tools and the time to really give it the once-over."

"I know that. Billy, you're an assayer and a damn fine mining engineer to boot. You can tell at a glance whether something's got potential. Tell me straight."

"I'm not a magician," Billy said. "I can't tell things at a glance."

"You see now that I didn't salt it, don't you?"

"I see that. But, Stern, you're away out here in the middle of nowhere, and it's costly to separate silver out of galena. You'll need to subtract either the cost of transporting your ore over those mountains, or building a stamp mill here on site."

"I guess you think I never thought of any of that?"

"People get excited when they think they've made their fortune."

"What would *you* do with it?"

"Sell it. And for a mighty pretty penny, too."

"They say it takes a gold mine to run a silver mine, don't they?"

Billy nodded.

"Well, don't forget: I've got a gold mine, too."

He shook his head. "No, you haven't," he said. "You've got a claim on a gold vein. You're looking at the same kind of outlay to develop that other site."

I nodded and bit my lip. "So what are you saying? I can't find buyers?"

"Oh, no, you'll find buyers easily enough. I just hope you haven't got your heart set on hanging onto these properties. If you do, you'll find out just what a headache that kind of life can be. Better you get your hands on your pile up front, easy, and spend it on the things that make you happy."

"Agreed," I said slowly. I didn't know exactly what kind of men Billy was used to dealing with, but a life of maneuvering around boardroom tables and placating investors, all just so I could say I was the owner, was not my idea of a dream. Cling to ownership? Not I. I wanted the very thing Billy was reluctant to counsel me toward—cashing out and going after what made me happy—except that the thing that made me happy was Honey, and she couldn't be had for the price of a gold mine and a silver mine to boot.

Two days later, having arisen at dawn and wended our way down the valley as the chill morning blossomed to a fragrant day glad with easy warmth, we at last reached the last bend in the river before Whitman's Gulch. I walked in the lead, my spirits a confusion of excitement and worry, marching with an eagerness that I couldn't quite master, tugging Ahab along more urgently than he would have preferred. Presently our camp fetched into view. And what I saw there froze me so suddenly in my tracks that Ahab had to turn his head aside to avoid ramming into me. Our camp was gone! Or at least empty.

Some remnants of the shelters still stood, a scattering of pallets with their leaning frames and scanty scraps of fabric, resembling nothing so much as the half-scavenged carcasses of animals. No trace of the laundry shed remained, and nothing was left of Jeff Bill's wooden kiosk, where I'd found Peter the Great that morning that seemed so long ago now, but for a couple of planks too unwieldy to have served for firewood. Not a person to be seen anywhere on the hillside, and off beyond the shitter where they'd buried the Tsar stood eleven freshly dug graves. I let fall Ahab's lead and sank to my knees. Johnny . . .

Behind me I vaguely heard the judge's ironic remarks about the value of these claims that so many had been willing to abandon. Billy was standing beside me with a hand on my shoulder, not saying a word, and Ford had begun to poke among the ruins in silent bewilderment. I don't know for how long I remained thus deaf to the world, but presently I heard Ford call out, "Whitman! Here's one over here!"

I stood and climbed over to where Ford was squatting. There lay a man sprawled on his filthy pallet trembling and pawing at something only he could see. He'd been run through with a sword or machete, scalped, and left for dead. I never smelled anything as awful as he smelled.

"Why, that's Green, Isaac."

"So it is," Ford growled.

"Green?" said Cutler.

"Peter the Great's pard," I said. "One of the accused."

"Hell on earth," Cutler said. "Do you suppose it was Indians did this?"

Ford shook his head. "It don't take red skin to cut off a scalp," he said.

"Another one over here!" Billy was hollering from the other side of camp.

We left Green suffering there and raced over to where Billy stood. This one had been shot through in dozens of places. So many places, in fact, that his palms were pierced where he'd held his hands up to protect himself, and you could look down at his belly and see an awful lot of the pallet he was lying on.

"Christ Jesus Almighty Lord and Savior of Us All in Heaven Above," Ford said. "Strain off your dumplin's just about with this one, couldn't you?"

"That's a Mexican," Billy said.

"Not just any old Mexican neither," Ford said, looking more closely. "I'm damned if that ain't the kid killed Peter the Great."

"Hell," I said. "Is it?"

"Looks like him."

"Good," Judge Cutler said. "We have both the accused parties present. We may proceed with our inquest."

"Inquest?" I said. "These men will both be dead in a few hours. Maybe minutes."

Stormy jerked his thumb toward the other side of camp. "Green's leanin' pretty far gravewards," he said.

"Which is why we must make best use of time," said the judge.

Billy and I looked at each other, and Billy cleared his throat. "Judge," he said, "I don't believe either of them can talk."

"That only tends in our favor," Cutler said. "An excess of colloquy is an obstacle to the speedy delivery of justice. *Et verbositate*—hell, no time. Just carry that one down to where the other one lies."

"Hold on, Judge," I said. I squatted beside the suffering young Mexican. *"Eres Joaquín?"* I said.

He blinked twice and seemed to nod. Then to the surprise of all he gritted his teeth and rasped out in a voice like dragging a dry stick through the sand: *"Sí. Soy Joaquín Caracas."*

The judge frowned. "I don't like all this talky-talk on the part of your client," he said to me. "Try and keep him in check if you would."

"Client? Hell . . ."

"You're the only one speaks his language. Stormy, you'll advocate for the other one."

"Green," Ford said.

"Green. Certainly. Now get this one down the hill that we may commence proceedings in good time."

We carried Joaquín, pallet and all, over the rough ground and deposited him gingerly beside Green. We tried to be careful, but that jarring ride down the hill must have just about finished him, for he lay silently, sweating profusely and clinching his eyes shut, for several long minutes afterward. But by and by he came back around some, and the judge began. "You'll each get to examine these two men," he said to me and Ford, "but I'd like a turn with each of them first."

Indicating the young Venezuelan, he said to me, "Tell me his name again?"

"Joaquín Caracas."

He cleared his throat and leaned forward with his arms clasped behind him. "Walking Carcass," he said, "did you or did you not on or about a certain day not very long ago, kill somebody?"

I translated the question to Caracas, who indicated his innocence. "No, sir, your honor," I said. "He denies it."

"Oh-ho. Well, suppose you answer me *this:* Where exactly

were you on or about that date and time?"

"Which date and time, your honor?"

Cutler stood up straight and gave me a withering look. "Oh, let me warn you right here and now not to play technical stunts with the likes of me, Whitling," he said. "I know the law inside and out, better than any man this side of the Rockies. Just *try* that game, and you're my meat, I promise you. Now get your client to answer the question."

So I asked Joaquín where he was the night Peter the Great had been murdered. *No me acuerdo.*

But weren't you here in camp? I asked. *Por supuesto.*

"Here in camp, your honor."

"Doing what?"

I got the answer: "Sleeping."

"All the whole night through?"

Sí.

Cutler clicked his tongue and turned his attention to the other pallet. "Counsellor Ford," he said. "Is your client still alive?"

"One second, Judge," Ford said. He leaned close to Green to feel his breath on his cheek, and I marveled that he could withstand the stench. The rest of us had our hands cupped over our mouths and noses. "Yessir," Ford said. "I reckon there's an ember left in him yet, if nobody pisses on it."

"Mr. Green," Cutler said. "Did you or did you not on or about that certain date, murder the fella whose name momentarily escapes me?"

"I don't believe anyone knew his proper name," I said. "We all just called him Peter the Great, or the Tsar."

"Well, that'll never do. Here on out we call him the deceased."

I nodded, but Ford said, "Diseased hell. If there's a disease caves your skull in like that, I never heard of it."

Cutler ignored him. "So," he said, "kill the deceased or not?"

Isaac Ford leaned over and poked at Green. "You the one made Peter so sick?" he said. Green, of course, made no response. His eyes had glazed over, unseeing. "He don't seem fit to answer, Judge."

Aside, to Ford, Cutler said, "Let me know if he cashes out during proceedings, Stormy." Then, to the assembled: "Let the record show that Mr. Green has elected not to testify. Mr. Whitling, you may examine the witnesses."

"Why, one of them is speechless . . . unconscious!"

"Correct. May as well begin with the greaser, then. And be prompt, lest he expire before we can reach a verdict."

Feeling like an ass, I asked Joaquín Caracas if he remembered anything unusual about the night when the Tsar was killed. I translated his answer: "A storm," I said.

I was about to ask Joaquín if he'd had any awareness of the murder before daylight, when Cutler interrupted. "The court instructs Mr. Whitling to ask Mr. Carcass if that storm didn't disrupt his sleep any," he said.

I didn't even have to ask. "Of course, Judge," I said. "It was a hell of a storm. Nobody could have—"

"Ask the defendant, Counsellor."

So I asked and got the answer I was expecting. "He says of course, your Honor. It was a massive, violent storm, so powerful that—"

"A-ha! We have our killer," Cutler said.

I felt my jaw swing open and just dangle there. "Just how is that?" I managed to ask.

"Just how is that?" the judge crowed. "I'll tell you just how that is. Not five minutes ago your client went on and on, swearing up and down he'd slept like a baby the whole night through. *Now* he tells us it was not humanly possible to have done so. Why would he lie about a little thing like that? I'll tell you why: because he's the killer, that's why!"

"Why, Judge, just because he forgot about the storm and then remembered it—"

"Don't you dare, boy! Don't you dare! I'll charge you with contempt so fast it'll make you cry for mama."

I wish I could say I put up a better fight for poor Joaquín, but I was no attorney. I didn't know the law. I hadn't been expecting a trial. The whole thing had happened too fast, amidst my utter bewilderment about what had befallen the camp, my anxiety over Johnny, my heartache over Honey. I was racking my exhausted brain for some rejoinder when Stormy growled, "It's all up with this one. Time to plant him."

Yes, Green had breathed his last. The judge removed his hat and held it over his breast. "Moment of silence, please," he said. All was silent around us, but for the call of a raven nearby and—Could that be? Yes: distant voices. Sounded like they were coming from up the hill.

When the judge was satisfied he'd sufficiently honored Michael Green, he pronounced sentence upon my client: "Walking Carcass," he said. "For the murder of—the Russian fella—I hereby sentence you to the death sentence of death by hanging by the neck until you are dead." He then looked at me and winked. "On a date not to exceed six calendar months from the date of this sentencing."

This changed the matter for me, and I suddenly came to view the judge in a different light. It was a fine piece of jurisprudence after all, I decided, Solomonic in its wisdom, maybe even. Anyway I figured it to be just about the most harmless sentence any innocent man had ever received—or the most meaningless, at any rate—and in the event, I was right, for poor Joaquín succumbed to his many injuries early the next morning. I buried him over beyond the shitter with the others, and on the marker that I fashioned out of the kiosk planking, I scrawled in the Spanish that was a mystery to all others present: "Joaquín Caracas, A Good Boy Wrongly Accused."

But I'm getting ahead of the story, for while Joaquín yet lived, I tried with Billy's help to attend to the poor child's wounds. But they were so many and so grave that I never saw a man looking more like a sponge, and we knew our work was futile. Before he faded away into that permanent mystery, I petitioned him for answers as to what had befallen our encampment in my absence, and though he scarcely possessed force enough to whisper, he gave me to know that bad men had come there, had stirred up trouble, and had caused a great battle in which many were killed and injured, and after which everyone had fled to the hills. What I most wanted to know, I didn't want to ask, but fearing that he would die at any moment, I forced myself to it. "My brother?" I asked him.

He closed his eyes and with great difficulty nodded toward the row of new graves where soon he himself would lie. *"Muerto,"* he choked.

I reeled away in the throes of a grief for which all others had been mere prelude. My childhood playmate, my companion through hardship and good times, he of my own flesh and blood, the finest, merriest, most guileless and kindhearted spirit I'd ever known, gone, buried, nevermore to be found among the living!

I staggered out past the shitter to the row of graves, wondering which held the precious bones of my brother. All were unmarked, hastily dug, by Joaquín's account, by men fleeing terror. So I sat amidst the little graveyard and wept and wept like a fountain until Billy Moore came and sat beside me. He, too, shed tears for Johnny. We mourned together in silence for the space of two hours or more, and at length Billy said to me quietly, "Stern. Point the way to your apex for me, if you would."

Scarcely conscious of the question, I lifted a hand numbly and stabbed my index finger toward the top of the hill and my ledge claim.

"It's as I thought, then," Billy said. "I know you're grieving, and I am, too, Stern. But if you want what's rightfully yours, you've got to set aside your mourning and fight for it right this very minute."

"What's this about, Billy?" I said, irritated at being disturbed.

"There's two men up there have jumped your claim. Say it's theirs now and anybody who tries to take it from them is a dead man. Why, they've built a breastworks and everything, like they're spoiling to fight."

I sighed. "Let them keep it if it means so much to them," I said. "I've had my fill of trouble."

"Stern," Billy said. "This isn't even about the gold. It's those two caused all this commotion. I don't know that they're the ones who pulled the trigger, but they're sure enough the reason Johnny lies here in this cold ground."

He meant for that to get my dander up, and it worked. "Give me a minute alone with Johnny," I said quietly. "I'll be with you presently."

Billy wandered off, and I tried to steady my voice so I could address my brother like a man. "Johnny," I said to the general area. "I might be minutes away from joining you, but I'll be damned if I'll let these miscreants wreck everything and walk away from it all rich and fat and impudent. If I live, I'll see to it that Mama's well taken care of, which was always your concern. And if I die, why, we'll clasp hands again there up yonder and wait on Mama's time when we can all be together again."

I walked over to where Ahab stood patiently, still loaded, and took down my long guns and ammunition. As I sat there cross-legged on the ground loading my pistols and guns, Ford and the judge came and stood over me.

"What are you fixing to do, Whitman?" Ford said.

"That pair of bastards up there has jumped my claim," I said. "I aim to march up the hill and take it back."

"Why, you stubborn fool," Cutler said. "There's thirty or forty abandoned claims all over this valley. Help yourself to any one of them and go on living."

I stood up. "Judge," I said, "my claim is the apex of a very rich vein of gold. It's the only one here worth a damn. And in fact it's worth a fortune."

You should have seen the judge's eyes bulge out and his face go red as a cherry. "The hell you say," he croaked.

Ford was just as thunderstruck. "Whitman," he said, "you ain't tuggin' our peckers?"

Just then Billy walked up to the group with his rifle over his shoulder. "He sure isn't," he said. "I've assayed the ore. It's almighty rich, too. That apex isn't the sort of thing a fellow shrugs off in exchange for some used-up placer diggings. Now, I don't know about you two men, but nothing in this world rankles me quite like a claim jumper, so I aim to march up that hill with Stern here and return that apex to its rightful owner."

Ford was already on his way over to Jezebel and was sliding his rifle out of its scabbard.

"Now, just a minute, you hotheaded young pups," the judge was saying. "This is a legal matter, and you've got the law right here, in my person. Why bring on more bloodshed when you could just as easily settle this with a hearing?"

"No thanks, Cutler," I said. "I've seen the way your trials go. I'd rather take my chances with bullets." I glanced up at the sky and then turned to Billy and Isaac. "You haven't got to go up there with me," I said, "but if you insist upon it, let's wait till nightfall when they can't see us coming."

So the judge sat by the fire, daubing Joaquín's white lips with whiskey, as we three crept up the side of the hill, spaced far enough apart that the pair of claim jumpers could never do better than to be facing two of us head on at once. The stars were jangling and sizzling overhead, and away off in the mountains a wolf was hollering and hollering to its lover but getting no answer. Far beneath me I saw our fire swaying and bobbing in the night breeze, and up ahead of me, on the crest of the hill, the squatters' fire lit an orange mound of sky above the black band of the makeshift breastworks they had built.

Our plan was simple: we would wait until certain that all three of us had found secure cover within easy pistol range, at which point I'd call the claim jumpers out. If they refused, we would fight for a spell, then wait. We each had enough ammunition and water to last us the duration of a lengthy siege, and I doubted that the squatters had water enough for more than a day.

It was no more difficult for me to navigate this terrain in the dark than it would be for a farmer to find his way around his own barnyard without a lantern, for I'd crawled all up and down it enough times prospecting that I could have drawn a portrait that left out no boulder or depression. Ahead of me, I knew, was a granitic slab just thick enough to hide behind if I lay perfectly flat. I began to wriggle my way toward it, quiet as a deaf bat. And then I heard Isaac Ford's voice calling cheerfully through the night, "It's all right, boys! Come in!"

I peeked up at the apex, and there loomed Stormy's hulking silhouette, perched monstrously upon the breastworks, waving one hand broadly back and forth over his head to signify that the way was clear. "Come on in, boys!" he repeated.

Well, if there was one thing I'd learned about Isaac Ford, it was that he was never quite as stupid as he meant for you to take him for. He had cast greedy eyes upon my silver find and resented me for my good fortune, and now here he was sitting on my apex, calling me out into the open. Was he in concert with the claim jumpers? What treachery did he have in mind?

Billy called out, "Don't go, Stern! I believe it's a trap!"

Stormy stopped waving his arm and hesitated there in the fire's glow for a long, still moment. I lay behind my rock watching him, panting with anxious disquietude, ready for any villainy. Then he growled: "Trap hell!" Abruptly he stooped out of view down behind the low wall, and when he stood back up, the firelight showed him in silhouette holding a squatter in each hand by the hair. "Here's your goddamn claim jumpers," he said, releasing them and letting them crumple to the ground behind the breastworks. He stood empty handed, palms outward, peering into the darkness, waiting.

Not entirely without misgiving, I walked slowly up to Isaac with my rifle at the ready, and across the pool of firelight I could see Billy Moore doing the same. I stopped within a few feet of the wall.

"Oh, put your pieces away, you jittery pair of kittens," Ford said. "Stormy Isaac Ford don't jump no claims. Been out here since Forty-Eight, when it was men only, none of you sniveling bald-face whelps, and no Irish need apply. There lays your claim jumpers. You'll know 'em, Stern, by sight."

I stepped in and peered over the wall, and sure enough I did know them: Pockmark and Lizard, snoozing peacefully or stone dead, I couldn't tell which.

"Friends of yours, aren't they, Isaac?"

"Friends hell. Stormy Isaac Ford don't call no claim jumpers friends."

"How did you lick them, Ford?" Billy asked.

"There warn't anything to it," Ford said. "Walked up and clobbered them is all. It's a pair of snakes all right, and I allow they did a bang-up job stirring things up to a boil around camp here. But they ain't no fighters, either one of them. You seen that yourself, Stern. Why, you watched with your very own eyes while that little pussycat of a missionary bested the both of them. No, no. Take it all together, they never was anything much more than a pair of Forty-Niners."

"Did you kill them, Isaac? Are they dead?"

This seemed a novel and interesting question to Ford. "Now, that, I don't know," he said and took to nudging at them with the toe of his boot. "Nah, look," he said. "They're breathin' all right."

We dragged them, none too gingerly, down the hill and deposited them by the fire, where the judge had fallen asleep next to the unconscious Joaquín Caracas. Cutler awoke at the clatter and said, "Did you fetch your men, Isaac?"

Ford grunted, flung himself down by the fire, and addressed himself to me: "If you ain't planning to kill 'em," he said, "these rapscallions will need to be tied up. Also: the fire's gettin' low. And: I could do with some supper."

I begrudged him no favors this night.

Chapter Ten

Bittersweet recollections—Gray brings counsel—Loss of a quarter share—Bungled negotiations—Legal threats—Re-enlisting the judge—A gallant gesture.

Billy and I split the watch. I sat up first, and when I reckoned the night was about half over, I nudged old Billy awake, not because I wanted any sleep but because I knew I ought to try and get some.

But it wasn't any use. I doubt that anyone sleeps who has that day learned of the death of a loved one. I scourged myself with rebuke for leaving Johnny back here among all this danger, and cursed the heavens that my good boy should have been taken instead of me: he, who never shook his grounding in Christian faith and was even too Christian to stop my scoffing at him and others for believing.

On the way out to Placerville with Honey, I'd had a foreboding about Johnny and had seen flashes of our past together, but that wasn't shucks next to what I went through this night. Hour upon hour, I stared blankly up at the merciless stars, seeing all the old times with Johnny, even the very oldest times, scenes of my earliest boyhood, images that had been lost to me for years and years. That awful night of grief was a window on the very mistiest past: I could see two-year-old Johnny trailing his little linen frock in the dust around our yard back when our house was still a simple cabin. I could see our father, who died when

Johnny was only three, coddling him on his knee (and behind them on the table my mother's wooden butter churn from that era, with the triangular chip in its cap, about whose existence I had long ago forgotten). I could see Johnny holding my hand as we explored the river bottoms together in a world of emerald leaf and golden sun. And when I remembered whipping Johnny for stealing carrots from the garden, it pierced me through to my heart, and I sat up gasping in the firelight.

"You all right, Stern?" Billy said.

"I reckon I will be," I said.

"You were a good brother to him," Billy said.

Lord God, I wished he hadn't said that, for now the fire began to blur, and my throat set in to aching and swelling. I lay back down with my back to Billy, for no one on earth wants to see a grown man cry even if he can't help hearing a sob or two.

I awoke at just daybreak with the red sun right before my eyes and with a sickly strange feeling come over me. Billy had fallen asleep, a thing unforgivable (ask any military man), and yet quite understandable, especially at dawn. For the same military man will admit that the night and its terrors are sufficient stimulants to keep a fellow at his attention a good long while, but when he begins to see the purpling of the eastern sky he senses that the world is not so hostile after all—senses this throughout all his fibers, I mean, not simply in his conscience—and relaxation and relief invade him same as would cold or fear. And before he knows it he is awakening to his punishment or his ruin. Well, I knew how it was, so I didn't say anything to Billy, just sat up and examined things.

Pockmark and Lizard lay bound and tangled together, each with a clump of dried blood in his hair where Isaac had thumped him. Ford and that judge slumbered on their backs, head to toe and shoulder to knee, dreaming, no doubt, of magnificent whores. Sometime during the night, poor old see-through Joaquín had finally gone into the good light, which must have shone through him like a punched tin lantern; and I was glad for him, for I don't believe any man was ever comfortable that was perforated quite like he was.

Beyond our little fire circle, at a space of about thirty yards, lay the repugnant body of Michael Green, still spoiling on his pallet. With all the commotion and turmoil of the previous day's events, we had not gotten around to burying him but had deposited him there only temporarily, to keep the smell off us. Some early-morning ravens were pulling at him, and I resolved not to put off his interment much beyond breakfast time.

Yes, all appeared well around me, and yet that uncanny feeling wouldn't quit me, so I stood and looked down the river. And here came two men leading a single pack mule.

"Billy, Isaac," I said, "get ready for a little trouble maybe."

They were up in a flash, making for cover with their guns in their hands. That judge went on snoring. Pockmark and Lizard began groaning and tugging at their bonds, fussy to have been disturbed. Me, I sat back down by the fire right in plain view with my rifle across my legs and waited for the strangers' approach.

It didn't take long for me to note something awfully sickeningly familiar about the mincing gait of the one in the lead, and as the pair drew closer I saw with a groan what we were in for. "Hell, Isaac!" I called. "Come on back out. It's Philemon Goddamned Gray!"

Yes, sure enough, here comes old bald-headed Philemon, with his peaky shoulders threatening to tear his canvas shirt through and his belt cinched too tight, just as infuriating and petulant as ever. He marches straight up to me and surveys the scene and says, indicating Lizard and Pockmark, "Well, well, Mr. Whitman. Still in the habit of keeping innocent parties in chains, I see."

I'm not usually much of one for spitting, but Gray always had drawn out the ruffian in me, and I got a little theatrical this time around and flung a nice cool string into the coals, which fetched me a pretty satisfactory hiss. "Gray," I said, "for some reason there's a series of folks keep looking for trouble by me, and I'm beginning to think that tying them up is an insufficient approach."

Gray turned to his partner. "Note that," he said to him. "Hear the way he threatens a man's life without a hint of provocation?"

I had never seen the other man before. He was what you call *undeniably* handsome, with a lustrous black moustache that followed the edges of his full-lipped mouth, shiny, dark hair, and a set of black eyes that appeared he was thinking of all the matters you in your ignorance were overlooking. His clothes, crown to heel, were black and neat and fine, as if he'd been picked up in town and set down in Whitman's Gulch by magic rather than having traveled hard to get here. He appeared disinclined to say much, just stood watching proceedings with that knowing look in his eye.

By this time Billy and Isaac had approached the fire.

"Mr. Ford," Gray nodded icily.

Ford grunted.

"A shame you didn't partner with me when you had the chance," Gray said to him. "For I've come to recover my rightful interest."

"Your rightful interest is a shallow grave," Ford said.

At last Cutler had awakened and sat up blearily. "Blazes," he said to Gray, rubbing at his eyes. "I thought I put you in jail."

Gray smiled. "Your keeper's scruples could be bought," he said.

Well, if old Cutler had been startled to see Gray, you ought to have seen his shock on recognizing the other fellow. "Luke

King!" he said, visibly recoiling. "What in holy hell's name are you doing away out here?"

The man named King smiled then, and the modesty and warmth of his gaze stood out starkly against Cutler's evident apprehensions toward the man. "Representing the interests of my client," he said in a smooth, soft voice.

Cutler shook his head. "Hmmf," he sniffed. "Lie down with a dog in the manger, and you're liable to get fleas," he said.

King rather blandly eyed our chaotic encampment. "I might apply the same adage to your circumstance," he said.

That was good, I thought: unhurried and calculated and well-targeted.

I said, "Just what matter is this client of yours about today?"

"My client—Mr. Gray—is owed one half possession of an enormous silver claim," King said, "and we've come out here to have a look at the site and to make it official."

"Go ahead and look at it," I said, "if a pair like you could ever find it."

"Oh," King said, "that isn't any trouble. We've already looked it over, since you so kindly led us to it, and all appears satisfactory. Of course we'll force the discovery of Mr. . . ." He looked down at a sheet of paper held in his hand. ". . . Mr. Moore's assay, and we'll require his deposition as to the prospects of the site. Now, is there a place of shade where we can . . . ?"

He was handsome, all right, but every bit as crooked and treacherous as Gray. I stepped closer to him and lifted a finger in his face. "Listen to me, you underhanded little snake," I said. "That galena is mine and mine alone, and the only way you or Philemon Gray or anybody else is going to take it from me is a fight—not a legal battle, a *fight.* Have you got the balls for a fight, or do you just mean to flap your jaw about depositions and discovery?"

King lowered his head during this little tirade, and, with a diffidence approaching shyness, he said quietly, "If I'm not mistaken, Judge Cutler will have a word or two of advice for you just about now, if he's your friend at all."

Sure enough, the judge's head was bobbing like a busted spring. "Come over here, boy," he said.

"Come on, Billy. Come on, Isaac," I said.

The four of us stood off to the side and hunched together in a little circle. "Now you listen to me, Whitling," Cutler said. "Haven't you ever heard of Luke King?"

"Name sounds vaguely familiar," I said.

The judge might have been a little disgusted with that, for he flung up his hands and snorted.

"I've certainly heard of him," Billy said.

"I've heard of him," Isaac said, "and a fella called Napoleon, too."

"You idiot," Cutler said to me, "Luke King is going to be president of this country someday—if they don't hang him first. He snuck around all over Veracruz with Winfield Scott, wrung more Mexicans' necks than any battalion of men. They wouldn't have made it to Mexico City without him, they say. Invisible, silent, everywhere at once. Comes home and reads the law. Kills six men in duels. Or maybe it's eight by now—been several days since last I saw him. Robbed a bank—everybody's sure of it—to set up his law practice. Come out here to get richer off the miners in Sacramento and never lost a case. But I'll tell you what: you want to tangle with Luke King, you'd better choose the legal tangle, because at least you and your friends might live through that."

"You mean to tell me you believe him and Gray could take that claim by force from the lot of us?"

"Lot of us your grandmother," Cutler said. "I won't speak for these gentlemen, but I sure know I won't die at the hand of Luke King so that you can be a tad richer than what you are already. But to answer your question: yes, of course; if Luke King wants to have that mine, why, he'll take it, even if you camp an army on top of it and fix bayonets."

I looked at Billy, but he was scowling and shaking his head. Ford had walked away, whistling.

"Well, how in the deuce am I going to beat them back legally?" I said.

"With me representing your interest," Cutler said. "For a consideration, of course."

"Of course. What kind of consideration?"

"A quarter share of that silver."

It was all so hazy and speculative. How much money did a quarter share represent? How unreasonable was Cutler's demand? And, in the end, how much choice did I have in the matter?

"Just a minute," I said to the judge.

I walked over to Gray and King. "Gentlemen," I said, "I'll engage with you on the question of ownership, but I prefer to do so back in Placerville or Sacramento, in more civilized conditions."

King nodded rather sadly. "That's quite impossible, I'm afraid," he said. "My client has pressing ecclesiastical duties in consequence of which we must dispose of this matter today, here in the field. I regret the inconvenience."

"Why, how can there be a trial without a judge?" I said.

"Oh, well, one hopes these things never proceed to trial," King said. "These are merely negotiations, the tidying up of contractual considerations, things not requiring the intervention or oversight of a judge when two parties meet in good faith."

"Good faith hell," I said. "I'll be right back."

I returned to Cutler. "One-eighth share," I said.

"One-eighth share hell," he said. "Lose a quarter of it, or lose all of it. It's up to you."

"Quarter share," I said. I could just as well have slapped him.

"Perfectly well. Shall we proceed?"

"No," I said. "See if you can't secure us an adjournment until after we've had breakfast and buried those two fellas on the pallets."

"Good," he said. "Gives me time to put our arrangement down on paper."

That afternoon I sat there disbelieving as that imbecilic Judge Cutler opened negotiations on my behalf for a galena mine that belonged to me by any source of rights imaginable. Ford and Moore, Pockmark and Lizard (somewhat recovered but still bound) sat observing the proceedings.

"Now, then," Luke King began, "it appears my client bears a contract, signed by Mr. Whitman, granting him one-half ownership of the mining claim in question."

"Let me have a look at that," Cutler said.

"Of course."

While the judge was reading, I whispered to him, "See here, Judge. Even if this thing was valid, it's only for the lead, not the silver. And anyhow, he got this out of me at the point of a gun. That isn't valid, right?"

Cutler smiled complacently and handed the document back to Gray's lawyer. Then, with a dismissive toss of the hand, he said, "Tell me, Mr. King: where did you obtain this *forgery*?"

King raised one black eyebrow. "I beg your pardon?"

"There, there," Cutler said, raising a finger. "He that's slow to anger is better than the mighty, and he that ruleth his spirit goeth on and taketh over the town."

King smiled indulgently and folded his hands.

"I warned you about manger dogs," the judge continued. "My client will swear to the ends of the earth he never signed any such piece of rot as you've churned up here. Why, this Gray of yours has taken you in like a very child, and here you sit with a forged contract in hand acting like it's the will of Great God Almighty."

If King was nonplussed any, he did a good job not showing it. "Why," he said pretty casually, "is this not your client's signature?"

The elated judge just about pounced. "Oh, it may *look* like his signature—may look a *great deal* like his signature, gentlemen—and yet—and yet! Why, the scoundrel who forged it seems to have forgot that my client . . . *always produces a flourish beneath the* G!"

It was awful still around there for a long moment, as when a deathbed vigil sees its culmination, and then Philemon Gray sets in to smirking. A forest fire came spreading up my chest, and it was getting a little bit hard to breathe. King, though, he never for an instant loses his composure. He just says, as low and peaceable as anything, "And what *G* would that be, your Honor?"

This bewildered the judge some, I could see by his blinking. He looks around for a second or two, gulps once, and blurts out, "Why, the *G* at the end of his name!"

I jumped to my feet. "You confounded old fool!" I shouted. "My name is Whitman! *Whitman!* It's an easy enough name, you biggety old bumptious braying jackass!"

Well, the judge just about shriveled right to nothing then, all the color gone out of him and a kind of day-after-the-funeral look in his eye. For a goodly moment it appeared he couldn't go on—not that I much wanted him to. I'd seen I'd squandered a quarter share of a silver mine on a man entirely without resource.

But damned if he didn't try to redeem himself!

With me fuming at him, and Gray snickering in his face, and Luke King calling on some fathomless reserves of manly discipline to keep his face straight, the judge begins shaking his head ruefully, as if shocked by the shoddiness of his company. "You misunderstand me, gentlemen," he says, and even though his voice has a new squeak to it, I can see the pluck coming back into him with each syllable. "I never meant to indicate my client's *family* name, but rather his *given* name. I'm surprised at you gentlemen. And at you most of all, Sterling."

This capped the climax. I'd been threatened and cheated and claim jumped, but I'd never so badly wanted to kill a man as I wanted to kill that judge. I lunged for him, but Stormy Isaac got himself between us, and I bounced harmlessly off Ford's belly.

"Steady now, Stern," Ford says. "Nothing rash."

I stalked off and kicked up some clods and let fly with the very choicest profanity I could muster, coveting Clarissa Gray's facility of language, and pretty soon I cooled down to where I could tell the judge that his services were no longer required. He slouched away and moped by the fire, and I sat next to Billy Moore across from my adversaries.

"All right," I said. "That bewildered old goat had it dead wrong: the contract was no forgery. But I tell you what it was, Mr. King, in the event you aren't aware: it was gotten at the point of a gun, on threat of murder. Now you tell me what kind of contract is enforceable that was come by in such a way as that."

"None indeed, Mr. Whitman, if such an assertion as that could be proved true. Now I suppose you're able to produce some evidence in support of this alarming and, frankly, slanderous claim?"

"Yes, I can, matter fact. Isaac Ford here heard your client confess as much."

King pulled at his moustache, very lightly. "I see," he said. "Now, was this before or after Mr. Ford assaulted and kidnapped my client?"

"Assaulted and—hell. Gray there was fixing to kill us all. He couldn't draw a breath that day without sticking his gun up somebody's snout. Why, even these two miscreants here can vouch for that. Ask that little one there, the one looks just like a skink."

King gazed disdainfully upon Lizard for a moment and then looked back at me, heavy-lidded and calm. "Mr. Whitman," he said, his tone awash with solemn pity. "You are quite beyond your depth. Allow me for just a moment to illustrate to you the tenuousness of your position. What you wish to have me—and, should it come to it, a court of law—accept as a final proposition is that you did not enter into this contract willingly, the burden of proof of which rests entirely upon your shoulders, I must inform you. Your evidence in support of this statement is the yet-unheard hearsay testimony of my client's assaulter and kidnapper. You further wish to explain away the kidnapping through outrageous accusations of belligerent behavior on the part of my client—a missionary of God!—behavior out of all keeping with his reputation as a man of the firmest moral fiber. By contrast, let us consider the mere outward appearances of *your* morality. Consorting with squaws and married women, conspiracy to kidnap, the evidence of which lives and breathes and struggles in its bonds here beside us. Murder? Oh, I don't know: depends on what we uncover when those fresh graves yonder are opened. No, Mr. Whitman, you may plead that you were forced into that contract, but you will never convince a judge or jury of it, and if by your hard words you haven't destroyed all hope of future intercourse with the Honorable Judge Cutler, he will explain as much to you."

Well, people have said some very harsh things to me in my time, but this slow, emotionless speech of King's left me feeling like the floor of the gallows had swung open under my feet and I was falling inside the noose.

Billy leaned over and whispered, "He's got you licked, Stern.

I can't see a way around it."

But I could.

"All right," I said. "Let him have half the lead—but that's *all* he gets—lead—for if you read it closely you'll see that I never said one word about *silver* in that contract."

I folded my arms.

Luke King smiled beneath that fine jet moustache. "Close reading is a long-instilled habit of mine," he said, "and the curious wording did not escape my notice. It was rather duplicitous of you, wasn't it, Mr. Whitman, to try to disadvantage my client through your misrepresentation? I suppose you were rather proud of yourself, in the moment, for disguising the real value of the claim from your counter party?"

"I don't know that I'd say proud. But the silver isn't rightly his, so I thought quick."

"You 'thought quick.' You also thought in direct violation of contract law, Mr. Whitman. Now, I don't wish to wax overly technical here, but there are some things you must understand. So I will set out for you, in simplified language, the many swords upon which your argument falls."

I blinked and gulped.

"By your own admission just now," King said, "you have made an obvious, deliberate misrepresentation in the drafting of a contract, omitting information to the detriment of my client. Any reasonable person would agree that your conduct—and indeed the resulting contract itself—'shocks the conscience,' a legal threshold for rendering a contract null and void."

My mind began racing for an answer, but King continued on in that same relaxed tone.

"Next," he said, "in the unlikely event that judge or jury failed to recognize this standard, you must be made aware that, as your one-time counsel, Judge Cutler, can attest, contracts are construed against their drafters, particularly when that drafter is a sophisticated party, holding technical knowledge beyond that of the draftee. By which, of course, I allude to your superior knowledge of minerals and mining as compared to that of a simple and honest churchman. I could cite a mountain of case law in which such ambiguities are resolved in favor of the draftee."

"Well—"

"Third, howsoever this particular issue is disposed, your conduct in the drafting of this document gives rise to a separate claim on my client's part of 'unjust enrichment,' a claim he will surely pursue should you foolishly persist in your feeble attempt to deny him what is rightfully his and hoard it for yourself."

"But—"

"Finally, and most—not least!—significantly, this debacle of a so-called contract is a radical departure from the industry standard, in which contracts dispose of *ores* and not of their constituent minerals. To put this bluntly, Mr. Whitman, if you hand this travesty over to any honest judge, he'll merely strike your 'lead' language and replace it with 'metal,' or add 'and silver,' and send you and Mr. Gray along on your way. Oh, and one other thing: deliberate misrepresentation—a kinder name for fraud—may also expose you to criminal penalties. We would not want that, any of us."

He was done now.

Well, hell and hell and hell again. I'd thought I'd had a pair of deadly arguments that would just about reduce this King to tears, and here he'd dumped a wheelbarrow load of even stronger points all over my feet.

It was all too many for me. He'd explained it clear enough, and it all sounded logical and by the book. But what did I know? I looked over at Billy. He only shrugged. Mining and minerals were his line, not the finer points of contract law. I could feel my heart coiling cold and tight like a pig of iron. The devils had me, didn't they? I couldn't bear to look at Gray. I feared that if I did so, I'd be driven to the kinds of actions that would *expose me to further criminal penalties.*

King had a very fine calfskin pouch, and from it he drew a document that he'd evidently prepared in advance. He rattled it a little bit in the air and then laid it down on the blanket smooth and soft and said, "Do you wish to consult with your counsel or will you sign over half the claim to Mr. Gray?"

I'd rather have eaten glass, but I said bitterly, "I'll go talk it over with Cutler first."

Cutler was sitting next to the campfire's ashes, whittling on a stubby little piece of cottonwood, trying to get it into the shape of a woman. He gave no notice of my approach.

"Listen, Judge," I said, feeling a little foolish after the way I'd spoken to him. "King there says I haven't got a chance of proving that Gray forced the contract. And he says *I* broke the law in how I set it up to be all about lead. He's got me talked right into a corner. Am I licked?"

Poor old Judge Cutler didn't even stop whittling. "Young man," he said, "it appears to me you were licked the moment you peeped your bloody head out from betwixt your mother's heaving thighs."

"That's not a very nice way to talk, Judge."

"No, I guess maybe it isn't. Neither is calling a man a buffoon and a muggins and a circus clown."

I hung my head a little, I felt so repentant. "I'm sorry for that, Judge. I am. Even though that isn't quite what I said."

He set down his whittling for a few seconds, then picked it up and cleared his throat. "Yes," he said, still not looking at me, "he's got you licked every which way, just as I knew he would, which is why I rejected both your lines of argument and tried for forgery." He stopped whittling and looked straight at me.

"You want me to have a look at what he wants you to sign?" he said.

"I'm afraid I do."

So the judge sort of slumps back over to the blanket, not looking too very proud anymore, and he huddles with that Luke King for the better part of an hour, wrangling over the terms of the contract. I left him to it, and he likely did a good job for me, although for all I understood of it, they might as well have been discussing astronomy and doing it in the Armenian.

At last the judge appeared satisfied with the language, and so he leans over to me and says, "Here it is, boy. You may as well sign."

I read through the thing and could find nothing to object to, apart from its very existence. Before I signed, I said to the judge, "Then this means nothing more nor less than my granting him half my interest in the galena claim, correct?"

"Yes, yes."

So I signed and thrust the paper across the blanket at Gray. "Here, you smirking jackal. You're rich. Now I've got to sell my quarter share quick as I can so I never have to look at your face again."

"Quarter share?" Gray said smoothly.

"The judge here is your other co-owner," I said.

"I see," Gray said. Then he turned to Luke King. "Speaking of Whitman's remaining interest, that reminds me: we have that other piece of business to attend to."

"Quite right," King said. "Though I hadn't forgotten."

Oh, no, sir. I didn't like the sound of this.

"What's this other business?" the judge said warily.

King began talking as he rummaged through his panier, and every gentle word of his landed like a blow to my stomach. "Your Honor, my client seeks damages flowing from the adulterous congress between your client and Mrs. Gray, which has resulted in loss of income, loss of spousal comfort, damage to reputation professional and personal, and severe mental anguish. We are seeking damages of eleven million dollars but will be satisfied with your client's remaining quarter-share interest in the Gray Galena Mine. Ah, here it is: contract for your client to sign, waiving any present or future interest in said mine in exchange for indemnification against charges and claims related to the adultery."

I stared and stared at Gray with my chest heaving and fists balling tightly. "Why, you filthy little turd," I said when I could speak. "You know I never touched your wife, and you're a cowardly, creeping maggot for saying I did!"

Gray burst out laughing: an awful, tinkling cackle.

But Judge Cutler was smiling and holding up a hand toward me. "Easy, Whitman. Don't get riled. Burden of proof is on the plaintiff, and I can't see how they can ever . . ."

Something in the reptilian grins of King and Gray gave him pause.

"Why, what do you have?" Cutler said, his face darkening.

Luke King touched his moustache once with the tip of index finger and thumb. "Only the testimony of my client," he said thoughtfully, "an upstanding man of God with a sterling, unimpeachable record of righteous conduct."

"Horse *shit,* right there," Ford muttered.

King ignored him. "Oh. And, if need be, the testimony of Mrs. Gray, the details of whose past, to put it as delicately as possible, will not bear up well under the scrutiny of a jury—or a public—concerned with matters of decency, propriety, morality; in short: character."

It all went black before me then, and when I'd recovered myself I found that I had marched off clear to the graveyard. That lawyer's ugly words rang and rattled around in my brain, galling me worse than anything I'd heard yet. Lies, such *filthy* lies, and supported by the law and threat of violence both!

I was hamstrung, laid right over a barrel. I stopped there among the fresh graves and heard myself muttering to Johnny: "It isn't *our* concern, is it, what happens between those damn fool missionaries? Traipsing all over the Far West never leaving folks a moment's peace. All peremptory and superior, condescending to decent folks and Indians that act more Christian than they could ever hope to! Well, you're right, Johnny, that goes for him and not for her. She's awful good hearted, you're right, and she doesn't deserve to have her name drug through the mud. Of course it's true what you say, that there she is out there in the world, looking to set things right for herself and shrug out from under an unfortunate past, and here that low creeping thing comes along looking to soil her worse than ever. And for what? To make himself just a little bit richer. You're right, Johnny: we *aren't* like him. We *are* better than that. Are you sure, Johnny? Is that the right thing to do?"

But I knew straightaway that it was, because I could feel that weight coming up off my chest just as sure as if a good stout angel had a hold of it and was flapping for all he was worth. Johnny was right. Maybe I'd never see Clarissa Gray again this side of the veil, but she had been kind to me and decent to all others, and it would never do to see her subjected to the cruelties of that rattlesnake of a husband of hers.

I just about flew back to where they were sitting around that blanket in the evening shadows. "Does that thing look all right to sign, Judge?" I said.

Cutler nodded sadly. "I hate to see you do it, son, but—"

I waved him off, seized the lawyer's pen, and scrawled my name across the bottom, big enough to make old John Hancock's ears burn some. "There, damn you," I said.

Philemon Gray chuckled. "So gallant," he said. "But if you

think this in any way prevents the details of Clarissa's past from—"

"Enough," Luke King said sharply. It was the first he'd raised his voice, and it tended to make a body's blood feel chillier than it had just been. Gray held his tongue.

I glared straight at Gray. "I don't believe it's too late of evening for you two gentlemen to be setting out upon your way," I said.

Gray began to answer, "Why, we'll go just as soon as we're—"

But again King cut him short. "I reckon you're right, Mr. Whitman," he said quietly. "We'll be shovin' off, just as you say." All the learning had gone out of his voice now, and he was drawling like any backwoodsman.

Ten minutes later, the pair were gone, and my silver mine with them.

Chapter Eleven

A period of rest—Artistic frustration—Prisoners—Merits of trial by jury—Gold's true value—Sickening news—Fond adieux—Joyful reunion—What happened in camp—Off to do battle.

After the labor of crossing the mountains, the horrors of what we found in the encampment, the shock of Johnny's death, the hard work of grave digging, and the mental exertions of the contractual dispute, I sorely needed a day or two of quiet. The judge did, too. He looked to have aged five or ten years over the course of recent events, and I felt a little sorry I'd dragged him out here. Ford, though, his cabin having been razed in whatever chaos had decimated our encampment, quietly led Jezebel down the valley and came back dragging four skinny logs, which he plopped into something very much like a square and went back to working his claim.

Billy scrabbled up and down the hillside, sinking little shafts, chipping at the rock, measuring, calculating, assessing. He was of that species of manhood that is so readily admired: expeditious, capable, intelligent, equally at home indoors or out, and perfectly ordered in all things within his sphere of control. Men like Billy never appear out of sorts, their effects never want for organization; they never scatter tools or equipment around. Billy's office, his bedroll, his laboratory, his mountainous worksites, the very clothing upon his person: everything was in its place. In the field, be it swelteringly hot or forty below, when others around him suffered beneath the elements, Billy quietly and effortlessly made shift for himself and did it looking like he'd stepped out of a catalogue, too. I always wondered how he did it.

For two days, I mostly sat around, keeping a fire going despite the heat, snoozing and mulling, reconciling myself to all that had happened. The judge sat opposite me, puttering over his nude figurine, which was both a pleasure and a trial for him. What plagued him were the ample bosom and ampler buttocks. Or I should say the bosom and buttocks *meant to be* ample and ampler, for the judge's artistic undoing lay in an inordinate interest in those particular elements of his sculpture. This excess of attention resulted in excess application of his blade to those parts, which invariably reduced one of these features (a breast or a buttock) past his liking and introduced an unacceptable asymmetry that could only be answered by trimming off more of the *other* breast or buttock. And when balance was restored, the aesthetic effect was so satisfying as to command his eye a little too long—and where his eye went, so did his blade; and so the cycle was repeated until the poor woman stood destitute of all female charms, smooth and uninviting as a stripling, at which point she was tossed into the fire with a curse and the judge waddled off to fetch another stick.

Sickened by their very sight, I removed Lizard and Pockmark to a spot along the river where they were shaded and could drink freely, like livestock, and I carried them two meals a day. Each was bound wrist and ankle and tied off to the trees where they couldn't reach each other but were close enough for company. Whenever I came near I had to be cautious to avoid their teeth. They snapped like a pair of wolfhounds and rained curses upon me for making them prisoners. But I couldn't see a better course, unless it was hanging, and told them so. They understood that in a day or two they would be carried back to Placerville and tried, and they knew well what the final result would likely be. So it was hang now or hang later, and, being nothing if not patient, they allowed they could put it off just a while longer.

Isaac had been for stringing them up straightaway, whether they'd ever been friends of his or not, but the judge allowed that to do so would be uncivilized and immoral, that the situation wanted a trial if ever one did. His extemporaneous comments to this effect sort of blossomed out into one of the finest speeches I'd ever heard on the topic of justice and civilization. I was a little sorry that Luke King hadn't stuck around to hear it, for I believe it would have impressed even him. Afterward I calculated that the day of that beautiful patriotic address might even have been the Fourth of July, give or take three or four days, which kind of makes a body's spine tingle to think of.

Well, the only one unmoved by the judge's remarkable oratory was the man who'd triggered it, Ford, who, when it was all over, mumbled, "Still seems to me we ought to hoist 'em."

"Why, Stormy," the judge said, "a man *deserves* a fair trial, doesn't he?"

"Ain't a trial meant to show they done what they done?"

"Yes! You have it right."

"Well, Judge, you and me and Billy and Stern, we all *saw* what they done."

"But a trial, you see, is what separates us from the barbarian."

"Thunder and lightnin', then *give* 'em their trial and *hang* 'em! Ain't you a judge?"

"Of course I am. But I'm also a witness. In such cases, a judge must recuse himself from the proceedings."

"Why, then, you're excused. Sit over there and we'll trial out just fine and string the pair up without you."

"Ah, but that would be extrajudicial. You see the dilemma now, don't you, Stormy? Not to worry, though. We'll fetch them back to Placerville, where another judge will try them. Paul Fletcher is his name, and I know him well. For that matter, there isn't a potential juryman in all Placerville who I haven't shared a drink with one time or another, and there's a great many of them owes me favors. I'll serve as principal witness for the people, and believe me, those two *will* swing. Why, it's as good as sewn up. You'll see."

Well, Ford grumbled that it was the height of absurdity to go to so much "pison trouble" for a pair of claim jumpers that everybody *knowed* was claim jumpers and allowed that the whole thing passed all comprehension. And he stomped off to his new cabin saying as much, though he never raised the issue again.

After Stormy had gone, the judge clicked his tongue and shook his head sadly and dished us out another splendid harangue (though this one was shorter and less comprehensive), holding up Ford's benighted ignorance as a caution, and as an argument for that noblest of ideals: free education for *all* the young white males in this great country.

After supper on the third day, I walked up to the apex with Billy to hear his report. We sat on the low breastworks that Lizard and Pockmark had made. I always had liked working up there. A breeze generally blessed it, especially of evening, and tonight a stiff zephyr was wafting down out of the high peaks, filling our lungs with air so crisp and fresh that it felt like we were cheating summer. Down below lay that pretty gold-embedded stream, with the trees clumped along the shore looking from up here about the size and color of turnip greens.

Billy says, "Well, Stern, I've got to tell you: everything's as you said it was."

"We have a likely prospect, then?"

"Only if you think the King of England does," he said. "Hell, you ought to have been an engineer, Stern. You calculated it all out just the same as I've done."

I shrugged. "Had two winters with nothing to do but read," I said.

I was looking west, toward the faint pinkish rind where the sun had set. Billy's eyes were on the eastern sky, already dark, where the first star or two had burned through the curtain of the new night.

Billy seemed to be in an awful wistful mood. He said, "You know what gold is, Stern, where it comes from?"

"Bowels of the earth."

"Sure. But how did it get there?"

"Get there? It didn't *get* there. It just *was* there."

"Wrong, and don't tell me God put it there, either. It came from the stars. The stars burned it off eons ago, and it was one of the many metals from which the earth was formed. But it's rare; oh, it's rare. Unspeakably rare, and precious. A single part per *trillion* in the universe."

That was a pretty fat number, although I knew I didn't have a decent sense of the real difference between a billion and a trillion. Billy must have understood this, for he said, "Imagine if you could build a machine to sort through the atoms of the universe at a rate of one atom per second. About how often would you expect to hit upon an atom of gold?"

"Hell, I don't know." I decided to pick an outrageously large chunk of time. "Fifteen minutes?"

"No, Stern," he said. "You'd hit gold about once every thirty-two thousand years. The number of years it would take you to amass an *ounce* of the stuff at that rate is too unwieldy a figure for me to express: a number with twenty-six zeroes at the end of it! Yet here we sit upon a *ledge* of it, Stern, *tons* of the stuff. And it belongs to *you*."

Well, I had read up on minerology, all right, but this business about the stars, and about the surpassing rarity of gold, was too many for me. Strange to say it, but hearing him talk the way he was actually sickened me slightly, made me feel kind of all-overish. It even kind of put me in the valley of the shadow, if you understand what I mean.

Billy said, "Have you decided what you're going to do with it?"

"To be honest, Billy, there's more of the sublime in what you say than I can feel myself equal to; I can't quite meet it with my mind. Now, cash—there's a thing I can fathom. So I'll answer you same way I answered you last time you asked: my plan is to sell out of it; sell out and go tell Mama about Johnny and see what comfort our riches can bring."

He nodded. "I expected nothing different, nor would I advise you any otherwise. I've written a preliminary report. People might know we're friends, but they also know we're honest, and my name is good in Placerville, so no one will question my objectivity. I've already had the judge legalize your claim; he'll give you that document. And if someone offers you cash, don't accept a penny less than seven million but don't blink if they offer you a hundred, either."

I chuckled a little bit, as merry as an undertaker burying his own mother. "Seven million," I said. "I always thought a figure like that would make me giddy. Yet all I can seem to think about is Johnny. And Honey."

At the mention of Honey, Billy kind of jolted up. "Stern," he said. He seemed to be hesitating about something, but then he brought himself to say, "There's another thing yet that you don't know about her."

"I know she took up with Ward Carson. There can't be anything worse than that, now, can there?"

"Well, yes, there can be," he said, looking me straight in the eye, "and I guess I'd better tell you before I lose heart. You say she took up with Ward Carson, and for all I know that's true. But it's just as likely he may have simply *taken* her. See—All right, well, here's the story. Long before you ever met her, that old pustule Carson had taken some notion of prospecting all the way up along the Humboldt. Months and months go by, and we've got him presumed for dead, or at least to have drifted on to other pastures. But he surprises us all by coming home. Empty handed, of course, all except for this pretty little Crow that he all but dragged back by the hair."

"Not Crow. Blackfoot, you mean."

Billy gave me a funny look. "Blackfoot hell," he said. "If I'm an American, that gal's a Crow. What in heaven's name would you or Ward Carson be doing with a Blackfoot?"

I had no good answer to that, except that everyone had always called Honey and the other washerwoman the Blackfoot sisters. "Anyhow, go on," I said.

"Well, so Carson came through Placerville with her. With her belly out to here *with his baby.*"

I felt the life-giving wind go right out of me.

Billy continued straight along. "He hauled her forthwith out to his cabin, and that was about the last any of us ever saw of her. A few months later he's coming in and out of town with another woman, towheaded Irish gal, who's pulling this little half-breed baby along by the hand. Not hide nor hair of the Crow. We'd all just figured he'd got tired of her and finished her off. But then Ward gets pretty admirably drunk one night and starts blabbing as to how his Indian slave gal tried to sneak off with the baby one windy night, how Ward tracks her to where she's bedded down with the child out in the woods, and he horsewhips her, draws his revolver, and tries to shoot her, but she's not very much slower than an antelope, and she skips off into the night. Well, in the scuffle he'd got hold of the baby, it seems, and now just to spite her he decides he'll take it by the ankles and swing it into a tree and let her find its brains and everything in the morning. So he grabs it by the leg, and it starts to bawl. And you should have seen him there, in the saloon, Ward Carson, of all people, telling this, how that damned old alligator starts dripping tears all over the bar! Says something just came over him, and he can't bring himself to kill his own son even if half the kid's blood is vile Indian. He figures she's watching him from the trees, so he hollers out to her that if he ever lays eyes on her again he'll smash that baby all to pieces. Says he's sure she understands, for she's the cleverest Indian he's ever met yet. When you said her name—Honey—I said that's got to be Ward Carson's Crow. Got to be. Far as I know, that baby is still up there at Ward's place and that other woman of his is raising it for her own."

I just sat there numb as a fieldstone for a while as this all sank in. Poor Honey! Why, the whole time she'd been in our camp, her heart had been breaking for her little boy, and at last she'd been unable to bear it a moment longer, had seen me headed for Placerville, and had been incapable of staying put. And then I had killed the sheep. Oh, I saw it now, what it had meant to her to see those lambs' mother taken from them. Yet she had forgiven me. And I had squandered that forgiveness because I'd worried what the world would think of me! Oh, the fool I had been!

And then on the road to Sacramento she had helped me to my feet and spoken tenderly to me, but the unheard cries of her long-lost child were louder in her ears than my declarations of love. And then—oh, what came to me next just about brought up my supper: why, she'd been on her way to . . .

"Christ, Billy, why didn't you tell me? Am I too late?"

He was looking at the stars shining golden on the horizon. "I think you must be," he said. "It's days and days now."

But I had already jumped to my feet and was looking down the hillside. Before I could speak, Billy said quietly, "Yes, you can take Grandee."

I was all for shoving off that very minute, but the night was moonless, and my friends easily convinced me of my folly. I would leave at the very first light. Billy agreed to stay and watch over the apex and to continue his examinations of it, and the judge and Stormy Isaac resolved to depart in the morning, just after me, to escort the prisoners to Placerville. Ford was not in the least discommoded by this chore. Oh, he grumbled about how much trouble the claim jumpers were, but he enjoyed the judge's society, and, as I have pointed out previously, he seemed to appreciate any distraction from his chosen calling. I wondered who among that exalted party would shoulder the many low tasks attendant upon a cross-country excursion, and I wondered further whether Pockmark and Lizard would survive Ford's impatience. But, such concerns being far beyond my ability to control, I set them aside and focused on my journey.

In the morning, I shook Billy's hand. "Don't get yourself killed, Stern," he said. "It would be an awful shame for a man of your net worth."

"You're a good friend to me, Billy."

The judge handed me the deed he'd written up. "Give this to Alexander for him to stamp," he said. "There's a letter here, too, instructing him as to same. He can be mulish."

"I thank you, Judge. Now, I know I owe you another four hundred for coming out here."

"No, you don't," he said with a wave. "I'm quarter owner of that silver mine, without heir, and with no great store of remaining years in which to expend my riches. What I've got is quite sufficient."

I turned to Ford and put out my hand. "Isaac," I said, "I

believe I'll miss your company."

"Christ Jesus Almighty . . ." Ford began, then paused. "I've lost track," he confessed.

"I believe we left off with Christ Jesus Almighty Savior of Us All in Heaven Above," I said.

Ford nodded. "Well, Christ Jesus Almighty Savior of Us All in Heaven Above and Lamb of God," he said, "you've become almighty spongy for a man that still wants to call himself a miner."

"I'll see that you're justly rewarded for all your troubles," I said. "You're a good man."

He looked up the hill at the apex and then back at me. "Tell you who ain't a good man," he said slowly. "Ward Carson. A sure-enough slinking little Forty-Niner, but wily and dangerous to boot. Can't help but think you're setting out to meet your end, riding into battle with the likes of him."

There wasn't anything very much to say to that. I'd have liked to disagree with him but knew how hollow it would sound. Stormy just walked off, shaking his head—sadly, I almost thought.

The sun came creeping up over the trees in the east. Without another word to my friends, I mounted Grandee and spurred him for the crest of the Sierra.

There was a world of difference between tugging a mule over that terrain and crossing it astride a horse as tireless and sure-footed as Grandee. That animal appeared to think of nothing besides proving his worth, and each time I'd get to thinking that he must slow, why, he'd perform some new extravagance—charge up a knoll, say, or jump clean over a log that he could just as well have stepped over like a conservative. After a time, I got used to it and more or less let him have his head, for he seemed to be a rip when it came to navigation, as well.

I had never been in a gunfight before, having always found better pastimes with which to amuse myself. But I had witnessed a few and had known some pretty regular contestants in the sport, and from what I understood of it, success or failure in that pursuit hinged very much upon a simple willingness to be the first to pull the trigger. Now, in dime novels, the opponents will stand steadily at a few paces' distance, scowling bitterly at one another in a stirring tableau of masculinity, perhaps exchanging exquisitely wrought and colorful phrases, until at some signal—sometimes overt, sometimes imperceptible—they will unsheathe their revolvers and fire. The winner is he of the quickest "draw," with the entire contest centering on speed of the unsheathing.

This is, of course, a preposterous fiction, and a thing that has never once occurred in the history of gunpowder.

In a real gun battle, a hot-blooded mutual displeasure tends to choke off whatever theatrical flourishes the participants might have inclined themselves toward. Blinded by fury, each rages bluntly forward with a pressing, burning urge to snuff out the life's flame of his opponent, without more ado than going after a horsefly that's munching on your shoulder. The two will close upon each other in a mad, headlong rush, no different than if they had only fists for weapons. As a general thing, just as in a fistfight, whoever is angriest—whoever's fury thrusts him into the affray with the greater and more immediate force—wins the day.

These were the thoughts with which I concerned myself as I let Grandee carry me precipitously along; I studied them out, rehearsed them in my mind, preparing myself for my bloody and smoke-filled encounter with Ward Carson. I wanted to see it all in my mind's eye beforehand, acquaint myself with it intimately in advance rather than be startled by reality.

But each time I tried to envision it, each time I saw myself marching resolutely up to accost him, those blasted dime novels interloped, and I heard myself crowing some perfectly jackass thing like, "Ward Carson! Prepare to meet your doom!" In my reverie—as would surely be the case in life itself—such an outburst was sufficient warning for Carson to draw his revolver and shoot me clean through the belly.

I do have an awful fear of being shot through the belly. If you ever come after me, kindly aim for the forehead, just between the eyes.

On my third afternoon, up on the very spine of the Sierra, traversing a little northward the better to make an easy descent, and cogitating nervously on these matters, I looked far ahead of me along where the broad purple flank of the mountain curved like the body of a fish with its great back fin arched against a hazy, blue sky. And there I beheld two people, specks at first, leading a mule.

They were picking their way my direction along that lofty crest among the coal-black rocks and boulders of this nether realm. A little afraid, I reined in Grandee and sat my saddle and watched with the wind thumping and ruffling in my ears. The strangers, too, halted, for they had spied me. As yet, they were too far off for me to ascertain whether they were white men or red. I patted my weapons and nudged Grandee forward along the ridge, keeping my eye skinned. By and by I began to discern that the strangers were man and woman—white man and Indian woman—doeskin tunic—Honey?—Carson?

No, not Carson. Too short, wrong color hair. Familiar, though . . .

Well, hold on to everything. No. It could not be.

I never thought I believed in ghosts, never thought there was room in my thinking for any such truck, but apparently it was so, for now I froze in the saddle, looked away, blinked, looked back. And still the apparition came on. A coldness ran all through my flesh just the same as if I'd been dipped in a February snowbank. Why, up here in the ether, in this lonesome, empty place of rock and sky, where no sound is ever heard save the moaning of the scouring wind like the crying of tortured souls, here in the realm of spirits, I beheld the ghost of my dead brother, Johnny, coming up the ridge, smiling and waving in joyous reunion!

Oh, he looked and acted just as he had done in life, his strong teeth flashing and his dark hair tossed by the wind. This was a vision more vivid even than those that had visited me back at camp, and though it terrified me to behold, still I knew how precious it was to receive this final witness, and I sat and trembled and drank it in.

His ghostly companion was not Honey but the other Blackfoot sister, who must also have been killed in the melee at the encampment. She, too, looked just as she had in life, though perhaps now she appeared a bit friendlier, perhaps a bit less guarded, for she was more than half smiling at me. With her ruddy cheeks and her tossing lustrous hair and her bright tunic flapping hard along her thighs, she appeared very beautiful there among those summits, which seemed a fitting place for her wild spirit.

I waited for the end of my blessing, for the two of them to fade away against the azure sky, but still they came, closer, closer, until I could hear the clop of their mule, and their laughter, and the very scrape of their feet upon the gravel! And then the spirit of Johnny handed the mule's lead to the spirit of the Blackfoot sister, and he ran to close the distance. Many times in my dreaming, ghosts had hurried at me just so, and always at the last moment, just before they touched me, I awoke sucking for air, and so I watched, petrified and wide-eyed, as Johnny's apparition glided straight up to my horse. I must have gasped and twisted in the saddle and yarned on the reins, and it must have made Grandee nervous to have been rushed upon like that. Anyway he shied awfully, and in a twinkling I was unsaddled and sprawled on the rocky surface of the mountain-top.

"Stern," Johnny was saying. "You all right, Stern?"

When my eyes came open, my head was in the lap of my brother's ghost, and the other was squatting beside me, poking at my ribs and spine.

"I'm sorry I ever whipped you for the carrots," I said, "and I'm sorry I ever left you among such a nest of scorpions. Now, if you'd forgive me and release me, and get along back to the spirit world—"

"Why," Johnny said to the woman, "poor Stern is lost his reason. Stern," he said. "Don't you know me?"

I sat up and scrabbled away from him like a crawdad. "Of course I know you. You're my dead brother Johnny, and I'm begging and pleading with you to let me alone!"

"Dead hell," Johnny said. "Where in the nation did you get that kind of an idea? I ain't dead, nor never have been yet in my whole life."

"Not dead? Could it be? Oh, Johnny, don't play tricks on me. Swear it's true. Swear you were never killed by that passel of idiots back at camp."

"Well, of course I swear it, Stern. Can't you believe your very own eyes? I'm standing here, ain't I? How could I be dead? You say so yourself all the time that there's no such thing as spirits."

Well, I'll just leave it to you to imagine how I just smashed into a million pieces then and grabbed right hold of him and pulled him hard against me and kissed him all over his head. Describe how good he felt in my arms? How could I? His muscle and bone, the thumping of his heart, the warmth of his blood in his skin! A brain inside that handsome head of his still performing its mysterious function, not yet food for worms but, for a precious season more, still directing the organism, still housing a universe of perceptions and judgments, most of them tender and bighearted. Miracle! My boy, my baby, intact, unscathed, complete! Oh, I just held him and held him, and poured out my tears all over his head and shoulders. You never saw anybody half as happy as I was that day up on the mountaintop, and I don't expect ever to live a happier day than that one, no matter how long I may persist on this earth.

To Johnny the reunion was quite a bit less emotional, which only stands to reason. He was powerfully glad to see me, of course, but had never thought me dead, nor himself either; and so my extravagances must have struck him as a little whimsical.

Well, I didn't mind about that, not even somewhat. In a tongue-tied rush, I laid down the barest outlines of my adventures, omitting only the existence of the apex, and when I came to the part about Joaquín telling me that Johnny had died, Johnny said, "Why, that explains your confusion, for poor old Joaquín never *could* tell me and Charles Benson apart—and Benson got killed not thirty feet from where Joaquín was holed up."

It wasn't right or moral of me, but I rejoiced some to hear that the young man Benson had fallen in the fray. Not for the thing itself, you understand, but because, in a strange way, it sort of clinched for me the fact that Johnny really was still alive. Yes, I'd be making myself out for a better man than I am if I pretended to have paused one second to grieve that Benson boy. In truth, I would have given a dozen young Bensons for the life of my Johnny. That shows you how hollow it all is, when it comes to noble sentiment, for Benson surely had a brother or a mother who would have sacrificed a dozen Johnnies for their boy, and I've no reason to doubt but what the Bensons were a fine religious lot.

Johnny explained to me more or less what had befallen the

encampment, though he himself was a good deal confused by it. After I'd left, things had gone passably quiet for a day or two, almost as if the miners had come to their senses. But then two men called Croat and Gunsen—Lizard and Pockmark, I knew—had arrived and, within a matter of hours, had set the stage for stirring those factions back up worse than ever. Having been briefed as to the recent troubles, they held themselves out as the providential saviors to the encampment, as the solution to the dispute over Peter the Great's death.

Their idea was that they, being perfectly neutral, with no interest whatever in the outcome, save for uncovering the truth, could do the men a great service by shuttling from faction to faction, hearing evidence from both sides in an unbiased way, and so coming to a reliable and unimpeachable conclusion regarding who had killed the Tsar. To give physical manifestation of their disinterestedness, they'd ensconced themselves away up on top of the hill, on my "useless" claim, and had prohibited all others from trespassing there, since to allow visitors would be perceived as granting favor to one side or the other.

But rather than shuttling back and forth and listening, they mostly shuttled back and forth pouring poison into the ears of the miners, whipping them into a mutual loathing even more desperately attenuated than what had obtained during my presence. The entire business of mining had fallen out of all consideration, with the factions becoming less metaphorically and more literally a pair of small armies preparing for contention. Men freely abandoned the claims that, just days before, they had guarded as preciously as the lives of children, in order to encamp alongside their likeminded fellows. The two parties had become as physically segregated as Washington's and Cornwallis's men, with most of the vast breadth of hillside become a veritable no-man's-land, where to wander was to expose oneself to the fire of the enemy.

As the days drew on, the atmosphere had grown so fevered that Johnny expected to hear the battle commence at any moment of the day or night. He slept with our gun by his side. Our gun and, it should be noted, the other Blackfoot sister, who had taken up with him about a minute after I'd left with Honey. On the last night before the killing began, Johnny said, he lay awake listening to the screams of insults being hurled through the darkness, and he felt more strongly than ever before that the long-awaited bloodletting was but hours away. Fears An Antelope (for that was the name of his beloved) had not slept a wink, either, and let him know that she, too, expected apocalypse at sunup.

And so in those wee hours, with the camp having at last fallen silent, they had arisen and stealthily loaded Fears An Antelope's mule and slunk off downriver by starlight. They had not gone more than a mile or two when the sun broke across the valley, and very shortly thereafter they began to hear long bursts of gunfire, dread fulfillment of their shared prophecy.

Now, as relieved as he was to have escaped the senseless fighting, Johnny was not above a quite natural human curiosity, nor exempt from feelings of sympathy toward the Mexican side, to whose cause he had been originally drawn. And so they had turned back, approaching the camp from a neighboring ridge that afforded a perfect view of the battle. Having achieved this vantage, Johnny found his curiosity intact but his sympathy quite severely diminished, for as they lay and watched, the whole day through, it was impossible not to find wholly repugnant this bloody scene of men with no legitimate quarrel shooting and cutting each other to ribbons, for no greater reason than that they had made up their minds about something, and no stronger moral compulsion than the ancient satisfaction that comes of coalescing around a pole.

Yes, it had been an awful hard thing for Johnny to watch, but he lay there bearing witness—and he noted that Croat and Gunsen had watched, too, safely from their breastworks—until sundown, when the handful of remaining Mexicans had fled downriver, pursued for a few halting steps by a handful of their wounded enemies. Some of the men from both sides had been killed in the shallow river, which had carried them haltingly away, bumping and scraping bottom as they went. Who knows but what the friction of those lifeless bodies along the stream's gravel bed hadn't dislodged a nugget or two of that gold that had been sent down from the stars before the earth was made?

By dark of night, Johnny and Fears An Antelope had risked all to steal back onto the field and crept into what had passed for a headquarters for the pro-Green faction. Believing all its inhabitants to have perished in the slaughter, they had helped themselves to an item or two that they judged of greater use to themselves than to dead men and, calculating that they had gambled sufficient for one day, had fled back into the mountains with their mule.

They had wandered like children for the space of several days, avoiding signs of men, letting the high clear streams, the pellucid sunlight, the impossibly verdant hillsides, and each other's loving touch purge their eyes and hearts of the human evil they had seen. Their peregrinations had carried them northward; they had crossed the mountains near Mono Lake and, coming to their senses at last and wishing to intercept me upon my return crossing of the Sierra with the judge, had taken to patrolling this stretch of the crest for days. And now here I was.

Well, of course they were all for coming with me to do battle with Ward Carson, but—as much as it pained me to leave my brother behind after retrieving him from the tomb, as it were—I had a fast horse under me and could not bring myself to shuffle down to Placerville at the pace of their overloaded mule, not when seconds might matter in saving Honey's skin. Besides, I had gotten Johnny killed once already by exercising poor judgment, and I was not about to repeat the error. Well, neither Johnny nor Fears An Antelope was very happy with me, but I made a hard thing of my heart, remounted old Grandee, and clattered off over the spiky fin of that fish's back with their shouted remonstrations lost to the snatching wind.

CHAPTER TWELVE

Alexander again—I visit the prisoner—The disturbing case of Judge Paul Fletcher—Enlisting the opposition—I confront Ward Carson—How it all ended.

Well, if I was weary and rank when I'd first arrived in Placerville with Honey all those days ago, then you should have seen and had a whiff of me when I fetched up in the place this time.

In front of Judge Cutler's office, I swung down out of the saddle—or tried to, for several of my lower parts appeared to have grown fused to the seat during the long incessant ride, and the tearing free put me in mind of an incident when, as a child, I grabbed the frosty brass doorknob of a church after throwing wet snowballs barehanded: things seemed to cling for a long moment and then to strip free. Worse, my legs had gone all to applesauce, which makes for paltry vertical support, ask any carpenter. It had rained down here, recently, and the street was a mire, but under the mirthful gaze of the citizenry, and without any choice in the matter, I sat me directly into it, like a boar hog, where I slapped and punched at my own thighs and calves until function was restored.

When I could stand, I leaned up against Grandee and pawed around in my bags until I produced the deed Cutler had written, and the letter for Alexander, and then I stumbled up into Cutler's offices. The assistant was not at his station, and I at first despaired of finding him in, but on an instinct I proceeded to Cutler's chambers, where I found him napping with his feet up on the desk amidst the leaves and stumps of what must have been nearly a peck of raw carrots.

"Alexander," I said. "Here—Alexander!"

He snoozed on, happily dreaming of whatever it is that officious clerks dream of when their bellies are full of carrots.

Louder I said, "Alexander!"

No effect.

Then I crossed my arms and said in a low voice approximating that of the judge: "Alexander."

Why, you never saw a pile of carrot leavings explode with such terrible sudden force, or a blurrier flailing of clerkish extremities. In less than an instant Alexander was on his feet, bowing and scraping like a serf, and I believe it took him five or more seconds to understand that I was not the judge, after which, like the smart turning of a page, his attitude transformed from panicked abjection to haughty self-importance.

"May I help you, *sir*?" he said when he'd recovered himself.

"Yes, you may," I said. "I'm Whitman, and the judge gives you these instructions to stamp this document."

"You may leave them on the desk," Alexander said.

"Leave them hell. I need you to sign them instantly."

"Sir," Alexander said, "this is a busy law office. I'm not at liberty to drop everything and—"

"Drop your pile of carrots, you mean, or drop your feet off Cutler's desk?"

Alexander cleared his throat. "You mustn't surrender to the appearance of things," he said. "It may have *seemed* I was idling, but I assure you—"

Being of a generally pacific constitution, and yet in a god-awful hurry, I seized the clerk by the collar and lifted him clear off his feet. "I haven't got any time today for dithering," I said through clenched teeth. "You'll stamp that paper, and you'll do it without a second's delay."

Five minutes later, he handed me a fresh copy of the stamped deed. I folded it neatly and tucked it into my pocket. "Thanks, Alexander," I said.

Pretty quietly he says, "Anything else, sir?"

"Matter of fact, yes. Do you know a man called Ward Carson?"

"Well, not personally, of course. But everyone's *heard* of Ward Carson."

"All right. Do you know where he lives?"

"Certainly I do."

"Well, then, tell me how to *find* the place, you utter simpleton."

Alexander appeared to take no offense at this, and it occurred to me that a requisite of his occupation must be the ability to maintain a generalized sneering disdain right up until evidence showed him he was in presence of a better, at which point he could surrender all dignity and never even miss it once it was gone. "Certainly, sir," he was saying now. "Nothing easier. Go out the Sacramento road six miles or so, and you'll see a little grassy road come down off the hill to your right. Now there's other such roads out there; you'll want the one that goes straight up over a steep hill with a white oak atop of it. That's Ward Carson's road. His place is at the end of it, I mean."

"Thank you."

"If it isn't urgent, though, you might save yourself a trip. I'm sure he'll be in town tomorrow for the trial. Certainly for the hanging."

Hearing those words, I felt for all the world like the devil had just clapped his clammy old left hand on my shoulder. My own words sounded like they were coming from somebody else's sore throat as I said, "Which trial would that be, Alexander?"

"Why, that squaw that shot at him and tried to steal his child."

I sank into a chair.

"Mr. Whitman? Something the matter?"

I waved a hand at Alexander and sat biting my lips, trying to swallow down the bile that kept rising in my throat.

"You appear unwell, Mr. Whitman. Let me fetch you a little water."

He left the room, and during his brief absence my head began to clear. Live through enough shocks close together and you'll see they don't hit you quite so square after a while. A plan began to take shape in my mind.

"Drink this, Mr. Whitman."

"How can there be a trial while the judge is away, Alexander?"

"Oh," he said, "we have another judge, Paul Fletcher. He'll hear the case and see to the hanging."

"Do you suppose they'll let me see her?"

"Why, I would imagine so. But why in the world would you want to do a thing like that, Mr. Whitman?"

"Because," I said, "she's my wife."

That jail was just about the most unpleasant place I ever set foot in, and I've been to New York; it made our squalid little mining camp look like the Buckingham Palace. It was dingy and ruinous and felted all over with mold, and it boasted no greater aperture than the tiny slot of a missing brick high up on the wall to let in air and sunlight, neither of which succeeded much in finding their way down to that filthy, maggot-writhing floor.

It took me nearly a minute even to make out Honey in all that gloom, but she knew me straight away, of course, and rushed over to the iron bars and plunged her hands through and just felt me all over, she was that glad to see me. For a good long moment we stood there hugging at each other through those ice-cold bars. When at last I could discern her features I saw that her face was puffed and stained from many long hours spent weeping in her solitude, and I knew that in all those hours she'd shed nary a tear for herself, nor likely one for me. It was all for that child of hers, and what was to become of it without her in the world.

She cooed and jabbered at me like a mother pheasant for a good long while, and of course I understood not a word of what she said, at least not specifically, although even a dog could have got the gist of it. When she slowed up a little, I started making promises to her about how I would stop this hanging or die, and about how no matter what happened, one way or the other, I'd care for that child of hers and raise it like it was my very own. She just smiled at me then like a church painting—she always was better at understanding my jabbering than I was hers—smiled a world of sorrows upon my brow, smiled as if she had already been cut down from the scaffold and stretched out in her grave, and that terrible peaceful smile just ran me through with an awful dread.

I said to her, "Honey, I mean it, now. You're not going up on that platform, because I'm here and I can stop it, and I *will* stop it." Again she reached up, just as she'd done that day on the road to Sacramento, and she laid her palm against my cheek and then dropped it.

I turned to go. "I mean it, now," I said, tipping a scolding finger at her. "You're my woman, and I'll not let you hang. They'll kill us both or neither one of us, that's how it'll be."

She put on an awful brave face, but when that venal clodhopper, Fuller, was closing the door behind us, I heard what I'm certain was a tiny, dignified, half-stifled sob.

Now, in my time I have traveled widely and met with nearly every manner of person there is to meet with, from wretches so derelict as to sleep amongst the hogs for warmth all the way up to some pretty quality folks, with linen tablecloths and butlers and imported glass eyes. Once, I even sat on a train not three cars away from the future governor of Arkansas. But I have never yet and likely never will encounter a man as singularly strange in personality and appearance as Judge Paul Fletcher.

As an author, I do not generally tend toward overwrought physical descriptions of my characters, calculating such portraiture to be of greater interest to me than to my reader. But in this instance, novelty compels me to sketch Judge Fletcher out in somewhat greater detail than is my custom, trusting that the singularity of the result will render the indulgence evidently justified.

Judge Paul Fletcher was a stooping, flabby man of some seventy winters, clad in a boxy, drab suit of clothes that draped over his unimpressive frame as if he'd borrowed them from a man whose physique he admired. His outlandishly styled hair was of a most unnatural golden hue: not the blonde mane of a healthy young bravo but rather a jarring travesty thereof, undoubtedly achieved, at pains, through some use of chemical. And chemical, too, appeared to have been applied to his skin (though to what aesthetic purpose was anyone's guess), which glowed a piercingly uncanny orange. His teeth were as obviously false as his hair and skin, and by their square and white perfection only served to underscore the weakness of his chin, his tiny, pouting mouth, and his advanced age. A pair of yellowed, piggish eyes glowered out from that rubbery, otherworldly face, at once accusing and ingratiating, a combination I had theretofore believed impossible.

A chill ran through me when I saw him, that natural dread attendant on any encounter with the insane. The clerk Alexander had warned me that Fletcher was "hell on Indians," and my heart sank to think that Honey's fate rested upon this man's reason, for it required no more than a few minutes of the judge's company to conclude that he was completely destitute of the article.

For half an instant, though, I took heart, for upon noticing my appearance in his doorway, Fletcher straightened himself in his chair and struck a pose of such comic Napoleonic grandeur that I took it for an ironic gesture of self-deprecation. This was a good sign, for a man who can laugh at himself must necessarily be equipped with those qualities of self-reflection and human sympathy required of those who would wield authority responsibly. But alas, I was wrong, for my appreciative grin was in no way reciprocated. With a horror intermixed with disbelief, I understood that the jutted-out schoolboy chin; the puffed up, feeble chest; the labored, twisted glare meant to suggest the glint-eyed gaze of the man of action but instead communicating insouciance and confusion—these things were all in earnest, fashioned in a hopeless and embarrassing bid to intimidate or to impress (two things which I guessed to be equivalent in Fletcher's view of the world).

More alarming, the tall piece of furniture beside his desk was a full-length dressing mirror, as out of place in a judge's office as would be a chamber pot, and it was only through great force of will that Fletcher periodically averted his gaze from his reflection in the glass.

"Well," he said, stepping around his desk, adjusting the mirror to keep its image in view, and sticking out his hand. "Here's a man who needs something."

I reached for his hand, but before I could secure a grip he seized my unprepared fingers between his, squeezing as tightly as he was able, while pulling me aggressively in toward him and then pushing me away, all the while flashing those fake teeth while his eyes, from second to second, changed from a crazed generalized hatred to a childlike pleading for adulation, darting back and forth between me and the mirror. Normally when a man disrupts polite human intercourse for no better reason than to make a puerile show of his masculinity, my dander rises, but owing to Fletcher's office, his advanced age, his physical weakness, and his obvious cowardice—not to mention his power of life and death over Honey—I subdued the urge to pummel him.

"Yes, sir," I said. "I understand you have responsibility for the trial of my wife, Honey, the Indian gal who's accused of trying to kill Ward Carson."

Still clutching and pumping at my hand, Fletcher said, squinting hard, "That's your wife?"

I tried to release his hand, but he wasn't done with his childish display of power, and insisted on continuing to pull and push against me like he was working a hack saw, proudly watching his own performance in the glass, delighted to have convinced himself that he had overpowered me.

"Yes, sir," I said.

At last he relinquished his grip. "Interesting," he said, wiping his brow. "Now, I thought she was Ward Carson's wife."

"No, sir. He may have said so, but she isn't."

Fletcher shrugged. "No matter," he said. "I know how it is with these Injuns. No ceremonies, no paperwork. You look at her wrong, you find out you've married her. And then you look at her wrong again, and she's set her moccasins outside your tent, and you come to find out that you've been divorced during the night."

He peered at me expectantly, pleased no end with this show of wit, but I made no reaction, it being in fact witless.

"Well," I said, "I want to see what I can do about getting the charges against her dismissed."

As if pulled away by a force too powerful to resist, he had turned back toward the mirror.

"Dismissed?" he said, looking himself bravely in the eye and turning at the hip for a more flattering angle. "Now why would you want to do that?"

One time I happened upon a railroad construction site just after a gruesome accident in which a worker had been impaled with an iron rod, and had overheard a foreman ask the victim, "Does it hurt much?" Still, I decided, Judge Fletcher's question was the stupidest I'd ever heard.

"Because," I said, as if he were a child, "she's my wife, and I want her to live."

"Ah!" he said, smiling through clinched teeth, first at his image and then at me, "you feel *that* way about her, is that it?"

"I do, sir. I want her to live."

"I know why you want her to live. You don't have to tell me. They'll do things a white woman never would. Trust me. I know. I'm hardly immune. What, you think being a powerful man makes it go away? Believe me. It doesn't. Makes it worse, because they all want something from you, plus they're dying to rub their crotches all over your greatness. Get the scent of it on 'em right where it counts. Right where it does the most good. I get it. Believe me."

I hardly knew how to respond to this strange outburst. "Well, Judge," I fumbled awkwardly, "all I wanted—"

"Listen," he said, "don't you worry. I know you've already heard about me, because everybody talks about me. It's all they talk about. They're obsessed with me. It's sick. They're sick people. They love me. Great. But just in case you haven't heard about me, you can ask anybody. Because they're all talking about me. In the history of this Republic, there never has been a more impartial judge than I am. Okay? That probably goes back to the Greeks and Romans, actually. Believe me. All over. Exceptional. You are going to love this trial, all right? And you know who else is going to love it? Your wife. Straight. Big. It's going to be an incredible trial—incredible—and everybody's going to be very, very happy with the outcome. Trust me."

All during this barrage of queer assertions and non sequiturs, he had only glanced at me for a fleeting second or two. The rest of the time his fascinated gaze had lingered upon his image in the mirror, utterly enraptured by what he saw there. The astonishing incongruity between his objectively repulsive appearance, and the worshipful regard with which he beheld himself, suggesting as it did a deeply impaired ability to perceive the simple reality of things, left me disoriented and not a little nauseated. Now he was folding his hands across his flabby gut, perfectly satisfied that he had given me more reassurance than anyone could reasonably require. And yet I confess to feeling, just then, a persisting doubt or two.

"But Judge," I said. "How can *everybody* be satisfied with an outcome in which only one side can possibly prevail?"

Fletcher looked back at the mirror, renewed his smile, and then transferred the smile to me: a smile meant to appear portentous, as if he possessed some secret knowledge or clandestine plan, although he was such a patently vacuous person, and there was such an obvious dint of intelligence in those fevered, jaundiced eyes, that I knew Isaac Ford would have been more capable of formulating a complex scheme than he was. "Trust me," he said. "Okay? You'll see. Believing. Everybody loves me because I'm fair. I'm firm. But fair." He raised a finger, evidently pleased with this simple formulation, and repeated it: "Firm but fair. Have you asked around? Have you heard about me? People will tell you, because everybody knows: *Judge Fletcher is great.* That's the word they'll use, and believe me, they don't use it lightly. That's the word they used for Julius Caesar, you know. Did he measure up? It's fitting. Look, if it fits, it fits. There's a meaning to that word. *Great.* Your wife is an Indian. Ask her. The Indians love me."

"But I've heard you were rather hard on the Indians."

"Hard? Have you seen how the Indians live? Believe me. Disgusting. Lice. Smut. Illness. Trust me. They love me. Total filth. Have I had to string a few Indians up? Of course. You have to be firm. They love me. Ask any of them. Atrocious."

My head was reeling, but I dug deeply and found the strength to persist for just a moment more. "Have you ever acquitted an Indian of a crime?" I said.

I saw that I'd offended the judge, for his smile began to droop until the weak mouth coiled into a petulant little frown, the tiny bunched-up lips resembling nothing more closely than when a cat raises his tail and proudly takes his leave of you. "Listen," he said. "I don't like that tone. Nobody questions me. All right? That's greatness. But I'll answer you. Atrocious. I'll answer you because I haven't got anything to hide. You, on the other hand—of course I've acquitted Indians. Thousands and thousands of them. Possibly a million or more. Actually, yes. Three million of them, and you can ask anybody. Okay? That's just a fact. A lot of people are saying it. Don't believe the lies. Nasty people might say otherwise. The number is three million. Well, three million and something. I have a firm grasp of the facts, but the exact figure eludes me at the moment. But it's four million. That's what it is. Don't believe them. They're nasty. Have I strung up a few along the way? Of course. Hey. You can't please everybody. You of all people should know that."

"Me of all—? Well, hell, I *do* know that. That's the point I was just making, when you said that everybody would be happy with tomorrow's trial."

He shook his head disgustedly, as if I were completely obtuse. "But I never *said* that," he sneered, with a wave of his little hand.

"Why, of course you did."

Now his entire demeanor had changed. The longing for acceptance had gone, replaced by a shadow fallen hard over his face, one eye newly glazed with a bitter hatred that I found not just grotesque but alarming. "You know," he said through the cowardly pout of his narrow lips, "there's a name for people like you, people who like to twist words and spread dirty lies."

I couldn't resist myself. "But how have I twisted your words?" I said. "I've merely repeated exactly what you said not two minutes ago!"

On my shelf is a title called *Practical Oil Painting,* and I have been through it six times now in search of a name for the color my comments brought out in Fletcher's face: pale ham-pink mixed in with that already indescribable orange caused by the chemicals. "That is *such* a filthy lie," he said in his nasal whine. "*So* filthy. Dis*gus*ting. Fake. Atrocious. Get out. Get *out.* You're a nasty, awful person."

"Believe you me, Judge, I won't be leaving any quicker than I can," I said, moving toward the door. As I walked through it, I looked back. There Fletcher stood, directly in front of the mirror now, smoothing out his preposterous hair and saying to the hideous image that he found so alluring there, "Trust me. Everybody is going to *love* this trial. *Every*body."

I thought as I went down into the street what a shame it was that a man of Fletcher's unhinged cast of mind had somehow risen to a place of ascendancy over the dozens of people in that town; it was a thousand times more authority than was safe to grant anyone of his febrile constitution.

Luke King betrayed not the slightest trace of surprise when I stepped into his hotel room and removed my hat. "Mr. Whitman," he said in his coffee-and-cigarettes voice, smiling blandly. "Back from the hills so soon?"

"Yessir," I said, looking around the place. He evidently used the room as a Placerville office, for his name was engraved on the door, and the commodious space was appointed with all the trappings and accessories dear to his trade.

I found it to be just as difficult not admiring his tastes as it was begrudging the man's intellect his due. No brazzle in the place, only leather, wood, tobacco, all the materials becoming of a sober and full-throated masculinity.

"Where's that bloodsucker of a client of yours, King?" I said. "Lurking in the weeds as usual?"

He picked up the papers he'd been reading and slowly tucked them away in a drawer. "Well," he said. "I'm hardly obliged to share this with you, but Mr. Gray is on the road to San Francisco," he said. "Looking for backers to develop his mine."

"*His* mine. The one you helped him *steal* from me."

King leaned forward in his seat and raised a finger. "Caution now, Whitman. Your testiness threatens your errand." The words were serious, but the tone soothing, very nearly pleasant. "Now, what is it you want with Mr. Gray?"

I nearly spat. "I don't want a single damn thing with Philemon Gray. Why, if I lay eyes upon him in our thousandth year in hell, it'll be too soon."

There in Luke King's eye I caught just the slightest hint of a twinkle, a thing I've always been able to detect when others might not. See, a person like me, cursed with a sharp tongue and rebellious way, learns early in life to observe the subtlest effects of his words upon his audience, especially when that audience is a parent brandishing a heavy wooden spoon or switch of hickory. Yes, I took that semblance of agreement as a good sign that he was as disgusted by Philemon Gray as I was. But I was not about to let on as much.

"Why, then, do you come?" King was saying.

"To enlist you, if you're available."

"Enlist me? In what enterprise?"

"A dangerous face-to-face encounter."

He sat back and clasped his hands behind his head, and I

saw his muscles firm up under his well-cut suit. "Mr. Whitman," he said, "I'm a lawyer, not a hired gun. Sign on the door even says so."

I nodded. "I read the sign," I said. "Matter of fact, I'm aware that to employ you as a hired gun would be to violate the law. Which is why I've come to hire you as an attorney instead."

King yawned and then excused himself for it. "And what is the dangerous face-to-face legal matter you have in mind for me to help you with?" he said.

"Forcefully persuading a man to dismiss capital charges against the woman I love," I said.

He looked at me for a very long time, those shining black eyes just going all up and down my person. With the thumb and forefinger of his right hand, he twisted at the end of his ample moustache, tugging absently and drawing his full lip out away from his fine, white teeth. I wasn't overly comfortable under this prolonged scrutiny. At last, he says, "Does this involve Ward Carson, any chance?"

"Indeed it does, sir. He's the man."

"Figured," he said, bobbing his head up and down in short little nods. "Figured about as much. But listen, Whitman. Gray about cleaned you out. How do you propose to pay me, being penniless?"

"Here's how!" I said and slapped the claim deed down on his little writing desk.

Why, you'd have thought Luke King had read a whole library's worth of deeds for multi-million-dollar gold ledges, the way he perused it casually, almost disdainfully, and then handed it back to me with the steadiest of hands.

"I suppose we could make some kind of arrangement, then," he murmured. "When's your meeting?"

"Soon as you'll ride out there with me. The hanging's tomorrow, so we've got to be quick."

Slowly Luke King stood and stretched—yawned again—tidied his desk—ambled over to the broad maple cabinet that stood on the far wall—fumbled for a key—swung open the cabinet door—and from it withdrew two rifles, two revolvers, and a shotgun. These he laid across his bed, and for a moment he stood over them, petting his chin. He looked over at me. "How are you equipped by way of arms?" he said.

I gulped. "What I'm wearing, plus a rifle and shotgun of my own," I said.

He nodded. "You'll carry your shotgun, then," he decided. "I'll see to everything else."

That grassy hillock that Alexander had told me about, with the white oak atop it and the road running up it, was the cheerfullest looking, most picturesque little knoll you ever set eyes on—right until you crested that low summit and got a look at the other side.

Yes, from the road, the hillside's wet, rich grasses gleamed in the golden light of the setting sun, just as pastoral and inviting as any fairytale lea, but after we topped out and descended its north slope, we dropped to a swampy lowland slathered already in full shadow, still and dismal as a cavern, and the path kept to its own schedule, climbing its way back up out of there, too, so that by the time we'd ascended a little to a sandy pine forest, the day's light was all but fled. Ahead of me, broad shouldered and straight, black-haired Luke King sat, clothed all in black, atop his black horse, against the black tunnel of trail bored into the black curtain of firs. No insect chirred, no owl hooted, no frog called from the low places. Nothing to be heard but the rhythmic creak of our saddles and the soft footfalls of our horses. We bore no light into that gloom.

I meant, as I rode, to rehearse the gun battle to come, but my untamed mind reverted again and again to the tales I'd heard of

Ward Carson's wickedness. It won't do to compare him to any wild animal, for no animal was ever so cruel. He had, it was said, once taken off all ten fingers of an enemy by applying the muzzle of his revolver to those digits and squeezing the trigger, each finger in slow turn, taking his time to reload after the sixth, talking his victim through the procedure, keeping him conscious, ensuring that no detail and no moment was lost on the helpless wretch. Another time, he'd caught a Digger Indian stealing tobacco and had crucified him to a sycamore and spent the afternoon using the poor fellow as a target to practice his knife throwing on.

That was the kind of man I was going to meet, I who had never once been in a gun battle. Yes, I had Luke King with me, and while Judge Cutler and Isaac Ford had painted a comforting picture of his slitting the throats of multitudes down in Mexico, I wondered whether he could be any match for Ward Carson's cold-bloodedness, or for his skill along the lines of causing human suffering. In this I admit to being prejudiced against King's learning. Could anyone as well spoken and well read as Luke King ever answer the hardness of a man as ignorant and natural-born cruel as Carson?

The further into that dark woods we penetrated, the greater grew my doubt. A dozen times I resolved to turn Grandee around and swear off this foolishness, and a dozen times I rode on, haunted by the knowledge that Honey would not live another twelve hours unless I saw things through. The reins trembled in my hands, and my quaking knees tapped the horse's sides.

By and by King halted his mount in the thickening dusk, and I walked Grandee up beside him. Ahead a light shone through the trees, orange and faint, shifting. "That'll be Carson's place," King said.

"I suppose."

"Now don't you imagine you'll go charging in there shooting the place up," he said. "We'll start out by seeing if we can talk sense to him. I'll know it if he means to fight. And if he does, I'll let *you* know it in time. Understand?"

"I suppose I do. But don't you find it wiser, in these situations, to rush in and, without preamble, to—?"

"No," King said. "If I felt that way, I'd have said so. Will you do as I say?"

I shuddered. "I will," I said.

"You scared?"

"Jesus yes."

"Good. Then follow."

A moment later Carson's hounds scented us and came bawling up the track in the dark, and the sudden explosion of their baying in that silent dusk was answered by a quick hot jet from my bladder. Before I could note my embarrassment they were upon us, jumping between our horses' legs, barking raw their booming canine throats, making an awful infernal nuisance of themselves. I connected the toe of my boot to the jaw of one of the devils, and he yelped and reeled off into the darkness, which felt satisfactory. But from what I could tell, Luke King never paused but rode straight through the pack as if they were made of mist, and we came out onto Carson's spread with the animals all around us milling and leaping and bumping each other and howling echoes like it was the end of times.

Where the path finally quit lay the clearing on which Ward Carson's place stood. This was the sort of dwelling site that is not nor never shall be completed, whether it stands for one year or a hundred: sawdust and tools and wagons and carts strewn all about, half-finished buildings, makeshift animal pens, stacks of lumber, piles of brush, scatterings of bones and antlers, the chaotic clutter of man's feeble toehold in the wilderness, which crowds him all about.

I had thought that, what with the overly sufficient warning of the hounds, Carson might have shot us on sight or at least been crouched and waiting with his guns at the ready, and I had trembled still harder in the saddle, struggling for breath in anticipation of the first bullet. But evidently he was stingy with ammunition. And stingy with a glance, as well, for as we hove up into the yard he wasted not so much as a glimpse in our direction.

He was skinning a scrawny hog by no other light than a solitary lantern held by a woman in a shabby nightgown who I presumed to be the Irish gal Billy Moore had spoken of. A great wide pile of guts—yellow, white, and orange in the moving light of the lantern, seemingly too large for that little dangling pig—spread around their feet. Not far off a rifle and a belt of revolvers lay upon the bed of pine needles, just beyond the elongated stain of blood that had spread from beneath the hog. Shapes and shadows rose and shrank as the woman swung the lantern over their work.

"Hi, you dogs! You quit!" Carson shouted, and the hounds quieted so fast and thorough that you'd have thought someone had dunked all their heads underwater. Without so much as another yip, they ambled off to their porches and steps and secret nighttime places.

"Who is that, Mary?" Carson said now, in a low, easy voice, still not bothering to take his eye off his chore.

Well, I'd heard that voice of his a time or two and loathed it, feared it absolutely: medium timbre, medium volume, everything about it rather medium, but with some phlegmy edge to it, some graininess of texture, that left his cruelty undisguised howsoever banal his utterance.

King didn't wait for the woman Mary to try to answer. "Lucas King," he said in that low campfire voice of his. "And with me's Stern Whitman."

Now Carson turned around so his face showed in the light of Mary's lamp, so ugly I'd have rather stared at the pig dross. He wiped first his knife blade and then his bloody hands on the thighs of his trousers. He was moving slowly and steadily and smoothly over to where his guns lay on the bed of needles. Still King never stirred, so I sat there quaking and watched Carson bending to his weapons as I heard him say, "Stern Whitman. I more or less expected you. Wondered if you'd show."

My throat was clicking open and shut all by itself, but I got some words through. "Why would you have thought that?" I said.

"That squaw, she said your name, must have been six or eight times, while they was draggin' her off." Still moving snake-like, without so much as a hitch, he lifted the gunbelt and began strapping it to his waist.

It was awful hard to keep my voice from squeaking. "Well, I've come," I said. "Come to ask you if you'll let her go."

Carson laughed and shook his head. The light glinted on his silver hair. He had his arms folded now. "You sentimental god-damned fool," he said. "Come out here to get yourself killed, and all for what? Some nasty little squaw ain't worth a half a plug."

King cleared his throat. "Gentlemen," he said. "Let us choose our words carefully. Mr. Whitman rode out here to have a civil conversation with you, Mr. Carson, to see what can be worked out."

Carson never took his glittering eyes off me. "And you bring this little pin-hook lawyer out here with you," he said. "I guess probably somebody filled your ear with all that rot about him being a good man with a gun. Well. He ain't. As you'll soon see if you don't the two of you tuck tail and ride hard off my land."

"Please, Mr. Carson," I said, sounding more like an adolescent than I had since adolescence. "I didn't come out here looking for any fight. I just want to ask you, as one man to another—"

Without unfolding his arms, Carson took two steps closer to my horse. My spine got frosty, and I saw that the woman was easing off to the side with that lantern still held up high to give Carson good light to kill us by.

"Listen to me," Carson said, more quietly than he'd spoken yet. "What you're asking for is mercy, and you've come at the wrong moment; I'm fresh out of the article. Hanging is mercy enough for her. There ain't a reason in all the world why it ain't her dangling from this tree instead of that pig. Believe what I say: I wouldn't blink to skin her alive."

Oh, I hated him, hearing him talk so. Hated him for his wickedness, for the ugly crook of his nose, for the weakness of his chin. Hated his woman and his homestead and the very blood-soaked pine needles below his feet. But, good Lord, was I frightened of him.

"As I was saying, Mr. Carson," I said. "I didn't come out here for any kind of fight. What I came for is to offer to remunerate you in exchange for Honey's freedom."

Carson scowled. "Munerate?" he said. "Talk English, Whitman."

"Pay," I said. "Pay you. I'm willing to offer you ten thousand dollars for her release."

Carson uncrossed his arms abruptly, and I saw Luke King jolt a little, like it was all up and time to draw. But he checked himself when he saw that Carson was only reaching to slap his thigh with laughter. "Whitman," Carson said, "you haven't in your whole life seen *one* thousand dollars all in one place, never mind about ten."

"Ward," I said, "I give you my word that I'm worth it."

"*Your* word. I don't pretend to know you much from Adam, but I've seen enough of you to say this: *your word* couldn't get you a week's credit at the butcher's. So it's sure as hell not going to get you very far with me."

"I don't blame you for thinking so," I said, "but my station has improved. I'm good for it, I assure you."

"You assure me. You hear that, Mary? He *assures* me. Son, if you were good for it you'd have carried your ten thousand out here to bargain with. All I see you carried is a pile of armaments fit to get you killed, and the fraudiest little gun man that ever sat a horse."

If I hadn't heard it with my own ears, and seen it with my own eyes, I would never have dreamed that a man could speak so of Luke King in his presence and live on. Oh, it galled me, the way Carson talked. I wanted very badly just then to shoot Ward Carson, and I had a sudden, nearly irrepressible urge to try it with or without Luke King's help. That rage roared up in me like someone had left the damper open and the wind had gusted. But then, strangely enough, it floated off pretty quick, replaced by a new clarity of thinking.

Suppose I shot Ward Carson through the brain right here, killed him stone dead. Would that save Honey? No, she would hang, and so would I. I wasn't going to convince a flintlock like Carson of anything, not by argument, not by pleading, not by promises, and not by waving guns around. I was finished.

I turned to Luke King. He gave a tiny little shrug of the shoulder, as much as to say, *Do whatever you think best; you're beyond reach of* my *aid.*

"Carson," I said, disliking the hollowness of my voice. "If you'll allow me, I'll dismount and prove my worth."

He flicked his wrist. "Free country," he said.

Luke King sat his horse, still silent, as I swung down out of the saddle and took out the claim deed. "Ma'am," I said, "a little light, if you please?"

The woman stepped closer with the lantern and leaned down

with Ward Carson to look at the document, and her shift came open at the throat and I saw just about all there was to see of her swaying around inside. That made me pretty scared, but if Carson noticed, he didn't bother to let on, or perhaps he simply didn't care. I watched his eyes moving down the page.

"So you see," I said when I reckoned he'd finished, "I am about to become a very rich man. I aim to have my claim sold inside of a week, and will pay you your ten thousand the instant I get a buyer."

Carson laughed, an incongruously open, unguarded childish laugh and, for the first time, turned and addressed himself to Luke King. "Well, King," he said. "Is this thing legitimate?"

King only nodded. His eyes looked very black with the orange bark of those red pines behind him and the darkness backing it all.

Carson turned to me, his face still spread wide with that laughter that appeared beyond his ability to master. "All right," he said. "All right. You've brought something to bargain with after all."

Relief washed over me like cool rain from heaven.

"Very good," I said. "Mr. King, kindly write Mr. Carson an IOU for ten thousand."

Suddenly Carson was done laughing; he was dry wind over a drought now. "Ten thousand hell," he said. "If you want that woman, it'll cost you a hell of a lot more than ten thousand."

The light was moving all over because the woman Mary's hand was shaking so. I looked up to the underlit boughs of those high pines and sucked in a deep breath and let it out as slowly as I could.

"I'm not very much in a mood to haggle," I said. "I'll give you fifteen. And you'll give me that little boy, as well."

Carson looked at me as straight and steady as a snake watching a mouse. "Oh," he said. "You'd like to take that boy out of here with you tonight?"

"I would," I said. "The woman and the boy, fifteen thousand."

"Fifteen. Hear that, Mary? He says fifteen. Rides in here worth untold millions and thinks he can buy a man's son!—a man's own flesh and blood!—for what's to him just a pittance. You ever behold such cheek?"

"No, sir," Mary said.

"Mary," Carson said. "What's my favorite out of all these hounds?"

"Martha," Mary said.

"How is it with me and Martha?"

"Love," Mary said.

"It is love. Who sleeps with me more oftener, you or Martha?"

"Martha does."

"That's right." He raised his head. "Martha!" he called.

Out of the darkness the hound trotted up to him, nuzzling for his hand and swishing her tail and bending her hips toward him. And then—why, it chills me just to recollect it, and I won't put you through hearing it described, what he did to his favorite dog. Afterward there wasn't very much left of her, that's all I'll say. He stood there all bloodied up with his butchering knife in his hand, and he turned to Mary and said, "Now run fetch Jacob."

Without a word she ambled toward the cabin with the quivering lantern held up, leaving us in darkness. While he waited for the woman to fetch the little boy he said quietly there in the dark, "You think that was hard for me? Martha, I mean?"

"I reckon it ought to have been." My voice sounded like a pebble that had fallen into a pool inside of a cave somewhere.

"No," he said. "It wasn't, and it ought not to have been, either. We've all of us got to die, one time or another, and it ain't easy most of the time. We've about all of us got it coming, and the hard way, too, I mean. When that boy gets out here, I aim to do him just the same way."

"I don't know if I believe you will, Carson. I heard—"

"Ho, you don't think I will?"

"He will," King said to me.

There was a scraping sound and a sudden spurt of tiny orange sparks where Carson was standing. He was sharpening his knife.

"You kill that little boy, you'll hang for it, Carson."

"I suppose maybe I might. But, like I said, we all of us will go one time or another, and for most of us it'll hurt like the dickens. The boy'll go, I'll go, and that disgusting little squaw will go."

"Twenty thousand," I said.

Carson didn't answer me.

The lantern was in the doorway now, and here they were coming across the yard.

"Thirty thousand," I said.

"King," Carson said. "Are you just going to sit there sucking your tongue or are you going to explain to this imbecile what's about to happen here?"

"Whitman," King said. "He wants it all."

"Bring that little boy over here, Mary."

I looked one more time up into those treetops. It was dark beyond the highest boughs, and cool up there, cool and pleasantly dark in all that fresh night air, and if you could get up there you'd likely see the stars, still hoarding their gold, away up there out of all human reach. I thought about Honey and that night in the wickiup, and all those other nights, our stolen kisses along the trail, the strength and skill of her hands, the smile in her eyes, the understanding between us, her mothering of Clarissa Gray. I imagined her with her baby—and with my baby.

I looked down and saw Mary handing that little boy over to

the butcher, and I said to him, "You go to hell, Ward Carson. And take my gold mine with you."

Postscript

Well, I've about exhausted my pen, and there isn't very much more to tell. We rode out of there with that little boy in my lap and the swamp still and quiet, and my heart booming in my chest like I had just won a gold mine instead of giving one away. Luke King said later that he never expected any other outcome, that I'd been so blinded by love and rage that I couldn't even see that Ward Carson had had me right over a barrel straight from the get-go.

Judge Fletcher let Honey go. He had to, for not only did I have in hand Ward Carson's indemnification, but I warned him that Judge Cutler was a friend of mine, and he'd be rolling into town any day to keep him honest.

Carson didn't get the entire mine, though. King helped me stipulate that a one-sixteenth share of ownership would go to Billy Moore, another to Isaac Ford, and another to King himself. Carson, he turned around and sold his majority share in that apex just the same as I'd been planning to do, and it made him pretty disturbingly rich. So disturbingly, in fact, that he couldn't seem to live with the wealth somehow; it drove him even crazier than he'd ever been. I guess it was September or so that he sold the ledge, and he was dead by Christmas, having sunk into an awful pit of drink, opium, and generalized despair.

Stormy Isaac sold his share, too, but it didn't ruin him. Nor did it make him a quality gentleman, either; in truth, it had no effect on him whatever, for he immediately banked the money and returned to the hills to grub for the color and sleep with a knotty log for a pillow. As far as I know, he's out there today, irritating his comrades, smelling his own farts, and refusing to lift a finger to help himself.

It didn't take Judge Cutler any longer to sell out of that galena claim than it takes a fork to hit the floor when you elbow it off a restaurant table, and what he got for his share fetched him a lovely brick home in town and a pretty young San Francisco blonde who attached herself to him with something nigh unto love itself. To the surprise of all, she was a good and loyal wife to him, right up until the end, and now lives quietly and modestly in a state of mourning that appears to be both sincere and permanent.

Luke King was the only one to retain his share in the gold mine. Choosing to retire from the law, and from gunslinging, he lives on the stream of income from his equity in the mine, which affords him a lovely competence, and he'll be Nevada's next senator if I've laid my wager correctly and things go his way this fall.

Ward Carson never knew what a boon to him was Luke King's remarkable forbearance, for as King demonstrated to me beyond doubt some time after that night beneath the pines, he was gifted with incredible speed and skill where weaponry was concerned, and left me in no doubt but that the stories of his exploits in Mexico and beyond had all been true. Today, as I say, he is respected in high company as a perfect gentleman, although one hopes that when he reaches Congress, its fad for dueling will have faded; otherwise there will be a slate of special elections to fill vacant seats.

Now, out of all those who held shares in that galena claim, who do you suppose would be stubborn enough not to sell out? Correct: Philemon Gray. That persistent little wart would hear of nothing but to develop that mine himself—just knew in his heart that he could do it better than anyone else and couldn't brook the thought of ever having to share.

Well, he managed to get half a stamp mill erected out there before he depleted his credit, and by the time he could scare up enough money to finish it, the equipment had all gone to rust, and he had to begin again from scratch. Under his colossal mismanagement, Gray Mining Co. went bust after three years of bitter struggle, and, true to the psychology of mining, that hill developed a reputation as an impossible concern. Desperate for money, Gray finally sold his equity for a pittance to the experienced and considerably moneyed San Francisco outfit that was developing the gold mine not far away in Whitman's Gulch. They slapped a stamp mill up in short order and started churning out silver by the ton, and I do wish I could have been the one to break that news to Gray. Last I heard he was tramping up and down in Michigan or somewhere, selling Bibles door to door, and I do hope his life is awful slushy and cold, and his afterlife the perfect opposite.

Clarissa Gray? Well, I'll tell you her news, but first I've got to confess that I changed her name for this book, to protect her, for now she's a public figure: first lady of the great state of ________, to be exact. Before the governor was ever elected, Clarissa fell madly in love with him, a man of deep learning, tender sensibilities, and philanthropic bent. The doting mother of three beautiful children uses her husband's office to petition for fair treatment of Indians, the poor, and the aged. From her I received a beautiful letter not very many months ago, none of whose particulars I will share except insofar as to report that she is happy. Blessedly, deservedly happy.

So there it is. Yes, for a short time I held more wealth than nearly any living man in the republic and exchanged it all for the lives and happiness of two fine women.

But you needn't pity my poverty today, or imagine that my

only wealth is the spiritual kind; for after Johnny and Fears An Antelope and their overladen mule came plodding into Placerville two days behind me, they showed me a look at those "few items" that the dead men up at Whitman's Gulch "would have no more use for." It was gold! Four long and almighty heavy sacks of it, an enormous accumulation of placer diggings!

We carried that modest wealth back home to Mama, along with our new brides. It wasn't funds enough for us all to live in luxury, as we'd dreamed, but we're comfortable, the lot of us, and never need to worry about money—especially now that I've been admitted to the Missouri bar and have tried my first few cases.

No man was ever happier with his wife than I am with my Honey. There is a mystery in all this, which is that two people with almost no mutual language can tell by the crinkles around the eyes, by the twist of a smile, that they are wholly compatible one with the other. Our hunch has proved true. I've learned some of the Crow language, and Honey speaks good English now, but even before that, we never felt we lacked in understanding, for it was our souls that communed and not only our minds. She still dresses in those beautiful doeskin tunics that I love. She is a proud Indian, and I am a white man, and together we are something more than one or the other or both: we are human straight through, humans in love, laughing and teasing and cherishing our time. Evenings we walk down through the orchard holding hands and talking of the future.

Here in Missouri, it is late May, and springtime is breathing its dogwood-and-apple-blossom breath in through the open window up here in my office, stirring the lace curtains Honey has made. At long last my story is told, and after completing this sentence I'll stow my depleted pen and descend the shiny pine-plank stairs, for down in the yard unfathomable riches await: my little half-breed children somersaulting in the grass, and Honey and my mother laughing together on the step, hulling beans.

ABOUT THE AUTHOR

Derek Burnett sometimes jokes that he lived "the last nineteenth century childhood": hand-milking cows, chopping wood, riding horses, and reading more frontier fiction than is good for any tender young mind. He went on to a career in journalism that took him around the world and continues to write frequently for *Reader's Digest,* where he was a staff writer and is now a contributing editor. His debut novel, *The Skeleton Walkers,* was shortlisted for Western Fictioneers' award for Best First Novel in 2015, and his journalism has been honored by the National Press Club. He lives in rural North Carolina with his wife and two children, who cheerfully follow him to rodeos, county fairs, and powwows.

The employees of Five Star Publishing hope you have enjoyed this book.

Our Five Star novels explore little-known chapters from America's history, stories told from unique perspectives that will entertain a broad range of readers.

Other Five Star books are available at your local library, bookstore, all major book distributors, and directly from Five Star/Gale.

Connect with Five Star Publishing

Visit us on Facebook:
https://www.facebook.com/FiveStarCengage

Email:
FiveStar@cengage.com

For information about titles and placing orders:
(800) 223-1244
gale.orders@cengage.com

To share your comments, write to us:
Five Star Publishing
Attn: Publisher
10 Water St., Suite 310
Waterville, ME 04901